# COLD
# IRON

## also by Nicolas Freeling

*Fiction*

LOVE IN AMSTERDAM
BECAUSE OF THE CATS
GUN BEFORE BUTTER
VALPARAISO
DOUBLE BARREL
CRIMINAL CONVERSATION
THE KING OF THE RAINY COUNTRY
THE DRESDEN GREEN
STRIKE OUT WHERE NOT APPLICABLE
THIS IS THE CASTLE
TSING-BOUM
OVER THE HIGH SIDE
A LONG SILENCE
DRESSING OF DIAMOND
WHAT ARE THE BUGLES BLOWING FOR?
LAKE ISLE
GADGET
THE NIGHT LORDS
THE WIDOW
CASTANG'S CITY
ONE DAMN THING AFTER ANOTHER
WOLFNIGHT
THE BACK OF THE NORTH WIND
NO PART IN YOUR DEATH
A CITY SOLITARY

*Non-Fiction*

KITCHEN BOOK
COOK BOOK

# COLD
*Nicolas Freeling*
# IRON

 VIKING

VIKING
Viking Penguin Inc.
40 West 23rd Street
New York, New York 10010, U.S.A.

First American Edition
Published in 1986

LIBRARY OF CONGRESS CATALOGING IN PUBLICATION DATA
Freeling, Nicolas.
Cold iron.
I. Title.
PR6056.R4C6    1986      823'.914      86-40118
ISBN 0-670-81180-7

Printed in the United States of America by
The Book Press, Brattleboro, Vermont
Set in Ehrhardt

*To Andrea*

# COLD IRON

1 The Divisional Commissaire, Monsieur Adrien Richard, had retired six days ago. He could have been six weeks gone, or six months for that matter: it was as though he had never been.

His successor, a gentleman named, and well-named, Terranova, had occupied his space and breathed his air for that little time and Richard, that individual thumbprint upon everything, was fading like a breath on glass. In fact very little had changed, but any group of professional civil servants behaves the same way. There is little to distinguish the Police Judiciaire from the Inland Revenue: the moment the speeches are over, the champagne drunk and the chiming clock presented, there is nothing left.

'Well you'll be dropping in, won't you?' 'Keep in touch then.' Not quite clapping Richard on the shoulder; nobody did that.

Castang, a junior commissaire of the grade called 'adjunct', felt surprised. A little setback to one's vanity, discovering that one is of small importance. For he had imagined that the end of the Richard reign would see his own banishment. Was he not labelled as Richard's creature; henchman; any word of the sort that will sound derogatory? A new chief does not like to find such people under his feet. A posting, he thought, would be automatic. Jokes had been made about getting sent to the Ardèche, or the Ardennes.

He had been left here. Richard had been left here too. This city, now large and modern, a regional capital since antiquity, was not a mouldy or a dusty corner, but it was provincial. Richard had not been called to one of the half-dozen jobs in the directorate at Paris, although entitled by both rank and abilities. Yes, well; politics.

And Castang had been left, where he was, in a job where he came to no harm, and did none: a chief-of-staff post, administrative. He had lost his criminal brigade after a nasty episode left him with synthetic articulations in the left arm: one does not again command troops in the field. One can command, in a superior rank, of Principal Commissaire and above. Perhaps, if he rocked no boats and broke no china, he would achieve rank with the accumulation of years and seniority, until his turn came for champagne and

1

chiming clocks. It seemed a dull prospect. Staying still means going backwards. Is there no more to the job than this? At the age when disillusion sets in he was surprised to find himself still ambitious.

A civil servant, an 'under secretary'. Is it then just like England? Is it so very important to have been to a good school and graduate from the right university? And then to belong to a good club and play cricket? All the ridiculous shibboleths? Yes and no. Yes, France is comically like England. There are careers open to character and talent, though perhaps not very many in the state administration, where nepotism is more important. The intellectual élite does not choose a career in the police. You don't gain marks by being bright: as a rule, on the contrary.

In his case, every potential good mark was balanced by a bad one. A good start damped by a foolish marriage. Good work, occasionally excellent, thrown into the shade by indiscretions. Vanity might be soothed by the thought of being under a cloud and not giving a damn. Now it appeared that his superiors took no notice of the cloud, thought him simply not worth bothering about. What did one do then?

He could talk about it to his wife. Vera has grown out of her unbalance, her humiliations and imagined inferiorities. Her shame at being a refugee and edginess at being Czech: the years of partial paralysis of her legs: more years, of inability to produce children. Years of dependence, of hideously having-to-be-grateful. Now she stands upon her own feet – literally; she has a small limp. She has developed a sharp, peppery intelligence. She can indeed be very nasty! She has two small children and looks after them. She is quite a good graphic artist; makes occasional, small, but welcome sums of money with illustrations or posters. She has too ambitions, to paint.

Her loyalty is intact. If asked she will reply briefly, 'Where you go, I go.' She is fond of her little house, on which quite a lot of the mortgage has been paid off. It is not worth much, but the land on which it stands is building ground, coveted, worth a lot. She is not wedded to her little house. Mm.

Monsieur Terranova walks about, with a quick light step, silent upon crêpe soles that would squeak on a polished floor – but these old floors have seen no polish for a good many years. The building is old, with big lofty rooms and gloomy corridors; a sombre heavy block, palatial in façade and prison-like within, traditional to French public offices. He is shortish, baldish, brown; a big intelligent head between powerful shoulders, energy and ability manifest. He says little to Castang but 'Good, that's good' in exactly the same tone as 'Bad, that's bad' when he found that fire precautions had been neglected. The man didn't smoke, didn't drink. Plainly he would go far. He would be forty-four or -five; just right for the present job: might stay three years before a posting which he firmly intended should be Versailles, that traditional anteroom to a good Paris job. And would Castang still be here making good the deficiencies of the computer? Not good enough. What was the way out?

The inspectors of the criminal brigade had a new game. Lucciani likes crime novels, strictly in secondhand paperback format, and his new discovery had before devoting himself to literature been a luminary of the Police Department in Los Angeles. Naturally, they'd gone all Hollywood Division, talking of their dicks dropping off when Castang was disagreeable, threatening to Eat Their Pistol if neurosis loomed in the shape of an unpleasant job; leering at girls: they'd be going about on rollerskates next. Orthez could be heard now in the passage saying "Don't care what you dress up as" (Lucciani had a vulgar new pullover) " 'slong as y'don't change sex." Castang sighed.

He considered the papers on his desk. Not an inspiring collection. Typical of all the other desks in towns of some three hundred thousand souls, say half a million counting the suburbs. And Paris too.

Marriage bureaux frauds. Adolescent fugues and suicides. There are no statistics on suicide attempts. Real or self-dramatisation? The computer gets a coughing fit.

Hankypanky in a backwoods village. A gendarme had been assassinated by poachers? It was said, not very loudly, that poachers had been ambushed and gunned down, so that this was vendetta. Castang thought it likely that both would end classified as shooting accidents. There are plenty of them. A fairly reliable statistic said that fifteen per cent of the populace possesses one or more shotguns. There are no figures for the ubiquitous twentytwo rifle: he guessed you could double fifteen. The French love guns . . .

The relations – this came up every year and was known as the sea-serpent – between the police and the judges of instruction. There is a great deal to say about this. Better perhaps to stay within Richard's one laconic word. Umbrage . . .

A homicide. Not 'a case', since the man had walked into the office and told his story, and for once it had been true: he'd killed her husband. Paper had had to be blackened. Castang's summary was pinned to the top, less laconic than he would have liked. Destructive passion for a totally worthless woman. The man had cried bitterly in his office. 'I have done so much harm.' And the woman, who had done all the harm, scotfree, consistently and invulnerably pleased with herself. No legal charge could be brought against her. A sad story? A beastly story.

Outside his office the Regional Service was in the routine round, for the most part quiet. Typewriters tapping and voices murmuring. There might be a body in the detention cells downstairs, to be brought up and processed: one has fortyeight hours from the time of arrest, before producing case and bod before a judge. There will be witnesses, rambling and prevaricating. Paper, paper. A criminal brigade inspector has outside field work. But senior cops, ever more deskbound, slip easily into the habit of preferring paper to people. Richard's well out of this, thought Castang.

They had spoken briefly together just before official leave-takings known as the 'wine of honour'. They were friends: it had not come about easily but had been helped by an absence of family in both instances. Bourgeois France is startlingly stilted in its social relations and only in the most formal way does anything but Family pass its doors. The wives made a further bond; the one from franquist Spain and the other from stalinist Czechland – much the same thing and they didn't have Family either. Other things besides solitude and refugees had thrown the two men together, but it was an accidental type of friendship and was now at an end. Richard had sold his house and was going to live down in the Basque country. If asked why he would say, 'Suitable for retired cops. Nice seaside golf courses. Good climate for Judith's plants' – she was a tremendous gardener. And 'Basques you know – always in an uproar – helps to keep one awake.'

Smoke from thin cigar, and maizepaper cigarette. Why maize? Because when laid in an ashtray while typing they go out instead of smouldering.

"I'm glad to go."

"We've seen improvements."

"We have indeed. You may see more than I have. We've shaken a little that immovable French complacency." Richard loosening his tongue at last, on leaving day. Castang over the years had been terribly talkative, had begun to learn silence from Richard. 'Good occasion you lose there for holding your tongue.' Now that Richard was talking . . .

"The trouble with government work is that one's expected to be patriotic. We should of course have plenty to feel patriotic about. Plenty of space, good climate, enough soil, three seas. Excellent communications; we're the heartland of Europe. We've wealth and energy, and just look at us. The old man of Thermopylae, who never did anything properly. It shows up what could have been done and hasn't. We could have got rid of all these ridiculous weapons. Instead, we have incurred the hostility of every progressive opinion in Europe while increasing the distrust of every reactionary. I don't think we have much to be proud of. We copy everything American down to the language and we do it incompetently. We're a joke, and we risk becoming contemptible."

"Don't the English feel the same?"

"Probably. Not very good either at cutting back the dead wood. Like those bushes of Judith's that she prunes right down. Good, let's go and have a drink. I'm not having any farewell dinner parties."

No. One had always rather expected Richard to say 'I am going *Now*!' and disappear with a loud bang like Bilbo Baggins.

"Dead wood?" said Orthez, amused. "There's plenty about. Start with the Parliament, the politicians. Or," relishing it, "the Pope." Orthez was from the South and had strong beliefs. More Cathare than Catholic, said Vera: he had small use for the Polish gentleman in the Vatican. "Lots of people feel like that. Why else do we have so many groups nobody's ever heard of throwing bombs? Let's start a revolution. What this country needs is a Hitler!" Castang liked him. He gave an impression of stolid force, no brains at all, and had a great deal of common sense. "Wouldn't it be something, though, if we formed a secret cell of dynamiters. We'd know how!"

"Finance a problem?" suggested Castang. "We're all poor but honest."

"I know some people over in the tax office who'll fiddle their computer. Ten francs contribution added to each name on the list. What you need is a holiday. You're stale, like. Who's been giving you these ideas then – the old man?" Shrewd guess. "He talks like that because he has nothing to do once he's gone. What new wood is he likely to grow, down there in Biarritz?"

"He's realist enough," said Castang feebly.

"Realist!" said Orthez with a contempt that surprised him. "No, really! Realism, it's one of these words like clarity that everyone uses and means the opposite. Like those little Californian books of Lucciani's; I asked him what he saw in them and he said they were sort of realist. I told him, nothing of any use or value ever got done by realists." Coming from anybody else it would have been a banal remark enough. From Orthez, whom nobody had ever accused of imagination, it was striking.

It was near on a fortnight before Commissaire Terranova, with much politeness, asked 'if he might have a word'. Asked Castang into his office. Poured out coffee from a vacuum jug; his only vice, to appear so far that is, was sipping all day.

"I'm impressed, Castang, I don't mind saying. I didn't know Richard well. One of the old school, it was said, but labels, what use are they? Very able. Good administrator.

"However – I suppose you've been wondering. New brooms, as they say. New spades, turning over the new-found-land, what? I've a name that lends itself to jokes, of course."

It was his longest speech since the wine-of-honour. That had been lavish, and the PJ had been hilarious as was traditional. Everyone had made speeches, and all of them ridiculous. The French educational system encourages the people to be articulate. When they have anything to say, and still

6

more when they haven't. Richard had been witty, others had been maudlin. Terranova had been brief.

"And, of course, we must be realist." Oh, there was that word again.

"There's one basic truth about this country. With rare interludes, caused by exasperation, France is governed by deep conservative interests. We do well to keep that in mind."

"Yes." In even a monosyllable, uttered by a well-disciplined person, there must have been a note – of some acidity repressed? – because Terranova asked mildly, "That worries you?"

"No." There was a 'Richard remark' somewhere in memory that Castang was fishing for: something like 'one gets on well with the English: they combine liberal ideas with conservative instincts'.

"How," it was put delicately, 'floated', "d'you stand on this syndicate question?" Put that query as lightly and as casually as may be, it is full of thorns. A good few policemen are in trades unions. In the lower ranks and especially the plain-clothes crowd, it is quite a left-wing syndicate. The commissaires' union, as indeed one would expect, is rather far to the right. Whatever answer one gave would be wrong.

"I'm not a great joiner. Believe in freedom of conscience, I suppose."

"Conscience, yes, that's very fine. You're an individualist, I suppose you wouldn't quarrel with that definition?"

"I quarrel with as little as I can." Castang not at all liking the turn these remarks were taking.

"Yes," said Mr Terranova. Bland cross-examiner's manner. "We're thought of, rightly to my mind, as a highly disciplined corps of officers. That's as it should be, and one can then allow a good deal of latitude in the respect of conscience, among the junior inspectors doing field work. You'd agree? You've commanded this criminal brigade, you know them well; you know the job well. It can be pretty tough out there. What you call freedom of conscience is important to remember when dealing with them. Or so most modern thinking holds. I wonder would you agree? I'd be inclined to draw the corollary that senior officers must be relied on to know what they think. Or discipline would suffer. Am I right?" Oh yes.

"Richard – very intelligent man. Perhaps a little old. The rule of retiring commissaires at fiftyfive isn't all that stupid, perhaps. Now Richard was past sixty. Kept on because he was so good! And would it be fair to suggest that he became a little embittered? He should of course have been in Paris: merit is not always rewarded." The forensic manner, and skilful timing: an answer was expected. Castang, trying to be honest.

"Yes. There's a good deal in what you say."

"I'm glad you agree. Because you knew him so much better than anybody. How long is it, in fact?" Castang, forcing, doing himself violence in the effort to remain honest.

"Thirteen years. At the start I was a junior inspector." Mr Terranova did not 'wash' his hands. The fingers and palm of the one made circles upon the back of the other which was supporting his firm and well-shaved chin.

"Quite. Quite." There was a silence. Mr Terranova understood the value of silence quite as well as Mr Richard. It 'lets things sink in'. Christ, thought Castang. Thirteen years.

It showed all right because the big avuncular face looked well satisfied.

"I'm a one for putting my cards on the table." Yes! – when they're winners . . .

"Find me simplistic if you like, I'm a simple man. I've no use for the bleeding hearts. I hope that I'm no nineteenth-century reac. Nine tenths of our criminal violence work was among poor, uneducated, ignorant and frustrated people who deserved God knows no punishment. Heaven forbid that I should revert to outdated penal concepts. And times have changed. We've fewer of those. But anybody, Castang, who shoots up one of my boys. Who holds up a bank to finance a terrorist group. Who dynamites or assassinates. Who puts him-, and herself outside society. I'll have no mercy. I'll tell you straight, I'm not just a partisan of a death penalty for such, I'll pull the string myself. For those, Castang, who are found in possession of lethal weaponry, who have aided, abetted, or sheltered – financed – encouraged with written or spoken propaganda; I wouldn't subscribe for an instant to Californian bullshit costing a fortune, electronic aids and chicken on Wednesdays: I'd have a prison camp, Castang, and a prison farm.

Up there on the Larzac causse, throw the army out, I couldn't care less, but that's for me. Dartmoor. I'd make the buggers work, I'd have them out there in the cold and the wet with a pickaxe and spade, and in leg manacles, boy, right?"

"Absolutely," said Castang. "Very well put."

"This is a good sound department and I don't see that I have a problem," said Monsieur Terranova quietly. "Anybody taking over – the former incumbent had his own ideas and beliefs. The more with a man of the intelligence and character of Richard. Wayward he might be – but sound.

"I have one thing to bear in mind and it isn't any personality problem. That this department should exercise its given mission with the maximum result. Early days, but it's precisely on that account that each senior officer must give emphasis to a rather mechanical interpretation of discipline. I dislike the word, but we must watch for any appearance of laxism. The crim-brig now, young Lucciani, young whatsername with the red hair. I'd like to see them tighten up on procedure. There'll be time after a certain maturing process to allow ourselves a broader way of thinking. I'm glad you agree.

"Speaking of yourself for a moment – just between ourselves – I see that you have a lot of unexpected talents. Pity about that arm of yours; I'd have suggested setting up a gymnastics team which you could have trained. And you're a considerable linguist; that's too much of a rarity. But I mustn't allow myself to run on. We've had a good chat, I'll bear in mind all you tell me. Mustn't keep you longer."

No.


The man who had cried lived up at the other end of the town and had worked, in a responsible position, for a firm there said (by Orthez, the investigating officer) to set much store by him. It seemed to Castang that he could do with as many friends as he could get. All those people would be ready enough no doubt to appear as defence witnesses, and that was the defending counsel's job, which no doubt he would do competently. It has been known that such men – and women – have found their friends turn oddly lukewarm, and that it should be the investigating officer – Orthez was like that – who thought of visiting them in jail, with notions about latchkeys and laundry and insurance policies. The hard part of going to jail can be after you come out. Words from a commissaire of police, who in bourgeois France counts as a minor notable, can be of use.

It kept him too late to go home to lunch. He went to a big brasserie. He liked such places, the slapdash bustle and speed of work, the friendly feeling, the heavy victorian furnishings and the solid leatherbound menu, all so soaked in cosy smells. Cooks and waitresses have been here twenty years; there is no nonsense about nouvelle cuisine, calories or blood pressure. A gentleman can belch if he likes and loosen his belt.

There are far too few left, like this, inspiring confidence; where your plate and your glass get filled to the top and the bill holds no nasty surprises; where the table does not wiggle and you can screw your bottom into the chair. There is heavy worn old silver and a starched napkin: there is always stew and sauerkraut, and more bread is brought without asking. You are anonymous; nobody recognises a commissaire of police and wouldn't bother if they did. There is a vicarious sort of friendship that you can enjoy, with your neighbours.

These were three middle-aged ladies with hairdos, and jewellery, and some trouble with their stays. They were all girls together, giggling at each, frequent, visit to the lavatory. They were having a slap-up meal, with steak (and frites), cheese, and goldfish bowls of ice with fruit and whipped cream up over the top. They had a bottle of white wine, one of red, and kümmels with their coffee. They talked loudly whether their mouths were full or empty, and the waitress (bosomy, her dishcloth slapped over her left shoulder) knew at least one from schooldays and much broad humour passed. There is no feeling of class in such places.

Castang felt consoled. He sat a longish while. A brasserie is a good place for solitary thinking and momentous decisions; like shall one buy a new car? And if so can one afford a Mercedes?

He arrived back in the office after half-past two, after tearing up a parking ticket. Excesses of zeal were at a discount today. Monsieur Terranova was nowhere to be seen. During the afternoon there appeared no weirdos nor even crank telephone calls. Even the banditry brigade (officially Search and Intervention) was quiescent as though from a heavy lunch or a dose of narcotics. And on his way home he met Fausta wheeling her bicycle and got a gleam of smile, a moment of sunshine gilding a grey afternoon. Was it just a smile or better, a mark of camaraderie and kindness? In the parking lot she mounted, arranging her skirt and raincoat neatly, and rode off. Where to? Nobody knew. She was said to be married, or shacked, with a young doctor at the University Hospital, in Haematology. Castang stood swinging the car keys round his finger. Had it been a secret smile, knowing or conniving?

Fausta was the symbol of the old régime. She had come to the department years ago, as a very young girl, picked instantly 'because she was so pretty' as Richard's private secretary, and become a great power in the land; being also intelligent, being also hardworking and conscientious, being also a character of much strength. Of course people said she slept with Richard which was nonsense: they'd all tried themselves and got nowhere. Richard, with deliberate eccentricity, used her as filter and bulletin board: his wishes, inclinations, and also commands. Richard had been brought up in the old, hard, crooked style of police work. The PJ, he said, was not a soupkitchen. Being sorry for unfortunates is better left, if you please, to social assistants and charitable organisations. Sentimentalism is here misplaced. Dead right.

In practice however humanity prevailed. Richard knew how to close either eye or both. Social justice could be described as Fausta's Absence of Zeal.

And what did Monsieur Terranova now make of this exceptional secretary? He had already been heard to speak of the need for 'transparency', and to denounce 'occult influences'. Castang got into the car. Fausta, he thought, knew how to look after herself.

He stopped on the way home to buy new toothbrushes, marked extra-hard, meaning they'd be pretty soft. Like him. While he was at it he got some shampoo called Ultra Gentle. If Vera didn't like it, it would probably do to scrub sinks.

And outside his gate he stopped to stare. The desirable residence was not much to look at. A tumbledown cottage, modernised by the PJ's criminal brigade; with carpentry by Castang, electricity by Lucciani, plumbing by Orthez, painting and wallpaper by the girls. The mortgage had been arranged through a fiddle by Richard and a foot in the bank's door by the Financial Squad. Castang was grateful. These rural survivals in cities are not uncommon in France, where some tough and obstinate old woman has resisted all blandishments and only left her home feet foremost. The cottage was worth nothing, but with it went a piece of land, only a plot of overgrown meadow with a few senile apple trees, but that could become a block of twenty bijou apartments at the drop of a conveyance. Worth money: Vera's sheet-anchor in case of a nasty accident.

She liked it. She had flowers round the back and a place for the children to play. One could paint, though the light is not famous. Picturesque and awkward herself she did not mind picturesque survivals, like pitprops to stop the place caving in. She polishes the windows and leaves piles of dust inside: she is meticulous to fusspot point, and downright slovenly too. Take it or leave it. She complains a great deal, more and more. Proud and independent woman, but a loving one. Sticks to what she's got, including her man.

Vera was at home; where else would she be? She has a small girl, and a very small girl, and they take a lot of looking after. Lydia is given to taking a brush and improving a painting as a nice surprise for Mama. 'Put the children down the well,' Castang had suggested. 'They're only girls when all is said.' Shocking remark, scandalising Vera. 'Does it make you unhappy not to have a son?' 'Certainly not. I look forward to incest.' Her face cleared; it had only been police humour.

She often got tense, but this evening she was quiet. They had a pre-supper drink. As we get older we don't drink before sundown. At lunchtime now and then, three or four times a week. But no whisky. We must support the national economy or the French will starve. We'll drink French wine even when Spanish or Italian is both cheaper and better.

"How were things in China?" said Vera.

"Paris has sent us a born-again Christian Democrat."

"Up to their clever tricks, I suppose."

"I don't even suppose that much. There are lots of them and Paris has to send them somewhere."

"I meant to correct any left-wing tendencies Richard left behind."

"He's not the worst of reactionary blood-drinkers. We've plenty of them too. One has just to eat the banana from both ends."

"Does he bother you?"

"I'm more likely to bother him. Disapproval of occult influence, meaning me as well as Fausta. He must have put in a listening post directly he knew he was coming here. He has to show who's boss, naturally. The football team's new trainer, applies new concepts. But if anything goes wrong it'll be me."

"What makes you think so?"

"Double-barrelled shot. The arm will continue to unfit me for anything but desk work. And speaking a little Spanish I'd doubtless be happier in Bayonne?"

"Might Paris send you to Bayonne?"

"They would have already, I think, if they wanted to. I'm not important enough to be worth getting rid of. It's just a way of keeping my beak tied to a chalk line as I see it."

"You've survived worse black marks, myself the first."

"Oh I have quite reasonable marks, in Paris. But they don't send down the inspector, you know, unless there's some awful balls-up. I'm taped as Richard's dogsbody. It's an extra ten kilos of lead to stuff into my saddle."

"You still might get sent to Bayonne?"

"And if I were, I wouldn't regard it as a tragedy."

Vera thought about this and then said slowly, "And neither should I."

"And I've even been wondering, whether it would be clever to take it by the forelock and ask."

"Isn't that though to show yourself rebellious and of evil disposition?"

"A risk either way. Terranova would like to clear me out, all right: that gives him the chance to bring in a man of his own. He might be disposed to help, if I approach him right."

"Anything's better than having to grovel." That Vera had thought about it, often, was shown by the fluency with which she produced a famous quotation, frowning in concentration to get the words right. " 'From the whole business one can derive this moral, that the man who mingles with a court compromises his happiness, if he is happy, and in any case makes his future depend on the intrigues of a chambermaid.' " The French profess great admiration for Stendhal but it's the bloody foreigners who read him.

Castang burst out laughing.

"You're quite enthusiastic!"

"We yam what we yam. There's spinach too for supper, incidentally. Look – after the children are in bed we'll talk about this. Okay?"

"Yes."

"And it occurs to me," shrewdly, "that we might get a better sale on this house, if we don't leave it to the last moment. One always gets screwed, then."

2 Going north, in the car, with the children behind them, and the last of the luggage, Vera who was looking out of the window at the landscape of Artois began suddenly to laugh and said, "Porthos!"

"What?" asked Castang, who had to look at the road. But delighted. She had begun to laugh again, often.

"He looks astonished at the others and says, 'But now I understand what you're saying. I understand English now!' And they look at him and tap their foreheads, and say politely, 'That, dear man, is because we're talking Spanish.' 'Oh,' he says, 'that's a pity; it would have given me another language.'"

"And what made you think of that?"

"I have no idea, except that we're coming into a very Spanish part of the world, and will we have to learn Flamand?"

"I shouldn't be a bit surprised." He is happy, at her content. It is of course impossible to follow these thoughts of Vera's. They are too elliptical. A painter looks at things with a different eye, and enriches, like Vera, with a sense of history and a love of literature. Just as a writer illuminates much of his own thinking by loving paintings and looking at them.

Right now it is only entertainment. She is collecting the place names of northeastern France, tasting them. It is a childish game; no need to make a big aesthetic thing out of it. Proust did the same with all those Normandy villages ending in -ville. It is true that hereabout are some of the best names in France (look at Nice and Cannes, Grasse and Biot, and you will discover some of the worst).

Not a suitable occupation for policemen: Castang is busy with traffic. But the police does – should – have its childish side. They see too much squalor and do not look at enough pictures.

He would have agreed. He had learned through harsh lessons. As a young cop he had been frightened of walking in the country-side: he had nightmares of finding the strangled body of a raped child in the bushes. He had had to learn to look at paintings without bothering about their subject.

Our world is horrible and we cultivate black humour to match.

The people Castang is most afraid of are those who have none. Northern presidents and southern generals: rabbis and professors of physics. A police department is the same as a hospital. Suffering and humiliation become the norm: to laugh is the more needful. The threat on one side is brutalisation. On the other, intellectual sadism.

There is a terrible lack of humour in France. It frightens Castang often. It frightens Vera all the time.

They have arrived. It is a new job, in a new world.

The Lille region, called the Pas de Calais – mostly Artois with a piece of Flanders – is thought of in terms of battlefields and coalmines. There are less of both than formerly. For the Police Judiciaire, it is among the largest and densest of the Regional Services.

The French think of it as full of Poles. After the Russian Revolution a great many came and settled here. Most of them found work in the mines, then flourishing and a home from home. They're all French now though they do not forget: Poles never do. The nationalist and xenophobe type of Frenchman prefers to forget that the country has always been a land of asylum, a shore of refuge.

This particular part of it is commonly thought of as dreary and ugly. So say people who have never been there, and are not very well acquainted with Paris, either.

It is thought of too as cold and rainy. And of course it is: as the Dutch say 'If it's stopped raining you've left Holland'. Will bland euphemisms sound better? Shall we say damp and chilly? It is not quite the disadvantage that might be imagined. The heliotropes avoid this part of the world. Fewer Arabs than in the South. Fewer dress-designers too and fashionable doctors, faith-healers and crooked notaries: maybe even fewer pederasts.

A romantic history. It belonged to the dukes of Burgundy, wealthiest and most powerful sovereigns in Europe, not a very attractive family. The last heiress, kind and pretty and oh-so-rich Marie de Bourgogne married a Habsburg. Holland, Belgium and Artois became Spanish. These are the Spanish Netherlands, just about the richest and most interesting corner of Europe.

One shouldn't underestimate romanticism. Aston Villa owes

16

more than it knows to the splendid name and the claret-and-blue. One could say the same of Arsenal. So the Football Club de Lens is as good an introduction, here, as any. When you see the red and yellow flags – Spanish colours – you begin to understand. These people are warm. A musician or an actor knows that this is the quickest and most stimulating audience in France, as well as the truest to their friends and their football teams.

It is, lastly, the metaphysical part of a pretty materialist country.

So that Castang is content too. His wish has been granted with unexpected generosity. It is not a snub. Though this is complicated, like most things French, and needs a bit of explaining.

The SRPJ (Service Régional de Police Judiciaire) is at Lille, where you would expect it: biggest city. In the Tourcoing-Roubaix triangle: textile mills. Other towns in the area are smaller but of more historic significance (a 'judicial' example: the Appeal Court is at Douai). And as often in thickly populated areas the PJ, to use its own jargon, has 'satellised' into 'antennae'; smallish semi-autonomous groups. Castang has been given an antenna and his step, to Principal Commissaire.

There is not that much difference. He is under the command of the Divisional Commissaire: he is small fry in a small place. But Lille is big, and a hundred kilometres off, and that on these crowded roads is far. And a Divisionnaire is an important person, and human for all that. Unless he is a very unusual character he is often fatigued and more often bored. He may also be plain lazy or given over to worldly vanities. But in general he will rely upon an experienced and competent subordinate. After a period of proba-tion, when he is inclined to keep a beady eye out for rocked boats and broken china. With any luck, Castang will be left, quite a lot, to his own devices. If he is good at chatting up the Chef, but this art he should have learned by now. He is not particularly young for the post.

Size is not important; haven't we learned that small is beautiful? The new city has some sixty thousand folk: the 'old' had near half a million. Both were bishoprics: both have fine, noble, and somewhat decayed gothic cathedrals. The one had a ducal palace: so has this and oddly enough it was the same duke. The one had much fine Renaissance architecture. So has this: in fact – but oh, architecture

17

. . . Castang has not yet had time to absorb anything. There is change: there is no-change. Change, to mean anything, is not just a change of scenery; or a premature menopause . . .

Vera is richer, since a Principal Commissaire's emoluments are respectable, and she has found a flat that pleases her. So that she has started well, with jokes.

" 'I sprang to the stirrup, and Joris, and we:
I galloped, Dirk galloped, we galloped all three!' "

"Great leaping Jesus," said Castang, flabbergasted.

"So appropriate, mm, poppet?" galloping the baby, which enjoyed it. Vera is a treasurehouse of the cruder gems of Eng. Lit.

"What's that!?"

"A bit Victor-Hugo, terribly good if now thought ludicrous. How we brought the good news, from Ghent to Aix, that's us. We're in Spain!"

"What did they gallop for?" asked Castang, interested. It was somehow typical of Vera to have learned poems by heart while learning English.

"I don't know. Does it matter? What do we gallop for?" So typically cop to ask such boringly factual questions: he'd be wondering next what they had in their sandwiches.

" 'Waterloo morne plaine'," said Castang helpfully.

"Oh yes, right next door." Her Lit and her Hist are sound enough but Geog is shaky.

"A bit further east," with prim police precision.

Taking possession; it could be painful. Vera ached sometimes. Like Henri's smashed elbow, surgically impeccable but the cut nerve-endings went on hurting long after. She thought of the 'little house' (successfully sold!). She thought back further to the flat on the canal – poplar trees on the towing path. Gross nineteenth-century building with florid plasterwork on the ceiling (half giggling and half terrified she recalled how it all came down on top of her, shot up by a machinegun in the street). Deeper domestic memories of the plumbing that clanked and groaned: the pull-and-let-go with a chain to the ornate castiron water tank which Henri had painted crimson . . .

This house was a sober, solid piece of modern brickwork, uninspired but with the large windows of the north which gave her

18

pleasure: they looked to a gloomy little *place* with one depressed planetree where bourgeois folk meditated, walking their dog. But it was spring and the leaves were bright in the hard dark light. She would shed blessings on the planetree and it would become less depressed.There were nowhere near enough trees in this town but there was magnificent dark and grimy industrial brickwork straight out of Piranesi: great fortress-like factories, towering chimneys, superb bridges and viaducts springing with a boldness and power of arch that took one's breath away. Oh yes, this was a painter's town. And had not Watteau, incomparable draughtsman, come from Valenciennes?

She found herself longing to attempt things she had never done before. Birds . . . surely the coast was not very far away, and she has heard vaguely of bird sanctuaries. Curlews and sandpipers and uh, things – she knows nothing about birds, resolves to buy a bird book.

Portraiture she has tried in an amateurish way and not got on with: she is still too raw, lacks the confidence. That will be for her maturity. But she is filled with longing to draw the figure, to do nudes – she has made feeble little efforts, the children sleeping or Henri taking his boots off. It should surely be possible to find some girl to model for her.

The flat is nice: midnight blue, and a good off-white lacquer that will show the dirt terribly unless kept spotless: her heart sinks at the thought but she must become a Chtimi housewife, impeccably clean instead of a great slut. But I am the Commissaire's Madam now: I must have a cleaning lady – a Putzfrau, oh dear, terrifying idea.

And Castang too is taking possession; of 'the sociology', and that starts with a small, grim and bricky office with barred windows. But with quite a good desk, solid slab of hardwood that gladdens the heart. For he has started by remembering his youth, brought up by his auntie in the Butte aux Cailles quarter of the thirteenth arrondissement (not at all far from Hugo's Champ de l'Alouette), in just such a pinched dark street as this: she'd had an eye for a piece of second-empire mahogany.

Yes, it is a gloomy town, and much dilapidated. The traditional industries, mining, metallurgy, textiles, have all fallen upon hard times and there is a hideously high unemployment rate. But there is, too, a tough inventiveness. The French as a rule are very functionary, not very entrepreneur – strange that there is no English for this French word. They do of course have a gift for every imaginable combination of moonlighting and the parallel economy. But Flanders, and even more Holland, has the entrepreneurial gift (decidedly it is a clumsy and ugly word) to a high degree. There are lots of inventive, skilled little businesses.

He has taken possession of a lot of files. These he knows well to be worthless: the previous incumbent will have taken pains to see that there was no juice there. Malice is mostly inspired by a sense of failure? I have nothing, so he shall have nothing either if I can help it? And that will be a comfort to me in my old age? One can, be one cop, magistrate, or the Keeper of the Seals, do very little for the man, as often as woman, who pours weedkiller at dead of night upon the neighbour's dahlias. We used to think that education was the answer: we now know better. There is no arguing, reasoning nor pleading with solid bone from the neck up. And that as the cop must learn the hard way is the lot of well over half the human race. It might make us more miserable to reflect that intelligent malice also exists aplenty. Perhaps the shrink can help us there? One in ten, maybe. But we can always laugh. The more you kill me the more I survive. Poor Hitler, poor Stalin. Poor Herod.

One cannot use the word 'take possession' about subordinates. To inherit is likewise a dodgy concept.

Oldish mostly and set in their ways. So hasten slowly, Castang, because your two principal inspectors are older than you are. And one is called Campbell.

Hereabouts one says Cam-belle. Pronounce it hereabout like Cambronne. That's the legendary general who when summoned to surrender by the English said 'Merde', and if you start giving him orders he's likely to say the same to you.

Reddish hair going grey. False teeth that do not fit very well. But he knows his job.

The other principal inspector is called Steelpath. The names one meets around here . . . nobody is called Dupont or Durand, Martin or Simon. One hastens there more slowly still. A bullet-headed type with little to say; that highly laconic. Another one who knows his job. I don't think I'm cursed in my staff.

Two inspectors. A young chap called Louppes. Be wary of that one because at meeting time he buttered me up, which the others didn't dream of doing. A disagreeable trait but means nothing save that he's a bit more intelligent, a bit younger and less experienced, less secure. One mustn't take it seriously.

"Have we no girls?" asked Castang with an assumed irony. "We need girls."

Yes, we've a girl. The first day she appeared very belatedly, with a tale of work that had to be done. There's a new chef? I don't feel concerned the slightest scrap.

This indisciplined insolence, calculated to annoy, does annoy. Castang mentally prepares his shoe for a sound kick to be administered to Miss – what's her name? Varennes. Like the Flight to Varennes? Really? And her first name? Véronique.

Irritation gives way to amusement. This name, thought up by some callgirl agency, simply can't be true. Without even having seen her he is entertained.

He has 'made his number' with his Divisionnaire, a Monsieur Sabatier, a handsome, silver-haired gentleman of much presence. Very well-cut shirt with the collar slightly starched and a striped tie. A look of being admitted to the inner councils of IBM. A modern desk in a modern office, the telephones and the presentation pen set in a neat semicircle, white cuffs and onyx sleevelinks on the black morocco blotter.

He looks with clear still eyes at Castang, from whom he is receiving quite pleasant echo-soundings. He has looked this fellow up, put his ear to the ground, and had a confidential service note from Paris. Monsieur Sabatier is a thorough, careful person, proud of his eye which is a good one. This is said to be a bright and able chap. As one can indeed see. With a talent for getting into the shit. As is well to know. Not a high flyer, not a coming man, no political affiliations. Sent here to the backwoods to file his awkward corners down a little. Apart from that, a competent technician and a well-schooled cop. Not, all in all, a major embarrassment.

And gives a good impression. The trousers are of good quality and properly pressed, and his shoes polished: oh yes such things are important. Clean fingernails, sits up straight, speaks when he's spoken to. Monsieur Sabatier puts on his expression of well-humoured detachment.

"Don't pester me, and I won't pester you. That place has got a bit run down, and I'd like to see it with the reins gathered up a little. Don't expect to spend any money," smilingly showing a gold crown in the upper jaw. "You've some good people out there. Use them intelligently and I see no reason to expect trouble. With that said, welcome aboard."

Castang wondered now who the listening-post was, out here. Either Campbell or Steelpath were such obvious candidates that it was a fair bet it would after all be one or the other. There is also an over-age but usable mystery figure called Metz, said to be an economics expert and said too to be an enforcer. It might be him.

These speculations, pretty futile at this stage, are interrupted by Varennes, a noisy interrupter as can be seen at once, with a preposterous excuse for not appearing earlier.

She looks like a real policewoman. Castang will cease to mourn for busty Liliane left behind in Terra Nova. There had long been a fashion in the French cinema for police stories, and for female cops played by the more undernourished kind of French actress; wretched little things who'd never get past the physical in any real police force; not tit enough to fill a coffeecup and if you met them on a park bench you'd give them a stale bun: need it more than the ducks. Topheavy of eyelash, if remarkably sparse of hair.

VV is a solid six-footer: thighbones fit to hold up the dome of the Pantheon. Majestic, what Vera calls a Big Bayerische Maid. She will run though like Atalanta and one will be surprised by her grace. Thick heavy hair, of that colour called brassy because one doesn't believe that so much gold can be real: straight, shoulder length and owing nothing to artifice. Police women do not want long hair. which gets in the way and can be pulled. Not even a drunk would pull VV's hair: the knees are massive and the elbows sharp.

A week or so, settling into routine while discovering a lot of things and turning blind eyes to others, and Castang has learned that she can be relied on. Plenty of tooth and claw, too.

Monsieur Sabatier has not exaggerated. The office had got sloppy. In an 'antenna' you're permanently short of staff and you don't of course keep a twentyfour hour watch: you work office hours. Emergencies and interventions – these are for the Municipal Police. The PJ is engaged upon a number of mysterious Missions about which they're highly secretive: god damn, it's a nest of one-man private espionage systems. They've all got their own private phone numbers with elaborately coded passwords and the recorder going. It is a delicate piece of dentistry to scrape these teeth without touching too many nerves.

Directives get issued in officialese, about abuse of communications and keeping private business out of the office. The secretary, Madame Chose, is far too apt to consider herself the linchpin of the PJ. With this, avoid giving (especially senior) inspectors the notion you're some kind of spy satellite, snooping on their devices. My calls will be logged along with everyone else's. And in my absence from the office the duty officer will be kept informed of my whereabouts.

Getting rid of secrecy – and of laziness. Involving a lot of hard work, being in first and out last. Paying with your person. It wasn't just sitting on your bum waiting for the phone to ring, because it might be Lille with a complicated affair for Johnny-on-the-spot. The local police has not the equipment or the training for criminal brigade work. So suppose something funny happens. It means getting on to Lille, which has an 'Identité Judiciaire' branch equipped (well, some anyway) for scientific tests and lab work – we are sadly behind other countries in this respect. But they have the resources of a university medical faculty, a teaching hospital and pathologists, for example, with some forensic experience. Get something tricky, and you can ring up Monsieur Sabatier. Or rely upon the local doctor, who knows nothing about police procedure and cares less. He would like to give your younger inspectors a few notions about the handling of evidence.

They have learned to put an elaborate mask upon their character as well as their activities. Louppes with his greasy smile is not as odious a faux bonhomme as you had at first imagined. VV's brash vulgarity conceals a spirit more sensitive than she lets on. The big noisy chatterbox can be quiet, is sometimes gentle. He looked at her typing, interrogating.

Is he 'taking a fancy'? No. Nor would one call her pretty, though her features are nicely put together, and her movements harmonious.

23

But he is pleased when his jokes, greeted by the others in stolid silence, get a healthy squawk of laughter from Varennes. The BBMs (big bayerische maids) are, says Vera, highly physical, their bodily movement saying 'touch me'; but this one, thinks Castang without sentimentality, is an antique, unselfconscious – like the Spartan girls who wrestled naked with the boys and thought nothing of it. It is to be presumed – ? – that some man catches her from time to time. But he'll have to deserve it. She's no bath-towel. Warm from time to time, but neither moist nor clinging.

She's pretty crude: the zest alarms him. In a bar, shaking down a large lout she suspects of passing drugs to minors, the lout (who is caught in possession) does not dare try violence, but calls her a filthy great les, and gets a slap that sends him across the room.

"VV," says Castang later, "stand up for yourself, but try to avoid violence; I don't like it." For he is trying to get some transparency into this opaque set-up by being himself transparent. He wants to show them that he has no intention of staying behind a desk wrapped up in paper: that he is going to work with them. They are still wondering where the catch is; suspicious and touchy and one must be careful not to get familiar.

She is the first to show some spontaneity.

"Town's full of whores," she says now. "The professionals stay in the bars and are quiet: the Colleagues" – she means the town police – "have no trouble. But there's too many been out of work too long around here. There are girls hawking it on the street, and that's from hunger. They're taking home a pay cheque to Dad. If I see a fellow trying to cut himself a percentage from those, or that fat boy who's passing drugs to them, I'll twist his balls for him, I mean it."

"I quite agree," said Castang, "but don't hit them first." He likes her for showing warmth. The police girls are often colder, and more vicious, than the boys.

He has a standing instruction that for anything beyond the misdemeanour level he shall be notified forthwith. No matter what or when. He has to pay with his person, if he is ever going to get a grip hereabouts.

So that he is lucky when one fine day no more than two months after arrival, it happens to be Varennes who is 'duty desk'.

3 Nicely timed anyhow. It is a quarter past eight in the morning. He has only just arrived at work himself.

"There's a fellow," said VV, "ringing up saying he has a dead body." Ears pricked. "So I ask has he rung Police Secours and no he hasn't, because it's one for us, he says, and decided about it, and he has good reasons for not wanting publicity."

"He said that? And you recorded this?"

"That's right. PJ, he says he wants, like that, so naturally I ask who're you then, and what d'you know, it's Lecat."

"The name's familiar," not placing it.

"Big-biz," relishing it. "So you wanted excitement, you're going to get some, mate."

Castang looked for a retort to crush this bumptiousness, found none, said "Well now", and "Get the car." Himself he went and got the vademecum, his Go With Me. A suitcase sort of thing, the product of recent thought. It held a few basic tools for the observing, collecting, and preservation of evidence. This was the job of the IJ. But the IJ is a long way off, along with Divisional Commissaire Sabatier, and the Criminal Brigade, and a lot more folk all inclined to be sniffy about the skills and competence of a police officer out in the Provinces. There might come a time for them. He might well find himself choosing to call for the technical squad: he might be obliged to do so. So far he had a death, and apparently something odd about it. Care in handling evidence was valuable in itself. It might also be valuable in the cause of simple self-preservation.

For Monsieur Castang has known a number of instances when negligence or carelessness – at times deliberate – has left the legal authorities high and dry. With a moral certainty that a crime was committed, and a pretty shrewd guess about the author. And no proof either way. The said big wigs can then turn round, lift their leg, and piss on the investigating officer; thereby no doubt relieving their conscience. Out in the country, the measuring and recording of accident or incident is a job for the Gendarmerie. It does so happen that between the Police Judiciaire and this admirable corps of public servants no love is lost. So like a prudent man, he was taking some precautions.

"What do we know about this fellow?" VV was driving.

"That one had better be careful about treading on his toes," without undue sarcasm. "I haven't rung up the computer to know if we've his prints on file. He's about forty I suppose. Said to be very fast. Y'know, picture in the paper all the time. Owns a lot of things: machinery, and chemical manures, and that big wine company. Snaps up anything that seems sleepy or moribund. A real entrepreneur. Must be bloody rich. We've never had anything to do with him – that I know of." Which carefully over-casual remark told Castang what he needed to know: that the Important Gentleman had had the ear – and better – of his forerunner. And, quite as likely, knew sympathetic and respectful people up in Lille. And Paris too, no doubt. Well well, one would see. The gentleman hadn't rung Police Secours. Mm.

The house was outside the town, nowise to be called suburban. A large desirable piece of ground, showing a great interest in privacy: high walls and prickly fencing. They had to ring at a big wrought-iron grille. A chauffeur type at a lodge inside took a good look before making the electronic pass that opened this, without asking questions: had been told to expect them.

Driving up to the house other interests showed. Trees, horticulture. A second lodge must be for a gardener, with that big glasshouse adjacent. The house was of modern design, with a conservatory holding palms, and orange trees now set out on a terrace. Money! An interest in making it doesn't always mean one has it. This chap had both.

And the gent in question opened the door. Butlers or valets there might be but they'd been banished. Casual trousers, shirtsleeves, a slim waistline, a dishevelled look. Certainly he was fast, and certainly highly nervous, pacing around like a panther, but he had himself under good control.

"Commissaire Castang. This is Inspector Varennes." Keen, pale eyes took them in.

"I'm Félix Lecat. You're the boss? I had an indistinct memory of an older man."

"I took his place." No further comment. The man found it natural that 'the boss' should come in person.

26

"Good – no, wait, come in the kitchen; I'll make you some coffee or something. I've told the house servants to clear off. Because this is serious." He busied himself measuring coffee, putting it to grind, running water into the machine. Castang said nothing. The man was collecting himself, using the precise mechanical gestures to set his mind in order.

"There's explaining to do," pacing up and down the kitchen. "One says on the phone somebody's dead. It's my own wife . . . All right; you want it as coherent as may be. I'll do my best. I got home late, half past four or about, it's of no importance and I'll say why later. I don't know where she was nor what she was doing. I'd expect to find her in bed and asleep. In the dressingroom I noticed the light was on in her room – we each have our own. I thought it funny and wandered in. She's lying on her bed dressed and looking very unnatural." He took a deep breath. "I thought she might be drunk and I thought she might be drugged, both unlikely but that – you understand – was all I could find to account . . . So, I thought christ, she's in coma. I was set to call the Samu, the emergency wagon for reanimation. She seemed to be lying so awkwardly that I thought I'd better straighten her out, you know to let her breathe more easily. And then I saw she wasn't breathing." He stopped pacing, poured himself a cup of coffee, apologised, poured two more, sat down. "I haven't been to bed, of course. I realise that I'm probably still in a state of shock, but I'm a businessman, I know how to handle myself."

"You called a doctor," said Castang in a mild, reasonable voice.

"What would be the good? I don't need him. And it's too late for her."

"But she may not be dead, man. She may, as you say, be in coma."

Lecat shook his head sharply, with the quick glare of someone not used to being contradicted.

"We'll have to have one though. If only for official confirmation."

"Mr – Castang, wasn't it? I think. I've had time for that. I see what I know. I decide whether it's enough. I make up my mind. It was apparent to me that what we needed here was police."

"Why?" asked Castang.

"You'd better inform yourself, hadn't you?"

"So we will," peacefully. "I'd like though to get it clear, first, what you think we'll be looking at. If I've understood you, a sudden death involving violence. An overdose is violence. You think it was an accident? You think it possible she took her own life? You think it possible," still in his 'reasonable' tone, "that someone else did?" Lecat drank the coffee in small sips; it was still very hot. He was coiled tight, holding himself in. He put the cup back in the saucer.

"I don't speculate, Castang, about such things. If I did, I wouldn't have called you. That's your job – to speculate."

"So we'll look and I'll ask you to leave us alone. We won't be pinching any jewellery." The glare again. The remark is in bad taste. Which it was. But deliberate, to release the tension a bit. "You'd only be in the way. So lie down, go for a walk, do what you like."

"You're right. I'd be in the way. I'll be out the back," pointing. "Across the verandah, past the pool. When you want me."

"Don't take any pills."

"I never do."

"We'll have a talk later," said Castang. "I might have questions then." Lecat shrugged, stuck his hands in his pockets, walked away; making it slow, showing how tough he was. When he was out of earshot, "For a man acting funny, he's acting funny," offered VV, finishing her coffee.

"Shock takes people funny ways. Where now? Upstairs, we presume."

"Why didn't he call a doctor?"

"Some people don't like them. Think they know better. Resent the authority. Here? Here. First thing, camera." The basic tool, the 35-mm. Standard lens and wide-angle. Humourless, Castang got down on the floor, climbed on a chair. Quite the little detective.

"You ever had a homicide before, Véronique?"

"No, but I'm not frightened of dead bodies if that's what you mean."

"Good, because there's a nasty part. No doctor, so we'll have to do some of the job: don't think I like it. Cold, yes, not rigid yet, the jaw. Mm, smells of alcohol but didn't choke on her own vomit. Get it close up. Marks, maybe bruises, wasn't strangled but."

"What's that mean?"

28

"Don't know, have to have post mortem anyway. At least we'll have a record. People can sometimes die if you grab hold of them suddenly. Not to be technical, reflex vagal nerve. Time, time . . . Can't say we will but we might eventually get a notion from her inside temperature of how long she's been dead. I'm sorry but we have to . . ."

"I'm really enjoying this," through clenched teeth. Thermometer.

"Véronique, do you know how to take a vaginal smear?"

"I've had them too," grimly. "You mean she may have screwed?"

"Crude but accurate. We now see the advantage of having women on the squad. Don't think I'm enjoying this. Doing it may save us a great deal of grief. Thanks, that's the horrid part over. No sign of force?"

"No. Where did you learn this?"

"I made a doctor show me," briefly. "People don't realise quite how much police work is looking up behinds."

"I prefer them live." He doesn't tell her so but she's steadier than plenty of veterans. They tell the recruits at police school how much of the work is going to be 'corvée de chiottes': scrubbing out the shithouse. It might be thought that this was the usual instructor-sergeant's lurid phrasing, done to make the greenies' flesh creep. There isn't any exaggeration. The mild bourgeois ladies and gentlemen who write amiable little detective stories full of corpses have never seen what Dickens called a demd moist unpleasant body: they wouldn't write with quite such tittering superficiality if they had. Today's world, remarkably insouciant about literary or cinematic death, is revoltingly squeamish about the real thing. Never before have we been so frightened of death. This is a classic post hoc propter hoc. We'd like to believe death doesn't exist. Draw a prudish, disinfectant-soaked veil. Call the cops. Let them clear up the mess. It's what they're for.

"Put in a new roll. Snap everything you see, every detail of the entire room. Now, how's your shorthand?"

"I did learn something at school beyond how to play with myself."

"Then I'll dictate, you write, and any observation you disagree with, say so." Homicide procedure is taking detailed and accurate notes. It's best to have two sets and check the one against the other. Even the trained professional is not the perfect eyewitness.

" 'Blood follows gravity and that can be the beginning of lividity and those funny little things can be a kind of skin haemorrhage you get with asphyxia. The path lab will know when they see the photos. Right, turn her over now.' "

"Sex was never like this before," said VV.

"So now the notebook again and the crossed knees and the skirt just covering because we don't want Lecat's mind to wander off the facts."

He has had a shower or a swim, because his hair is still wet. He looks tired round the eyes but healthy, and above all more relaxed. And Castang, soul of formality, goes into the professional patter. "This is a preliminary investigation. No evidential value. The notes are just for our memory. This is a violent death. Accident, suicide or homicide, we are careful to draw no premature conclusions. We have to have the doctor, who will certify death and give us his probably ignorant opinion as to cause. It remains an unexplained death by violence, which means a mandatory post-mortem examination. That's right, pathology laboratory. Likewise the Procureur de la République." A slight frown at this, coupled with a slight smile: a murmur came from the thin flexible mouth of which Castang caught ". . . utter bullshit."

"Who names a judge of instruction. Who in turn might come and take a look, as the law requires." When people said 'what utter bullshit' Castang would no longer say 'I quite agree': that would be held an indiscretion. But he had said this kind of thing so often that shades of irony crept in. Lecat was formidable, not least because there wasn't much he missed. ". . . official enablement to enquire and interrogate. You're not on oath. Let's say it's a help if your considered recollections are as accurate as possible. It isn't an interrogation." People who tell the truth to police officers deserve the Legion of Honour, rather more than most of those who are given it. "We don't need any lawyers at this stage."

"When I want any lawyers I'll let you know in writing, in triplicate and with fortyeight hours' notice," said Lecat mildly enough.

"Pending expert, detailed medical evidence, there are no indications of an accident, Monsieur Lecat. There is nothing consistent with suicide. There are signs of violence on your wife's body. These antiquated formalities may strike us both as ludicrous but somebody killed her and it's going to be my job to find out who."

Perhaps it is the 'business' habit; a scepticism pushed to the limit of believing nothing and nobody. The fellow is not worried enough. His wife is dead and now that the initial shock has passed he sits there looking faintly amused.

They were sitting by the pool. Pale green tiles for those who wanted to swim: wood and canvas chairs for those who just sat. It was like being on a movie set, resting between takes. VV sat secretarial and composed, showing a lot of leg but her notebook primly on her lap. Feeling a sense of unreality Castang went and telephoned to the Proc. There was a long silence on the line: a distant voice said, "Who did you say?"

"Monsieur Félix Lecat."

"I see . . . well, you'll exercise prudence. And discretion, Monsieur le Commissaire." A fine thing it would be to get told to exercise imprudence.

Let's just put a hypothesis for the sake of argument, thought Castang, walking back with a heavy tread. That this chap has killed his wife. Would that explain things at all? It appears that he is a notable in the commercial world, in the context of France and indeed of Europe; even Castang has heard of him. Which in a town this size makes him a very big fish indeed.

Oh, it has happened; still happens; in towns bigger than this. A notable commits an imprudence. Now the notables in provincial towns form a small exclusive club. Less than formerly. The world of Balzac, where the Commissaire of Police is married to the Judge's sister-in-law, who is the Proc's cousin; and they all assemble once a week to play bridge in the salons of the Préfecture – that, no. But one can still find a family atmosphere in shared interests. A few telephone calls, an elderly timid judge of instruction, a mysterious fudging and mislaying of material evidence. Against this there is only one real safeguard and that is the Press. And the Press . . . leaves much to be desired.

Richard knew how to handle these people. But Richard was a Divisional Commissaire of great experience.

Whoever killed Madame Lecat, it had better be a burglar after her jewellery. Or – or – dammit, a dismissed servant with a grudge. Or practically anyone provided it be quick, easy, embarrass nobody and the Commissaire can gain commendation by the prompt arrest of a penniless somebody, preferably one with a drug habit.

Véronique excused herself: that is to say "Where's the toilet?" Lecat, not bothered at all by the absence of servants, went off to the kitchen and appeared again with a drinks cart, tall misty glasses going clink-clink, a vacuum jug of – fresh – orangejuice. Left to himself, Castang had a strong wish to spit in the pool. Scriptwriters' conference, somewhere in a canyon off Mulholland Drive. Sunny Cal. The sun of early June in the province of Artois was slanting in, surprisingly hot. Lecat pressed a button: a canvas awning spread itself: Lecat smiled.

4 A green telephone rang and Lecat answered. He listened a moment and said "Let her in, idiot" and to the company, smilingly, "Madame le Juge will be vexed. Fool of a gateman thought she might be selling encyclopedias." This lack of tact did not appear to oppress him any more than the facts so far elucidated. The estate was very well guarded indeed. There were no indoor servants present at night. Madame Lecat, name of Marguerite, had a large and varied acquaintance, about this her husband knew little and apparently cared less. She might have been anywhere with anyone. And Monsieur Lecat had spent the evening and the early part of the night in Brussels: a matter easily verified.

The doorbell rang and they went as a committee of reception to greet Madame le Juge. Surprise for Castang. It was not the elderly throat-clearer of his imagination. It was a small, slim woman who had got out of a small, fairly dirty Seat car. She looked to be the same age as VV, who would be around twentyeight. She wasted no time.

"Alice Jimenez, Juge d'Instruction," holding out her hand. "You'll be Monsieur Lecat. My sympathies, and apologies. Good morning, Commissaire, we haven't as yet met."

"Castang. Inspector Varennes, PJ." She was dressed simply, even shabbily. She had not brought her clerk, she had no official briefcase, she hadn't even a handbag. Perhaps she'd left it in the car.

"So to work. I'm due at the office. This is a formality," to Lecat. To Castang, "You have a presumption of homicide if I understand."

"It's still to be determined but it looks that way."

"So there are indications and these are visible? Well, you'd better let me see. We're taking you on your word, Commissaire. You're in no two minds about this?"

"We'll have to wait for the conclusions of the police pathologist but I'd be surprised if his opinion differed."

"You haven't asked for the technical squad from headquarters?"

"I'll defer to your judgment, Madame. To spare Monsieur Lecat a lot of officialdom, perhaps some premature publicity, it might be enough if I say I have made a fairly thorough examination and a photographic record."

"I see. I'll look," with decision. And did, with VV to open doors. Castang and Lecat stood in the hallway with their arms folded. Busy with their thoughts.

"I agree with you," coming down again."Well, I'll speak to the Procureur. And we'll await, shall we, your preliminary report, Commissaire." She looked at Lecat. "One must not anticipate or speculate. We'll have to have her taken away now, and post-mortemed I'm afraid, and a seal put on the room." She looked at her wrist, at a square man's watch. "Perhaps, Monsieur Castang, since these things take a lot of time, to type up, and get" – did she too practise irony? – "into the proper wording, you might have the kindness to drop in and see me. At the Palais. At midday, if you could manage that? I'd appreciate it. Your servant, Monsieur Lecat." No irony. "I must run." And did.

"Brisk," said Lecat drawling a little. "Concise. Admirable."

"She's my legal superior," said Castang. "Comment would be improper."

" 'm I under suspicion, d'you think?"

"Ask her. She'll decide. In due course."

"I'm asking you."

"I don't think, till I've something to think with."

"Not wanting to be improper . . ."

"If the autopsy turns up homicide then everyone's on the same footing. You too."

"Okay. I know where I stand now. I liked the way you didn't try to hog the press. Owe you one for that."

"Bound to come out soon. And when they hear who it is . . ."

"Yes. Let's not misunderstand. I'm used to the press. Publicity is bread and butter. Get me right, it isn't lack of feeling. A simple professional judgment. You'll get them forming a logjam outside your door."

"I'm not looking for the great big hand with a view to personal advancement. Count on me, if I can count on you. If your office starts leaking little items about bewildered hick cops . . ."

"It won't. I know how to handle journalists. Then I make it I owe

34

you two. It might so fall out, I could say a word in an ear privately, wouldn't do the career harm. And if you understand," pointing a finger at VV, "yours neither, my girl."

"I'm not your girl, and I don't like fingers pointed at me."

"Good for you and I apologise. Right, Commissaire, if you've all you want at this stage, I'm like the judge, I'm due at the office. I'll leave word there and at the gate here, to give you access to whatever and whoever you want."

"I'll let you know," said Castang, "about funeral arrangements."

And when it's all done with, at last . . . The police do not think in terms of O eloquent, just and mighty Death. Administrative Death, rather.

"These maids, Véronique, you'll get after them. The gardener's wife, apparently, is the caretaker: you'll find all you need there. Better drop me in the town, first. I've got to go to the Palais – Madame le Juge seems to be the zealous type."

"Mademoiselle Jimenez." Emphasis a trifle sarcastic, so that he cocked the brow.

"Tell me." Since he'd been a thought taken aback himself. And let's see how VV is at a character sketch.

"Oh, she's ruffled our feathers a couple of times. She can be awkward, but she's straight, and once you know her . . ."

"The point," patiently, "is that I don't know her."

"Not just Spanish but workingclass and it's all based on that. The parents could maybe barely read and write so there's a biggish area of touchiness."

"Chip on shoulder? Poor but bright girl makes good?"

"No, that's not fair – too crude. She makes no bones about it – carries it lightly, you could say. You need to know, though, because she can be pretty outspoken, and her opinions are bright scarlet now and then. She's a thorn in the eye of a few of the old schnoks on the bench, as you can imagine." Castang could imagine. What he didn't quite get was the thinking behind the Procureur's naming her to what might well turn out a pitfall job. Hoping that she would fall into the pit? Too obvious, no? Still, Castang had known prosecutors, even Advocates-General, who were silky on the surface and pretty crude underneath.

*

"At your service, Madame."

"Call me what you like, if you feel that the dignity of the office requires it." She'd sent her clerk for lunch. "There's a pub round the corner where I often go for a sandwich. Or is that beneath the dignity of the Commissaire?"

"I'm new here, so show the way."

"It's quiet; we won't be overheard and they're used to me."

Alice Jimenez had pale, rather bad skin, a shiny nose, irregular teeth; eyes as intelligent, and as beautiful, as any he had seen. Dark brown hair, long and well looked after. A tartan pleated skirt on the meagre bottom half, a brown pullover (rather heavy for the time of year) on the likewise meagre top and a big leather belt holding the two together. The pullover, an expensive one, was darned at the elbows and she had a ladder in one stocking. Her shoes were low-heeled, plain, and needed polish. Her hands and feet were small. She appeared scarcely more than a child. She wore no perfume and no makeup. Sitting by her side she simply smelt clean. She was carrying, now, a handbag; saddle leather, much used. Rummaging for a cigarette she spilt a good deal of the contents, keys and things, and Spanishly a tube of toothpaste. He held her a flame, lit his own and said "Two lung cancers" peacefully.

"But look at all those anal cancers among the ones who don't."

Liking her he thought, well, let's provoke.

"What other vices have you got?"

"This is ridiculous, I'm the Examining Magistrate. However, I know more about you than you suppose, so let's be fair. I survive, and I try not to be sentimental about justice."

"You came out top of the class, in Bordeaux." The Ecole de Magistrature.

"Yes," thinking, as she has so often thought, about this. "I had a very strong motor, I had no idea how strong, chewing up all that mouldy old hay as though it were fresh lettuce. Been told I was bright at school, but a child has no idea. I only knew I was fiercely motivated. I dare say you've been told? My father is an illiterate labourer, my mother was a barefoot goat girl. And I was a redhot little anarchist: I've dropped a lot of that. It's a handicap, coming out top. Envies, resentments.

36

"I had to learn it was both good and bad. It's the hardest, to learn how bad you are.

"Most young magistrates out of school get shovelled into Instruction for four or five years: to knock their corners off. Being top, I had various choices. I thought of Bench. As Children's Judge. It's too hard, frankly, you've too much power. I didn't have the courage.

"I thought of becoming a prosecutor. That's very tempting, you know. But looking, there's so much mandatory crap. You find yourself continually pleading vindictive nothings that you can't duck, on behalf of a governmental obligation towards constraint of the subject. That's what anarchism is about: arche, the rule, is a bad substitute for people incapable of governing themselves and increases their incapacity.

"So I chose instruction after all, exactly as though I'd come out bottom, and that did me a lot of good. I'm learning.

"It's said to be so powerful: the horrible cliché of course is that Napoleon said it was the most powerful job in France and that's another huge truth/nontruth: learning the inseparability of things . . ." drinking her beer, carefully dosing mustard on to her ham.

"A judge of instruction – a good idea but a bad fact, say the English, since they've never had the idea, and any idea they've never had . . . well, their minds work differently to ours. Since the praxis is bad they're right to condemn it? – halftruth. Invert it and can we make a bad idea into a good fact?"

"Is it a bad idea?"

"It's maybe a false good idea. You can't get over the antithesis, cops and magistrates, it's the surgeon and the physician, physics and metaphysics: d'you believe in angels?"

"From time to time."

"Yes, it's easier, in Spain. Satan, being Chief-angel, fell from pride, as we're told. And so do judges of instruction.

"It's fine, being an angel. I am both prosecutor and defence, I accuse and I excuse. Liberties and constraints go through me, there's nothing worse than a bad judge. They want to do the cops' job. They think they know better. Those fellows, said Stendhal, who cannot see power unless it is cloaked in insolence. Law isn't very important really. One does have to have a bit of commonsense. So what are you making of friend Lecat?"

"That maybe he didn't kill his wife even if we think he did. And that it's going to be quite hard enough to find out even without the press." She laughed.

"The press is like the judge of instruction, the blessing and the curse. The difference is that there's rather more of it. We're going to get on all right, Commissaire. I know very little about Lecat, except that he's a coldhearted bastard: another one afflicted by the sin of pride. There isn't anything that gives them pause, you know. It's because they hold life cheap that they're all so fervent about the death penalty. She doesn't like the rich, you'll say. True, true. Nothing to do with socialism. Nothing even to do with religion, though it's too easy to forget how much law has to do with religion. But it's very difficult to do justice to the rich. They've stolen so much of the justice for themselves, you see, and you have to take some away before you can give it back."

Vera had found a model. When accosted in the supermarket this girl, well and indeed excessively brought up, had been struck rigid with horror. I'd have been the same myself, thought Vera, and was patient to the point of a formal visit to Mum, to establish bona fides. A fearful experience, with coffee, cake, and small talk. Upon learning that this was the Madame of Monsieur le Commissaire Mum became so enthusiastic that brakes had to be put upon her impetuous desire to please.

The girl was selfconscious, which infected Vera who had not drawn from a nude model since life-class days in Bratislava when she was still in her teens: a sad hash got made of the first efforts. Monique had now got cosy, indeed alarmingly familiar – going while naked for a pee, which was a bit much. They had afternoon sessions, when Lydia was at school and the baby asleep, and it was unlikely that Henri would walk in, but Vera found a kimono-thing and left it within reach.

"Well, he might. I couldn't very well stop him."

"Ooh. Would he be shocked?"

"No. He's seen a lot of naked girls. The elbow a little less – right. A lot that really is shocking." Much more so than Monique's tendency to part her legs when comfortable.

"But he might wonder what my bare ass was doing in his sittingroom."

"Perhaps. Mine too. Live and let live."

"You mean it's no business of his, you'd say."

"More likely what he'd say."

"Does it matter if I talk?"

"No." It did rather, since Monique was incurably talkative. But she held the pose well, and if forbidden to talk would get bored and fidget. As it was –

"Straighten your back a little more – one moment, I'll get that cushion a bit further down. Try not to curl your toes up." When it became wearisome she let the girl walk about, to rest her, and invented quick impressionist poses to amuse her. The drawings were not good but one had to stick to it, to learn.

"Here," putting the baby's bath on a chair, "these are the days before bathrooms. One foot on the floor and the other – right, as though you were washing it. Put the towel round your shoulders." She giggled at first, but caught on.

This of course was the moment when Henri did walk in, standing transfixed at running his nose – so to speak – up against this nubile bottom.

Castang carried this off, with only a fleeting irritation at Vera's tiresome tendency to keep things secret. The girl squeaked and upset the tub: fortunately there was no water in it. Castang picked up the kimono, handed it politely to her.

"Don't let me be a constraint. Only came to change my shirt, be gone in a tick."

"I don't mind," said Monique gallantly. "You made me jump, that's all." But stood there of course like a wooden doll, all awkward angles. He looked at the easel. There was the pleasant smell of paints in the room. The canvas began to have recognisable features. He felt pride, as though he'd done it himself.

"Oh, a maja desnuda, that's nice, but I won't stop the two of you working, I've plenty." He took a packet of cigarettes off the bookcase and vanished.

"I'm sorry," said Monique. "Shall I go back to the pose?" scrambling into her cushions. "I felt sort of constrained. He is a man after all."

"So you should feel constrained, from time to time – good, keep it like that – but he sees you with a detached eye, the same as mine." Boring old sex, but even painted by me she's supposed to come out looking desirable. You don't paint a nude just to look like a chair. One can always scrape the canvas. But I rather hope she won't.

Even if I was bare-ass, right down to my puss, Monique thinks to herself digesting her fright, nobody worries about that now. All the girls on the screen . . . well, if I were paid that much . . . but he must have thought me a right ninny.

Vera paints busily. Trained by austere methods to use few colours and no carmine she is not about to confuse modesty with prudery. Czech art schools . . . or the gymnastics class either. Displays either of emotion or bottom were visited with a bleak look. The whole thing was learning selfcontrol. All this chat about liberty, in schools and everywhere else – why, the very word 'schooled' . . .

"Liberty is an illusion." Monique might not be the world's brightest but didn't need it spelt out.

"Mum goes on and on. One gets so fed up. You know, decency."

"Now if I were to paint you with your pants on, that would be indecent, wouldn't it? It isn't what you show but what you suggest."

"Ever do gymnastics? Well, you've seen it on the screen. Even if you fall, you get up instantly, if you're in pain you don't show it, you salute at once with your arms to show you're free and in balance. That's a rule. You've a choice about some things and none at all about others."

Expression of puzzlement: Vera tried again.

"Say you suddenly get furious with me and sling an ashtray at my head. You didn't mean to kill me but you do. My husband marches in and puts handcuffs on you. What do you say?"

"I don't know."

"You'd say you hadn't done it on purpose, the way children always say. He'd answer that not being a child you can't use that as an excuse. You might say I'd made you furious and you couldn't help yourself. No good either. You might even say that everybody's free and you were only expressing your emotions. The answer is that you can't. That's a rule. We have to accept constraint. There isn't any choice. He might feel sorry for you but he wouldn't have any choice either. If you give your word you've got to keep it."

"Yes," said the girl, not knowing whether to be bored or not. Tja, thought Vera, refusing to sentimentalise it, whether she shows it to me – or Henri – or whether she puts it on a plate for some sweaty boy, my job is to paint it along with the rest.

Castang got back at 'a reasonable hour'. You have to keep yourself in control even of a homicide: there's no point in letting yourself get overworked. It happens anyhow, whether you like it or not. It's a rule, that you pay an extra percentage of injustice. Much like the rule that supermarkets put their prices up to cover the losses from shoplifting.

"Complicated doings," he groaned, changing his shoes – after all, what was there to do about it? This damn sandcoloured carpeting went nicely with the dark blue and off-white colours, but showed up every mark . . . As with the polished floor in the north, you put on slippers when you come in. Another rule.

Vera was not sentimental about homicides. Nor about any police work. Nor about being a cop wife. Nor about being a Czech exile. He had once brought her, well-meaning in a hideous if pathetic way, a book by one such: dubbed a genius by the newspapers. She read it, with an effort, and said she preferred watching the ice-hockey team.

"No good?"

"People have to make a living. But the place is full of these shysters, coming here and sleeping with tenyearold girls, on account of they're geniuses. Goodbye to the entrancing seacoast of Bohemia." He'd understood. It was like those little books of Lucciani's – this was still at the 'old house'. All those Los Angeles cops worrying about getting drunk and being neurotic. Enough to make you throw up and retire to Santa Barbara: what was Woody Allen's line? – that they've no garbage here because they've turned it all into television programmes . . .

Conversation now, over supper.

"So you've a nude. Very difficult?"

"Very. Probably no good. But one has to try."

"Where did you find it?"

"In the supermarket."

"You'd done babies."

"Yes, but one never gets them really right. They're nice to draw but that's just the trouble; they're mine, one is too involved."

"You could ask me."

"You! You'd never sit still. And can one ask officers of police to take their clothes off' Any more than I could take my own clothes off and sit in front of the mirror. Not so much narcissism as worrying about one's hair being dirty and that awful hip bone, and why are my tits sort of soggy: it doesn't work."

"Well, she seems a nice girl, and she's tits like Aphrodite."

"If you were painting her you'd be on top there in no time." One of those scratchy little spurts of jealousy.

"We've each our own sorts of detachment," getting up to clear away plates.

He must have been overtired because he found himself lying in bed, not sleeping, and his mind running. Not upon Lecat. That would never do. But as usual in such moments, upon a wellworn and painful set of memories.

Vera had been a turbulent teenager. Brought to France on the gymnastics team, but left on the substitutes' bench for being vain, and sulking. Ideas in her head about politics, and choosing freedom, but really she had flounced out in an attack of vexation and piqued vanity. He'd been there on crowd control, had her flung at him and felt sorry for her, because now she was in trouble. A fatal sentimentalism: he hadn't told her to turn straight round and go back because one thought better in the morning of these headstrong performances. Instead he'd wrapped her up in a blanket and given her a cup of cocoa: she was, of course, fatally pretty as well as pathetic.

She'd been so incredibly grateful. It had never occurred to her that a strange country, where she had neither family nor friend, might not be particularly pleased with this embarrassing gift. In fact, she would have been sent straight back like a parcel, if no one had taken responsibility for her.

And in a further onrush of sentimentality, he had. He had known a journalist who got a Russian girl out this way. A marriage certificate signed by a Consul, giving her status, and divorce papers the week following: a simple bureaucratic three card trick. But by then he was in love with her. And constrained.

For she had not caught up with the idea of a debt unpaid. To the man who saved and protected she'd give and never stop giving. An innocent resolve, seen by her in the crude terms that were all she knew, spending one's last breath in loving, darning socks and cooking dinner. That might have lasted a year or so, one supposes.

God or whoever, some sentimentally-ironic term like the President of the Immortals, thought up a better trick when she fell off the bars and hurt her spine. Poor girl, she sat in the wheelchair begging him to divorce her because she'd never be anything but a dead weight. One refuses these offers from no sense of nobility but because there is no choice.

So she'd had years more of having to be grateful and came to doubt her own generosity, thinking it mere obstinacy. And the obstinacy helped her. 'I'm going to walk, I'm going to.' The spinal cord was not broken; jammed in some way. Doctors will tell you anything that comes into their head.

Now she walked: good joke: little-orphan-annie threw away her crutch and danced, after years of devotion from a Good Man: very Victorian piece of fiction.

Vera slept deeply. A strong character, she had an individual way of winding herself tightly into bed 'like a dog' after which there was no budging her. At her most exasperating she has a monstrous sense of the comic. Refuses to take herself too seriously. One loves her because . . . what else can one do?

**5** As they'd started, so they'd go on. There are enquiries needing a hundred men, with telexing and telephoning all over the country, and sacks of mail with helpful suggestions from the public, all in a great glare and shout of publicity: such is the life of the Banditry brigades, whose commissaires simply love being interviewed on television. And there are quiet enquiries 'in the interests of families' where two is enough. Castang found himself with Varennes and was well content. They had an old car. Police forces everywhere in France have been kept short of money for a hundred years and are lamentably ill-equipped. They lament; everyone else is indifferent.

We are backward because we are a poor country. So we buy our cars secondhand from Albania. Everyone else can have fleets of BMWs. But you see, we have Intelligence to go with our old rattletraps. You have only a radio while we have our own built-in nightingales to sing to us.

VV drives, for Castang's mind tends to wander.

"Lecat's office. At the wine business." Another town, but not very far away.

"We'll need some petrol."

"We may have no petrol but we have ideas." This preposterous slogan was invented at the time of the oil crisis some years ago.

"Leave me out for a start: not paid to have ideas."

Castang gave his attention to the landscape, which was dramatic. A June day in northern France. Not a stupid day of unending drizzle nor that, equally stupid, of blazing sun; but a huge sky of towering dark cloud that piled higher and higher out there ahead. Another mass had gathered behind them.

"Going to piss down," says VV.

"Good."

"Yes, but the windscreen wipers will fall off again."

The road climbed a hill and in the distance they can see the town, upon which sunlight sheds a magical grey and gold harmony. The green of foliage, still young in early June, makes of the woods enchanted forests. The hell with discipline, with homicides and with Commissaires of Police.

His mutter draws a sideways glance from VV, mingling alarm and respect, sympathy and derision. Discipline must be restored.

"Let's hear about the maids," in official tones.

"Right. Well, there's only one man who works inside the house: that's the cook. Didn't catch him, gone fishing. There are three maids, who live out. The housemaid, Perrine, is a married woman, works nine to five: does the cleaning and things like answering the phone and the door.

"Madame, deceased, had a personal maid, also a married woman but older, hours irregular but mostly daytime, does – or did – the sewing, ironing, Madame's hair and underclothes, and so forth. Little beady-eyed blackavised soul, name of Victorine."

"Such real maids' names they sound invented."

"They're real enough. There's nothing much to say about them and they've little enough to say for themselves. Plain, honest, hard-working women. They both claim to have noticed nothing unusual. No irregularity in Madame's appearance or behaviour. Their mouths were pretty tight. No juicy gossip on offer. I'd say they know which side their bread is buttered. They saw little of the boss, but show a healthy respect. Both he and her were said to be autocratic, impatient, short-tempered: but on the whole kind, generally considerate, occasionally generous, he more than her. 'You had to take the rough with the smooth.' They were hard worked but well paid. If he was bastardly he'd make up with a joke and a big tip. She was the real madam and didn't even part with her old clothes. But they'd no ill to say of her."

"Good, and the third? I bet her name is Céline."

"Not far out, she's Caroline. Younger, unmarried. Thin, plain, serious. She's the gardener's daughter and lives in a cottage on the grounds with her ma and pa. You understand, I haven't made any big thing of interrogation. Just to get the picture, situate and get their routines clear."

"Quite right."

"Well, she comes in the morning, to help the cook, sort of kitchenmaid, and in the evenings she dresses up, after the other has left, answers doors and if there are guests waits at table."

"And were there any guests?"

"Don't interrupt with the obvious," sharp and female. "No there

45

weren't. That's just the point: often she's up till midnight, so the arrangement is that when Monsieur and Madame are out she gets an early evening and that's what she had. Went to the pictures, she's a great movie-goer; not much fun in her life I'd guess."

"And the other two?"

"I wish you wouldn't interrupt when I'm trying to concentrate," irritably. "They went off in the ordinary course of events. Perrine in the c. of e. knows nothing. Victorine being a personal maid would know her madam's little ins and outs pretty well. The lady simply said she was going out. She was wearing an ordinary day dress, which seems to indicate she wasn't going anywhere special. The one we found her in, so she hadn't changed later. Same goes for hair, jewellery, whatever. I described this and was told it was what she usually wore."

"Good work, Véronique," meaning it. "What are their reactions to learning of her death?" They were coming into the town. She knew her way: he didn't.

"Shocked, bewildered; it seemed genuinely. The usual how-could-such-a-thing-be-possible. An intruder, a robber? Chorus of agreement. But it's just not possible. The place is super-protected. Electronic whatnots all round the perimeter and closed-circuit television. The gateman is the chauffeur, that's the clown we saw. Even when he's not there the gate and the approach is watched by the caretaker, that's Caroline's ma: she's said to be very conscientious but I haven't seen her yet."

"So summing up?"

"Big mystery, mate. Happens in the best of houses. We're really going to have the press on our back when this gets out. As it will – has, no doubt."

"Of course. Be waiting for us this evening."

"So here we are," parking on a kerb where she had seen a gap and reversing smartly in. "So anything special you want?"

"Just eyes and ears. Be my conscience."

"Be my guest," said VV, acid.

Another town, but they resemble one another. Their names are in the history books. Battled over interminably and they have that look. Hitler's generals, and Hindenburg's, went straight through them. Rarely were they that lucky: burning and sacking, loot and rape have been the norm. You find apathy and cynicism: the only wonder is that there isn't more of both.

This people likes to eat, and to drink. They 'know a good glass'. Small wonder that Les Etablissements Barthélémy has been here a long time, with a solid reputation for giving value for money. A Name, like Boussac: people spoke of 'Monsieur Charles' the way they did of 'Monsieur Marcel' and when Félix Lecat snapped the firm up cheap people said that would never have happened in the old man's time. Simple people don't understand: they said the grandchildren had been brought up soft, and didn't know the names of their own employees. This talk about liquidity and cash flow: what does it all mean? Say this much for Lecat; the bastard is a sharp bastard and knows how to handle people. He has sure laid off a lot of staff. Times are hard, and when were they ever anything else?

The building is in typical style: solid, grimy brickwork, with the florid audacity of the Victorian entrepreneur. The warehousing of wine lends itself well to this boldness and arrogance; like railway arches. Splendid arcades of generous breadth and noble proportion.

No time alas for betjemanesque transports. The entrance had a large plain brass plate kept highly polished, with 'Vins Barthélémy' in curly lettering. One has almost forgotten the meaning of the word copperplate. The hall inside from grand and gloomy had become oddly cute. The old shop counter, magnificent and flamboyant piece of immense black cherry, was now a tasting bar. The wine business is easily made picturesque. Barrels and crates, a whole museum of antique glass and faience. The electronic cash register marries happily with old counting-house tools; the scales and the scoop for weighing coins.

A cleaning woman in an overall said, "The hostess will be here in a minute."

"Police," said VV wanting no hostesses. "Manager."

"I'll tell Monsieur Guillaume," unimpressed and unhurried.

Monsieur Guillaume when he appeared was a handsome fortyish, trim of figure in a business suit and waistcoat. Still, it was cool in here. An individual touch was given by his wearing an Anthony-Eden hat. Perhaps he was bald.

The announcement of police didn't bother him either.

"Ah, yes, the Patron told me to expect you. He's not here, alas: gone to Toulouse. Back this evening, maybe. The little plane, you know." A white hairy hand made an arc in the air showing how trivial was the distance between here and Toulouse. "Madame Charlotte, that dusting should have been finished a long time ago. So I'll have to do instead. Unless, of course, your business is personal."

"It is and it isn't," said Castang, used to this fishing. "But it is official, and it's confidential."

"Shall we go in the office then?"

This too was period, with panelling in the fine pale mahogany one could still get in 1850 and original furniture of the same, so that the IBM machinery drew rather pointed attention to its discreet palegrey self. Monsieur Guillaume sat down in a buttoned black leather chair, pulled an ear, thought of taking his hat off – balding would be the right word; the black curly hair had slid half way – smiled pleasantly and said,"The girl will be here in a moment: what would you like to drink? We've plenty!" a phrase as old and polished as the panelling.

"Not just now," to VV's regret, but the reserve held out promise. "Perhaps you haven't heard that Madame Lecat was found dead this morning."

"Great God . . . He never said a word. Behaved exactly as usual. Admittedly, that's quite typical, what I would expect . . ."

"Then I dare say that he would like you to keep the information to yourself until it comes out."

"Monsieur uh, Castang; we understand silence here. Believe me." I do. But . . .

"The press will almost certainly have it by this evening."

"One moment. Ah, here's Mademoiselle Martin. Sure there's nothing I can offer you? No? Thank you then, Aurélie." A stately figure Aurélie, and with splendid looks. Merits attention but to quote Vera 'blow your nose and avoid lechery'.

"So the question is, have you seen her or heard from her? – essentially yesterday, but make it the last couple of days. We'd like to know something of her state of mind as well as her movements."

"Nothing at all. She didn't make a habit of dropping in. We do, I should say did, see her quite often since there's no real cellar up at the house – the Patron thinks it a needless duplication. So that for entertainment which is – was – frequent she'd come in and consult about anything she wanted. The last time might be ten, twelve days ago. Absolutely as usual."

"And Monsieur Lecat himself?'

"Well I've answered that, haven't I? He could have any number of things on his mind, and might or might not mention them to me. He keeps things in compartments."

"I don't want you to invent things but I'm presuming you know him well enough to recognise any small sign of fatigue, preoccupation, nervousness."

"No. He's a very, uh, controlled person."

"So I should imagine."

"Let us understand one another, Commissaire, he's not that cold inhuman figure save in public. With people he knows and trusts, he's open, uh, hilarious – often very funny."

"That's what I mean. Was there any alteration in that?"

"To be quite honest, no. The only other person, call him a familiar, old Canetti, a fixture here, father and son seventy years between them; you could ask him. I'll show you around, we're a happy little family here . . ." Castang realised that there was no way of avoiding a practised sales' talk and a tour intended to dazzle.

First, the Thing, which sat in the back office, able to tell you where every item of stock was, day-or-night 'all over Europe'; how and where it sold; putting in its reorders. Dazzling and boring. There were a few human beings left too.

"Martin runs the shop, local sales – very good girl, got it up here in the head. But the real heart of the operation's in the handling and packing, wine's lovely stuff but a nightmare to move, bulky and fragile, heavy and delicate, costly: how d'you robotise that? And anything of any age must be handled manually which accounts for the prices you dear people complain of – now we'll look at the cellars: they're really something."

Yes. Vaults: sumptuous.

"We do well with Germany. Belgium naturally – they understand Burgundy there. Holland of course. England for Bordeaux: those dear people think they still own Aquitaine, which encourages them in that delusion.

"We've depots in Paris and Lyon naturally but the best stuff is right here." Castang, no more than tolerably bored with the prephylloxera chat, wondered why he took so much trouble.

"And here is our head cellarman, Monsieur Canetti. Always known as Canette. Now find something good for our friends, mm?" I've never heard the police called that before, but rank has its privileges.

The silent elderly gentleman did his act with the candle-flame and the pipette and the little tulip glasses. Castang who knows nothing about wine and cares less is surprised by the wonderful smell of the magic potion. "Good!" Mr Canetti has a knowing, crooked little smile.

"Hoo, spiders!" says VV and gets her share of the patter: fifteenth-century cobwebs, practically Gobelin tapestries.

The tour brings them back to the office where Monsieur Guillaume, still talking, suggests a nice glass of port, a nice little cigar, and – "Hallo, Roland, what can I do for you?" A young man has appeared in the doorway, frowns upon the company, makes hand signals indicative of urgency and confidentiality. "Excuse me, Commissaire, just one sec."

The girl Aurélie brought in a silver tray with a decanter. Her movements are quiet and self-possessed: she has a lovely smile. A very pretty girl – but Castang's attention has been caught by the newcomer. Who intends that you should look at him. A handsome young man, beautifully dressed and a bit too much so: creamy summer suit, luscious silk scarf. Castang sits lazily, draws on the cigar which is tasty. He's all for these sensual pleasures. The young man is talking to Guillaume in a professional manner, but is either self-conscious or – he keeps glancing sideways into Castang's indifferent gaze.

"Sorry about that – oh good, the girl's fixed you up. Monsieur Cesari just wanted a natter about some buyers. Is that cigar good?"

"Who's he? Yes, very."

"Pleasure to see you enjoy it. Oh, he's something between sales and entertainments, looks after people, you know. Roland Belle-Gueule we call him." Deprecating laugh. "Able young chap though, and the Patron thinks well of him. Great score with the women. Well now, where were we? Any questions you may have, Commissaire . . ."

"No, no, I'll just drink this."

"All a bit too much?" wondered Inspector Varennes, turning the car round.

"A lot too much."

"Cobwebs and Château-whatever and all that smarm. Like maple syrup poured over one's icecream. Hell, we were only checking up. Was that all just because the Patron told them to be polite?"

"We missed getting taken out to dinner, some nice little place that isn't in the food guides, by the elegant young man."

"Pah," said Véronique, shifting into top. "No doubt they're all on the fiddle and that's why they're so obsequious, as though we were the finance squad checking on the books."

"What makes you think so?"

"Nothing really, but a business like that – one of those common-market re-export larks: bottle of Algerian plonk crosses the frontier three times before getting sold as Margaux in Sweden. Well, on to the next Château."

"Far?"

"Quarter of an hour."

"Is it a château?"

"No, it's quite small. I've been past a few times – very Monument Historique. Contrast to Lecat. Old money. Beyond that I know nothing." And Castang knew only a little, from the homework done.

Of the rich he had experience. A good deal of police work is done among the rich. There is even a pretty close correlation between money and criminal activity, for money is power, and those who have it want more of it. When he had met the very rich he found that in general they used their wealth to manipulate those with less. They do at times quite outrageous things without even noticing, for they have become largely indifferent to the world around them. There must be exceptions: people of character, alive to the responsibilities of wealth, but he had not met them.

It didn't do, as the judge of instruction had told him, to form any hasty opinions about Lecat, having only just met him.

But the wife was something else again, of her he knew less still. She had been 'born': she was from one of the old land-owning families who take their names with the particle 'de' from the name of their estate; 'their' village with 'their' people in it. Going back to the time of the kings. The aristocracy.

Around these people in France there is a good deal of legend fostered by republican sentiments. He would need to make a real effort to disentangle myth from reality.

And such people had more than a simple-minded addiction to money. It was likely to be hideously complicated.

The wife had a sister, and the sister was married to an Army General – retired – named Laurens. Who owned, or anyhow lived in this place they were coming to. This was her family, 'the' family. It was important to her. That was all he knew, so far.

Such people would be ultra in every reactionary opinion. Monarchist or Orleanist, Boulangist or Pétainist: everything sounding frightful and even contemptible, when not just laughable. But careful there. They aren't base on that account. It is not through ignoble interest that they think this way. It is natural to them, they are born to it. Social attitude and political belief are to them unquestionable. Like religion. And that is the most basic of all.

The men went into the Army, or the Church. The women went into the Church too, when they didn't marry into the Army. Maybe they still do, because tradition is one of the most important factors in their life. Beware of complications, Castang, and beware of over-simplifying, too.

They were there. One caught no more than a glimpse from the main road, of a house masked by the contours of a rolling landscape, set among trees in pasture land. They had to go roundabout, up a side road, through a five-barred wooden gate and along a driveway little better than a cart track. Cows grazed on one side: if 'estate' there had been it was sold or let to a farmer. Much in contrast to the Lecat palace: far older, confident and serene, with none of that ostentatious obsession with privacy. There was not even an avenue or a gate. The roadway made a turn past a stand of larch, passed over a cattlegrid, and was gravelled only in the surround of a little formal garden directly in front of the house: a diamond of miniature box enclosing parterres in fleur-de-lis centering upon a fountain in a basin. Was that lead, or bronze, and how come that in three German invasions this had never been pillaged or destroyed? The house was a plain oblong in two stories, late eighteenth century, with tall windows opening onto a terrace. Everything was simple, direct, and without the least pretension. No servants! The door was opened by the mistress of the house, and nobody told the police they should have gone round to the tradesmen's entrance.

Writers, from Chandler on, have described the 'only thing that very much spells cop': 'the unwinking cop look'. It is a fact and they have it in common, the city-bred criminal brigade specialist and the country gendarme. Clear-eyed since in general they are healthy and active, cool since they are unemotional, and both since most of life is made of cliché and even threadbare adjectives have to do duty. It is their job to take everything in, to know you again: it is useful and may be necessary. They look thus first at the physical details that spell identity; hands and ears and the way your hair grows; the cut of lip and the orbits of the eyes. And then the social details: your clothes and the way you wear them, what they cost and the impression you are trying to make with them. The weakness of this is the liking to fit people into categories. The police is very category-minded. Like librarians. They feel bothered if you fail to fit one of their labels.

Bad policemen will even talk about a 'criminal type'.

Castang, who knows that folk who conform outwardly to a type often have strong antibodies in their bloodstream, tries to look with his wife's eyes. There is so much that dulls the ability to see. It is so very much in the interest of a few that the many should be uniform and predictable. So he tries to turn himself, exactly the way you turn a pencil in a sharpener: he invents blades that will peel him of blunt insensitivity. Most are small, even trivial. Thus a hundred metres in the car had given him six seconds in which to see that at the beginning of June the larches have already their characteristic colouring: but the spruce, that most boring of all trees, spreading its fat little fingers in the pale green of new growth, is suddenly beautiful because the shadows inside the pendent fan-shaped branch have found an intenser, darker green from the contrast. The one time of the year when the spruce is a blessing instead of a curse. Like a Russian soldier singing in a choir.

A standard technique is to 'see it' for his wife as one would for a blind companion. No different to Kim's game, in which you are allowed to look at a miscellaneous assembly of say twenty small homely objects for a given moment before they are concealed and you are asked to recall and name as many as you can.

"Tallish," he told Vera. "Taller than the sister and bigger boned. Not blonde but fair. The sister was brown. Some resemblance of feature: recall that the sister was not exactly looking her best at the moment I laid eye. Awkward legs, thickish low down. High heels to lessen that. A lumpy shambly walk but good posture, back straight, head up. Blouse and skirt, good but old, almost ragged. Big hands, nails short, no varnish. Wedding ring and diamond cluster, no other jewellery. In the evening perhaps or on formal occasions. Same with makeup. Neck, hands, arms freckled from sunlight. Hair pinned up. Active, hard-working women – time spent at the hairdresser is time wasted? It would be in bad taste? Being and behaving in good taste is very important, I should think. Meticulous? – no, fastidious – impossible to imagine these people yawning or belching or picking their nose: they're brought up disciplined."

"The house?"

"Perfect, apple-pie – why does one say applepie? Smoothly organised. One sees these people are not particularly rich. The furniture's old, probably inherited. Carpets and curtains worn, even shabby. No servants or luxurious gadgets. She has a daily woman no doubt but does the rest herself. But they behave as though they're very rich and everything were done for them."

"You saw around?"

"They show you about as though it were Versailles and it were normal to take an interest. Not the bedrooms of course. Salon, library, diningroom, morningroom – quite a small house. Perfectly proportioned.

"It isn't lordly or arrogant. It's the landowning class. 'Our people' when they mean the villagers. But perfect manners. They treat everyone as an old friend, be you an ambassador or the baker's wife, nothing staged or elaborate.

"Remarkable selfcontrol. I mean, the sister is dead, in sudden and hideous circumstances. And we come, the criminal brigade. That shakes anyone. You see the veneer crack and the paint peel off. But these people behave as though you'd come to read the gas meter. You feel that if the Russian panzer commander walked in he'd be asked to tea. 'Just wipe your boots though, there's a good chap.' "

"Were you asked to tea?" asked Vera giggling.

"Yes indeed."

"They seem to have made a conquest of you," said Vera.

"Yes. I admit."

There had been a simplicity, also. No trace of affectation or embarrassment. As though concealment and pretence were beneath them.

All this is infrequent in the experience of the police. He'd been talking about 'them' and hadn't even mentioned General Laurens . . . No need: they were a well-matched couple.

Army virtues, like courage or steadiness under fire. You didn't think of that because it isn't commented on, wouldn't even be thought of.

The early training in childhood? You do not cry, you do not flinch and you are told not to raise your voice. But this stoic formation was not enough to account for General Laurens.

Oh yes, Castang has been impressed, as he had not been by Monsieur Lecat. Or he would not be fumbling inadequately about with meaningless words like gentleness, sweetness. Goodness, damn it. These are not the conventional expressions one would use, in the description of a retired general of not quite the highest grade. Well, he hoped he was adult enough not to mind looking silly. It happened often enough, but would only be prejudicial to good discipline if VV found it too obvious.

General Christian Laurens e.r. (the initials stand for 'en retraite') was a small man – slim, silver-haired, fine-boned. Not even a moustache to give a military note. For all one could tell, he might have been a bank manager (e.r.). Heelless leather slippers and overall trousers: he had plainly been gardening.

With grave courtesy he offered Castang 'a glass of claret'. No? Rather have a whisky? Well, it's teatime and we're going to have a cup of tea. Miss Varennes? Both she and Monsieur Castang ('I'm glad I've got it right; Castaing is the more common form') would like a cup of tea.

No silver teapot either. Kitchen pot, odd cups, and 'English digestive biscuits. Aren't they good! To tell the truth, from Marks and Spencers.'

VV was sensible; put herself in a corner and kept still as a mouse, accepted her cup with a nice smile.

"There is a fact," said Castang. "That Madame Lecat is dead. So far it's the only one. There is a corollary probability. That she was killed."

"Lecat," said Laurens, grateful for the businesslike tone, "made it sound certain." Cécile, sitting very upright with her knees crossed, smoked a cigarette and looked steadily out of the window as though the two men were discussing a fall in the stock market.

"To my mind it is certain," Castang replied. "I have not the right to assume it unless confirmed by expert medical opinion."

"It is a hypothesis." The General held his empty teacup rigid in mid-air, balanced between two fingers of each hand. If he got it exactly horizontal, then an effort of willpower would suffice to keep it there unsupported. "But we must face it as a certainty." Fine-skinned sunbrowned hands, marked with the leopard spots of age. The hands as controlled as the face. My stocks have fallen badly. If I sell, I lose. If I do not sell, I risk still graver loss. "It is unimaginable and inexplicable."

"I'll put it formally," said Castang. "Can you suggest anything that would account for violence?"

"I can not." He looked at Cécile, but she appeared deaf.

"Very well. There is a further important factor. Monsieur Lecat is well-known and wealthy. The Press . . . you know that there is no limit to their capacity for brutal intrusion and vulgar innuendo."

"That's rather nicely put," said the General. His wife stabbed her cigarette out in a brass bowl.

"One feels so sorry for the poor," she said. "Sensation – they don't know how to cope with it and get in a muddle."

"I mentioned it only because it might not have occurred to you that by this evening we won't be able to keep it to ourselves."

"Poor Marguerite."

"Every kind of suggestion will be made," said Castang. "Contradicted or not, and over several columns. With photographs."

"It's kind of you to warn us," she said a bit distant. "We'll cope."

"In case some fragment of gossip should have even a bit of truth in it, it would be as well to tell me now. May I smoke?" The General was filling a pipe after two cups of tea.

"Oh my dear chap . . . You mean – did Marguerite drink? Have gigolos?"

"In that direction," guarded.

"Of course she did," striking a match. "Oh, with discretion – she made no noisy scandals. But things will be said now."

"And one will disregard them," said Cécile, "as one always has."

"Even the official side of a homicide enquiry is harsh and can be shocking. The examining magistrate will be . . . impertinent. So will I." She looked haughty then. Minor civil servants had better not show impertinence. But Laurens smiled.

"Let's not exaggerate, my dear boy," he said kindly.

6 If the news had reached Lille – and of course it had – no sign of this reached Castang. Obstinate silence from Monsieur Sabatier. And if the Divisional Commissaire shows no inclination to hold press conferences, then it's up to Johnny. With some trouble Castang reached the Mayor on the phone. He didn't like it either. Plainly the affairs of Monsieur Lecat were a delicate subject. It was not at all easy to persuade him that there's no such thing as bad publicity.

"You're not going to have them in the Town Hall!"

"Can't have them here – too small. These premises date from eighteen-fifty. Wouldn't want that on television."

"You're not going to allow television!"

"We're not imagining we can stop it, are we?"

"You're on your own, Commissaire. Strictly no comment from this office." So he wore a white shirt. Help the firing squad all you can. And had a stiff whisky. But only one.

And of course some clown was at it straightaway.

"In a relatively subordinate post, you feel able to handle this?"

"The question is impertinent and silly so we'll agree to disregard it." Just as well he'd only had one whisky! Act hostile and so will they.

"Pretty new here, aren't you?"

"The Procureur instructs me to enquire: I do not question his decision."

"And your Divisionnaire?"

"The same applies."

"And you've already concluded on a homicide?"

"An enquiry is designed to eliminate all but the truth."

"And you haven't even got autopsy results yet? is that correct?"

"If the circumstances were not ambiguous an autopsy would not be called for." Sounding weary. Feeling it, too. Looking, no doubt, awful.

"So you're making publicity for the department."

"No. Behaving with prudence."

"Your statements are provocative."

"I won't go beyond observable facts. At present there are few."

"Like Monsieur Lecat is a nationally-known figure."

"You say it, it's so."

"Your calling this homicide, is that with his knowledge and consent?"

"Ask him."

"Is he a suspect?"

"I won't answer that as you very well know."

"Your suspects seem pretty limited."

"You'll find out soon enough." Most of it was crude coat-trailing. The nasty one came at the end: a responsible Paris paper.

"Pending the results of scientific tests it looks as if you've got a family affair on your hands: would you agree?"

"A premature conclusion."

"But answer the question. A probability?"

"We'll cross the bridge when we come to it."

"And if the tests are inconclusive? Then you're stuck, right?"

"When I'm stuck," feeling the fixed smile must look pretty arid on camera, "I'm sure you'll let me know."

"Have you questioned Madame Lecat's family?" Local journalist.

"Ask them for an interview." They will.

Looking at himself was horrible. A June evening, humidity high, but he was still sweating too much. Lecat with the press was much better. Practised, easy.

"Do you consider yourself a suspect, Monsieur Lecat?"

"A suspect? Oh! That would make quite a nice headline. Then you'd all be rushing about, accusing me of using a calamity to promote sales. Come come . . ."

"But when the calamity is a homicide?"

"That is really two questions. So I'll give two answers. If the investigating officers found a possibility of homicide I would see no reason to doubt their competence. And whatever it's called technically it is a domestic calamity which touches me personally. I make no further comment."

"But murder – "

"That's an emotional word which I won't use."

"Can we take it you have confidence in the police findings?"

"The police findings can be left to the examining magistrate, and I'll respect her judgment."

"She's known, shall we say, for left-wing views. You're not afraid that her statements might make political capital out of your situation?"

"I don't suppose any such thing," said Lecat easily. "Or suggest it. And anticipating your follow-up, if any statement by a judicial or administrative authority were seen as open to a conjecture of that sort, then I'd take steps," showing his white teeth in a carnivorous grin, "to see it was not misinterpreted by any of you." He has kept his word, thought Castang.

"Impeccable," he said out loud. "Makes me sound clumsy and so very stiff."

"You weren't too bad," said VV kindly. "Should I keep the tape?"

"Oh yes, from now on we're Nixon, we tape everything. And no accidental leaning on the erase button."

Indeed. The television had hardly been switched off before Monsieur Sabatier was on the line. A friendly, low-pitched drawl.

"Good, Castang. That was competently handled. It would not look well – you understand me – if any hint were made that I were not confident in your ability to handle such a matter.

"Very well. As things stand, so we hope they continue. From what I've seen, no flak from Lecat. We admit, the situation is sensitive. I'm bound – you follow – to keep a close watch. But as things stand. Just a call to assure you of my backing. I've had the Proc on the line; reassured him there. All right? Sure you're happy? Stay that way, hombre."

As long as the Man is happy.

Very good, Castang, you're getting to make your enquiry. Just recall that me and my pal Lecat are like that, so make no unreasonable disturbances or there will be dire consequence. Make your enquiry in the sun of benevolent smiles. Make it rapid, logical (this is the country of Descartes as we're forever being told), and make it something that the halfwits can understand.

A crime of passion; that'll do us nicely. Silly little Mrs Lecat, feeling neglected (her husband has these important business interests), got chatted up by the chauffeur. Or perhaps the gardener. As Hanaud says with pardonable sarcasm, 'Quick, quick, the thumbscrews for the gardener, and in a moment we know all.'

Cécile had been tightlipped about her sister's little slips from virtue. General Laurens, like a sensible man, and quite aware that the Polizei would make it their business, had made no bones about it. Mentioned had been 'drank too much' and 'gigolos'.

The first had the merit of saying what it meant better than that coy and prudish euphemism 'problem'; but was still vague. A neurotic tippler with a gin-bottle hidden in the bathroom? It did not rhyme with what they had heard of Marguerite. A woman who now and then has one too many as part of a reckless pattern . . . restless becoming reckless after three shots of vodka: that would fit in.

And 'gigolo'; a pleasant, oldfashioned word. What would it be called now – a stud? But the same thing; the muscular young man about the swimmingpool. Well, one would find out. What have you got a staff for, Richard would say: summon the troops. Yes. Uh. Which troops?

One can forgive Castang for falling into the douce reverie at this moment. Commissaire Richard, often accused of intellectual arrogance, meaning impatience with his cripplewit gang, said that plainclothes staff were exactly the same as uniformed peelers.

'Line them up every morning; inspect them for boots-and-buttons. You'll find half in bedroom slippers and t'other with its trousers on back to front.' There had been many well-worn jokes about 'les sergents de ville' and 'Get fell in, the whistle's went.'

'You must shake them up every day. Laziness, apathy, taking the dog for a walk, are eternally uppermost.'

Castang was not exempt. He was pulled in every morning and sharply cross-questioned. 'I'll have none of this written report bullshit' – little bits of paper to explain why it had taken three and a half hours to get a haircut. Editorial conference every morning, for the Research and Intervention (holdups, terrorists, gangsterism, so that one was never sure which side of the law one would find them): the Juvenile and Narcotics: even the financial gentlemen who labour all day in unaired cellars at undeclared Swiss bank accounts.

Castang is wistful because things are very different here. Outside the big cities with their hierarchy of specialists the PJ cannot define its duties in this compartmentalised fashion. He might get to know about half of what his two senior inspectors were up to, however much he enquired into their murkier doings. They took an interest in little groups with fervent ideologies, in collectors of arms, inventors of deathrays, ingenious systems for defrauding the Social Security. It is more political too, often overlapping the parallel police, gentlemen jealous of their prerogatives who 'survey the territory'.

In the dim past, when even Richard was young, there had been an antiquated concept known as 'Enquiries in the interest of Families', covering adulterous wives, alimony-dodging husbands, runaway teenagers; with an attendant expertise in racecourses, casinos, and gay bars. Richard had had an old gentleman who did these 'private jobs', way past retirement age but indispensable, known as Monsieur Bianchi. You simply didn't find this kind any more: they belonged in the Maigret era. But Castang had learned the uses of an old cop. As a hatchet man, for being bastardly: expert in threats and near-blackmail while knowing just how to stay within the provisions of the Code of Criminal Procedure.

Thus, Madame Metz, the dame-pipi, the secretarial and telephone lady, an awful pest but indispensable, has a Monsieur Metz who is likewise. And when Castang decides upon a foreclosure of mortgage . . . It is a fearful hypocrisy, says Vera. Yes. Admitted. Alas, there are people who understand nothing but a twisted arm.

Monsieur Metz would do nicely to look into the private life of Madame Marguerite. It is an enquiry in the interest of a family. And in ours, too.

As for VV he has other duties for her. And for himself a series of friendly chats with the servants. Culminating, we all hope, in thumbscrews for the gardener. Because the criminal brigade can see a fact which serves as starting point. This rich man's house, the Lecat Palace, is damn well protected. The rich nowadays are paranoid about protection. And Lecat has gone the whole hog. In the old days – were they any better? – you closed all the shutters and if you had grounds you surrounded them by a high wall with broken bottles set in the cement. Nowadays you had the whole place wired. Being Lecat you have the high wall as well.

Castang had thought Véronique exaggerating, with her tale of the gardener's cottage stuffed with television screens on which the old lady who lived there could cover the entire approach to the house, and the surround. When the chauffeur was not there to open the gate she took a good look at you herself before pressing the button. This makes the job easier. Or in theory. Since you have the authorised list of all who are entitled to access. And she is so used to seeing them around that they come and go unnoticed. If you wish to assassinate a public figure, use for preference the body-guards.

Looking over this list, Castang decided to begin with the cook. A cook is a confidential fellow, and responsible. Exactly the one at the heart of the domestic hive, who is taken for granted, and who, unnoticed, notices everything.

Monsieur Rémy. Known to his intimates as Rémy-le-boulanger, for he started life as a baker. But he had talent and had got on in life. Castang is not an intimate but would like to become so.

A quick, pale man, with sharp intelligent eyes, thin sinewy features. Nothing, says Virginia Woolf, is more derisory than adding up lists of features. But she wasn't in the police.

He is ready enough to talk freely, because he knows he cannot be suspected.

"See, Commissaire, if there's a late party, I'm here. So is everyone here. Outside that, I'd never be around here at night. I'm up early for my marketing. I'd be seen, I'd be noticed."

"Who by? Madame Lecat?"

Rémy sat back in the 'comfortable chair' in the corner of his kitchen he used as office, and laughed. Unflustered.

"That I'd be playing patacake with the governor's wife?" amused. "You don't want to let yourself get carried away, friend. You want to play, assume I'm that way. Assume she's that way. Now look at the facts. I saw her every day. Sometimes in her bedroom – times she'd still be in bed. Gleam in your eye? Mostly in her office." He reached to a shelf. "Here's my books. My diary, calendar for days ahead, what guests and when, any special notes like Mrs Whosit, last time we gave her veal cutlets and remember she doesn't like bananas. My order book, everything I buy, quantities and prices. She kept a right close eye. You look in her office you'll find her housekeeping books, with the counterfoils for every cheque. I'm tidy. First I'm that way myself, second the governor sees to it I'm that way. He leaves me alone, doesn't nag, so long as I do my job, but he's real hot on expenditure.

"Now wherever and whenever I'm with her, not only is it known and all noted down, but there's maids all over the shop, in and out. Not much they miss, either. Don't throw no dust in your own eyes." It was exactly what VV had heard from Victorine. And when he looked at Madam's desk in the morningroom the housekeeping accounts were as meticulous as in any regimental orderly room. Those women had been brought up good and careful managers.

Her personal accounts were a different story. This was her private area, and it was as though she took pains to keep it so. There were her bank credit slips, showing a small, perhaps inherited income from investments, and the large regular payments one assumed to be allowance. She didn't seem to gamble or have any stock exchange interest. In this chequebook half the counterfoils weren't even filled in, and the rest with abbreviations, not even dated. A rough check, to avoid getting overdrawn. Nor was there a diary. There was a visitors' book, a desk diary with guest lists and notes about food, as Rémy had said, and the usual pop-up finder for phone numbers. But even in her handbag there was no 'little book'. Does everyone have a little book? Did she have one hidden somewhere? Her bathroom calendar was full of birthdays and anniversaries but beyond one or two notes of 'checkup d' – a doctor or dentist – there were not even the expected little crosses marking her periods. An unselfconsciously healthy woman or a secretive one. He cast about a while in the usual hiding places before realising that it was Victorine who so neatly folded and put away underclothes. The jewellery box stood on a shelf. There were no locked drawers or cupboards. There might be a hidden safe but Lecat would know of that. A woman at once transparent and opaque. Hard to know what to make of it.

Frédo, the chauffeur, was a familiar type, haughty with menials and crawly with an officer; obsequious and loquacious. Oh, a terrible lot of work he had, four cars and the gate. Well paid and wouldn't deny it, but the boss and the madam both maniacs, white gloves y'know, everything had to be spotless. Around here he mostly drove the boss. He did drive the madam sometimes, but mostly have it clean, tanked – that one, the little BMW – and leave it at the door for her.

No of *course* he wasn't complaining. Don't mind saying, Commissaire, nobody'd get a word out of him, being this was a really confidential job, only the boss gave the strictest instructions you was to be told and shown absolutely everything you wished.

Oh we're very conventional. The Rolls, the Ferrari, and the utility for heavy work, besides Madam's. That's right, the boss took the little one that evening, drove himself. Brussels? – that would be about right, 'cording to the petrol.

The gate? Easy, nobody can get through unless I open it, or the concierge checks on her screen, that's Violette, you ask her. In or out, check on everything, the boss is very sensitive about who comes in here. Nobody can let themselves in without a card. Like this, see, it's a credit card. Even if one got lost or stolen it wouldn't do no good. Voice-pattern goes with it, speak your name or the lock won't jump.

The family got cards. And the confidential staff. Like me, and Rémy Mathieu the cook, and old Georges the gardener. That's Violette's husband, ex-army, awkward old bugger. He maintains these security systems; saving the boss he's the only one knows how.

Maids don't have cards, nor outside staff, no not even Monsieur Guillaume in the office.

He was the faux-bonhomme, an unlikeable specimen but Lecat would have him sewn up tight.

This was like the locked-room mystery beloved of antique detective stories, and the point is that what seems foolproof isn't.

Hard to see how this would not be foolproof, because the servants are a check upon one another. The stranger breaking in did not seem at all likely. No. There remained this small group of servants – and whoever the family chose to let in. Accompanied, since a voice pattern is needed, by themselves. Lecat was in Brussels, as can be verified, and that left Madame Marguerite.

Well, better go and see 'the concierge'.

The cottage in the grounds. Picturesque, with trees around and its own little garden, all thatched-roof-and-wallflowers and there ought to be an old dear in a clean white apron, curtseying on the flagged path. And there was Violette, a thin tough woman of sixty. A lined face, a quiet voice. In no way grim or like Mrs Danvers; a gentle face and a kind mouth. Very much on the ball.

"I've my instructions, Inspector. Please come in." Slate floor and beams and not a speck of dust. War medals, framed; certificates of excellence from Horticultural Societies; silver cups for shooting. She showed him her surveillance system, complete as a bank's, with a monitor in the kitchen and an audio warning should she be anywhere else.

"And you're always here?" She smiled at the note of incredulity.

"Where would I want to go?" with simplicity. "Not but what we've plenty of holidays when the family's away, in the south or abroad. We've our own vegetables and fruit, and Monsieur Rémy gets me my bit of fish or meat when I ask. If I do have shopping then my man stays in. It's a constraint, I grant. But Monsieur Félix is considerate." Well he may be! thought Castang.

"And we're in good health, thank heaven.

"It's true that we don't get younger. But there's Jean-Baptiste, he lodges with us, a very quiet respectable young man and he's part of the family really. Sort of engaged to my daughter Caroline. We hope they'll get married soon and take over."

"Just tell me," said Castang, "whether you are satisfied. Nothing was missed, that night?"

"No," she said sadly, "nothing was missed. I've thought and thought, with that dreadful thing happening to Madame. But nobody got in. I'll put my hand in the fire for that, Inspector. I'm so accustomed to it, you see. Even if I'm in the you-know, there's the buzzer. My old man checked all the circuits next morning, the way he always does."

Damn it, he'd never met a witness who impressed him more. But as with a prison, there is still a key, and a man who guards it. There's no system so sophisticated it can't be perverted, by a chap who knows how. Ostensibly, nothing had been missing. But who knew what Lecat, a very rich man, kept in his house? There are business papers worth as much as any jewellery to the right person and whose loss Lecat might not be willing to admit.

He found the gardeners at work, and answers to his questions. Old Georges was in his greenhouse, in that thick rich scent that is more a taste. He was the ideal publicity photo for a nurseryman's catalogue. Corduroys and a stiffened leg, moleskin waistcoat and a Pétain moustache. But formidable. Slowed he might be, but the pale shooter's eyes that had won all those trophies in his kitchen had not lost their sharpness.

"I don't like strangers or snoopers, or any sort of official. But the Captain says I must talk to you. Leastways answer your questions. I been here a goodish few years now. General Laurens got me this job. I been with him in Germany. Before that – Indochina, all over. I was armourer sergeant twenty years. Show me the locksmithing or any precision metalwork I can't do. All electronics now, but the bolt still goes in the lock, boy, a firing pin in the action.

"For the circuits and such there's a young man comes down from Paris. Anything goes wrong – and it don't – I know where to look. Nothing gets by me, or my old woman. I check this perimeter every sunset, rain or shine. There's nothing," looking at Castang with some contempt, "you or any cop can tell me about guard duty."

"Do you carry a gun?" asked Castang mildly, and with the short easy movement of dealing a card off the top of the pack a 9-mm. parabellum was pointing its maw at his belt buckle.

"You want to see the licence you ask Captain Félix."

"Put it away." Lecat could have half a dozen. He would be on comfortable terms with the Préfecture.

"But you like flowers." He had hit the right note at last.

"I always did like flowers. Right from when I was a boy. I thought Georges, you're a man of war, and that you'll stay. But in a war – you ever been in a war? – there's bits sharp and sudden but between times you got a lot of farting about. You learn to look at flowers."

Police work is no different. Castang, who knew nothing but to point to a bunch in a shop and say 'those zinnia things', had shared Vera's attachment to dotty-Ju, Commissaire Richard's Spanish wife, Judith the Gardener. Dotty? So was everyone. There was nothing about old Georges to raise his eyebrows. The only query was where and how Lecat, with all his money, had found these amazing people; and now he knew: General Laurens had 'passed his word' to his by-courtesy brother-in-law.

One question still: could the respectable young man, almost part of the family, have been moved or bribed to turn a switch, perhaps, for a quarter of an hour?

The young gardener was manuring a bed; placid farmyardy atmosphere of pitchfork and wheelbarrow. Young only in contrast to the old man: thirtyish and perhaps more, a spare, taciturn man with a well-balanced look who wasted words as little as movements. A southern look, with close, fine black hair and eyes like ripe olives and small, neat ears. Simon – it's anybody's name. That and Martin are the commonest names in France. Castang had met somebody called Martin too around here; he couldn't think who; it was of no consequence. And as for Jean-Baptiste, there are fewer than the myriad Jean-Pauls and Jean-Claudes, but it's as anonymous as you could wish.

"Yes?" coolly. "I can talk, and work." Neither hostility nor enthusiasm. The same economy as the practised gesture of dumping each forkful just where it was wanted. His overall was clean and looked tailored to his wiry body. His boots were carefully dubbined. His hands had no grime beneath the nails. The sort of man who spends fifteen minutes cleaning his tools at knocking-off time, who takes his boots off at the door and goes at once to wash; then sits quiet and contained in a corner, reading the paper from end to end and folding each page neatly at the turn. One glass of wine. Maybe a pipe. Castang could see why Violette approved.

He answered questions in brief phrases, with a politely suppressed misliking for nosy parkers. Seven years he'd been here. Was that long? – time to see growth in a tree. It was a good job; why change? He liked music, liked a good glass of wine, a good football match. He was well lodged. Violette was a good cook. Georges was a good gardener. Monsieur Lecat was demanding, but a good boss. What more could one ask?

Madame? Peppery at times and impatient, but not with him; he'd had little to do with her. If she asked for something he brought it, as far as the kitchen; the rest of the house wasn't his concern. Never been in it; why should he? He saved his money, did as he pleased, bought what he wanted, minded his business.

He spoke with a slight accent of the Midi. True, he was a southerner, he neither knew nor cared where from. Orphan, child of the Assistance Publique, if that were police business. Did a hitch in the army, last two years as General Laurens' driver. It was the General got him this job. He hadn't known a flower from a cleaning-rag. But he could read and write and he'd studied. Nothing wonderful about that: he'd been a good apprentice who didn't let his mouth rob his ears: Georges was a good teacher.

He had not stopped working and the barrow was empty. Paying no further attention to Castang he wheeled it away. Big old wooden barrow with slide-on back and side elements. Fill that up with heavy stuff like manure and you really had a load. General Laurens had a good eye. And Monsieur Lecat was fortunate in his servants.

Confirmation came from Rémy Mathieu.

"Funny pair, aren't they? The old boy never stops talking. To trees or melons if there's nobody else. Jean-Baptiste he doesn't utter. Get on well together; they're both hardheads in their way.

"That's right. The General looks after his troops, as they say. Come up for Sunday lunch, once a month. Strolls out into the garden then for a chat with them – never misses. The ladies saw more of each other than that – natural, seeing they were sisters.

"No, Madame wasn't interested in the garden. Cut flowers for the house, the old boy brings them here and she'd do that duchess act putting them in vases – make a lot of mess, too. Otherwise I don't see them: it's Violette does their cooking. What would they do in the house? Those ferny things in the patio, by the pool, true enough they come and spray or whatever, 'bout twice a week. The General takes an interest, some people don't like that patronage act. Don't mind saying I do. He makes a point of coming in every time to thank one," mimicking, " 'Damn nice dinner, Mathieu, appreciate it' but not condescending you know, not hoitytoity. That's why everyone likes him. Hullo, Roland, looking for me?" It was the exquisite Monsieur Cesari, just like yesterday looking as though Yves Saint-Laurent had knotted his tie for him. A hoitytoity look at Castang, a curt "Goodmorning".

"Not seen Aurélie?"

"No. Why?"

"Some stuff the Patron forgot, she was supposed to pick up."

"Not seen," moving a casserole two inches; it was simmering too hard. His stove and his pots were well polished, ready for inspection by any General.

Cesari performed something between a twitch and a sniff, vanished.

"Belle-Gueule," said Castang, drawling it a bit. Mathieu looked up, amused.

"You've heard that? Find him a bit too perfumed myself, for kitchen wear. He's all right when you're used to him. We've all got our little vanities, huh? His real name's not even Roland. Toussaint. Decided that was a bit too countrified for the wine business. Don't get taken in though, by the lily look. Knows his job and works at it; wouldn't last long with the Governor if he didn't, right?" Rémy realised abruptly that he was gossiping, or that he was being pumped. "I'll excuse myself now, if you don't mind. You've seen about all of us there is to see. No offence meant but I don't much want people under my feet, when I'm working. Life goes on, you know."

Castang passed Mademoiselle Aurélie in the hall: she was floating down the stairs, decorative in a pretty frock. A remarkably pretty girl. She said "Good morning" with the beaming hostess smile and no interest whatever in the police, and sailed past: he heard Rémy's indifferent voice saying "Roland's looking for you," didn't catch her answer.

For a moment he hung about, to breathe the atmosphere. There was a bustling upstairs. He heard the voice of Madame Cécile, a brisk upperclass tone that carried. "I need a hand here, Perrine." One loses a wife, another loses her sister. And whatever else, there is upheaval and raw edges. It was human of Lecat, to have forgotten things, and sent the girl to pick them up. Cesari, with his air of importance, was a sort of dogsbody. A bit of a housefly? For a moment Castang allowed a notion to cross his mind. Was Lecat sleeping with that – highly attractive – girl? He rather thought not: the man would have plenty of choice and would surely keep his hands off the servants. She was there to entertain customers, business acquaintances: a feminine hand to do flowers, pour drinks and see to place cards. Marguerite had not been interested in 'office' entertaining.

Cesari, though . . . When the General, with his liking for plain speaking, had mentioned 'gigolos' – had that been what he had in mind? Castang thought he could dismiss that notion too. Lecat kept a pretty sharp eye on the servants' doings. Still, he might get VV just to brush Monsieur Cesari with an angel wing . . .

Well now, back to the office. There is a lot of work there.

The chauffeur was not at the gate but as he drove up to it the barriers opened and a loudspeaker clicked and said 'Thank You'. Old Violette, on top of her job.

7 "So where are these photos?" Castang, sitting down heavily. "Paddy got them done yet?" Mr Campbell had a sour grin for this characterisation as the tough Ulsterman. Typical that he should be the resident photo expert. Probably expert at faking them too, when needed. But was it work for a senior inspector, dear god?

Big sharp prints. Well, God Bless Nikon. He was unwise enough to say so.

"We'll write to Japan," said VV. "A glowing tribute to say but for them we'd all still be martyrs to halitosis."

Castang went on looking at them. Nice bright photos. Interesting conclusion. Anything else? That Paddy Campbell took his time about the job: a way of saying he didn't propose to be flustered.

"See anything in these?"

"To be honest, no," said Inspector Varennes, looking honest.

"Not even for the Tourist Board," added Inspector Campbell.

"Waste of a good roll of film, strikes me."

"We aren't intuitive enough."

Castang was in the position of the umpire being needled by a horrid tennis-player. Don't get involved in the backchat but fix them with the eye and say 'Fifteen seconds'.

"Early days yet," he said.

"D'you want me to get them mounted on a board that we can stick up?"

"We'll see," said Castang. "Thanks for the trouble." It would be nice to have had a quick answer. A good statistic. The underlings toeing the line. Sarcasms, be they from a snotnose girl or Divisional Commissaire Sabatier, eaten up quick with hot buttered toast and himself to pass the salt.

If only to soothe my own vanity.

Nice to have a big comfy clue; buttons torn off, Tibetan tobacco-ash or the print of a flatfooted size fortysix.

He hadn't any. What he had was a Lecat. Very brilliant, very polite, very rich and very influential. Fall in it, Castang, and Paris will say wow, you're really bright; we think these talents should be exercised Imperially. We need a good cop in Djibouti.

Castang went to the hospital. An autopsy is expressed in a lengthy written report. There was a time when you got this in twentyfour hours even if it meant the secretary sitting up all night. Not now. She isn't putting in overtime on account of a few piddling policemen.

A pathologist is a busy man; also an awkward one to handle. You are not important in his eyes. Be you the millionaire's wife or the alcoholic clochard you take your turn, you go on the table, there's a sharp knife and zip, you are open from larynx to pubis and he reads you. Mostly without much interest: you're yesterday's newspaper, you're a cirrhosis statistic: it comes to the same thing.

He has small respect and less use for a commissaire of police: to him you're just another crowd-pleaser. For these he has contempt flavoured with some sourness. Because his speciality does not make a lot of money from rich old ladies. He is unlikely to have a grand house stuffed with antiques, to be pals with important personages, to win prizes and give press interviews, worrying about the colour tie that looks best on television. He does no important Life-Saving, heart transplants or what have you. Even if he has a Chair in a university faculty he is low on the party-invitation list. Because Pathology is shit on a glass slide. He's the fellow whose completely colourless voice tells you that's quite a pretty little cancer there, mate. Even the man Auden hoped for, who

        'With a twinkle in his eye
        Tells you that you've got to die'

casts a certain gloom over the cocktail gathering.

Oh well, he takes them as they come, even police bureaucrats bringing paper in their wake.

"Let's see, the girl must have left her notes somewhere." There are no horrible smells. Just that lowering feeling. "Christelle!" The girl who has the bad news in an envelope. In Austria known as 'the-Christl-of-the-Post'. A jolly fat girl, dark with dark curly hair, a real Celt.

"Yes, of course it's asphyxia, much good may it do you," slightly irritable.

Castang got given a cardboard cup of instant, stirred it with somebody's ballpoint.

"She was found in the bedroom you say. On the bed? – then yes, a pillow would do nicely." It did do Castang good. Your professional but non-specialist diagnosis has been confirmed by the pro. It puts you solid with the Procureur and the Judge of Instruction. There won't be snide remarks in the Press, or from Monsieur le Divisionnaire in Lille.

"It matches a certain amount of bruising and scratching. Desdemona job." Of which I have an excellent photographic record. Takes the sting too out of having the piss took by my own staff.

"She didn't struggle much. Pretty high alcohol reading. She might have been fairly dopey though you'd expect a good tolerance. Healthy woman of that age, practised drinker. Moot point."

"Any chance of knowing what alcohol and how far back?"

"I'm with you, Inspector Lestrade, but can't help you much. Not altogether digested, so a meal some two hours previous. Wine, bread, cheese. Can't tell you what bottle the wine came out of."

"There was something about the food, Christelle, d'you recall? Little seeds."

"Like on bread? Poppy, or sesame."

"No, whatsisname, get it in a minute, detest them myself . . . Caraway," said the doctor and the secretary together.

"You get it in some kinds of German bread."

"No, more embedded in the cheese, I know because it struck me as funny."

Castang had a memory of Richard, saying 'Beastly little seeds, get in your teeth' and himself replying priggishly 'Good for your digestion.'

"Alsace," he said. "Serve it down there like that. Munster cheese."

"Sorry old boy, I'm not the Michelin Guide." But surely it would mean somewhere quite sophisticated? Memo, VV, search for restaurants with munster on the cheeseboard.

"Well, I've nothing much else for you. No pregnancy, no abortions and no recent sexual intercourse, so you can forget les histoires de cul."

"Passion doesn't always mean sex." Castang, prim.

"Does to a pathologist." At last, a laugh. "Trace of semen, at

74

least you know you've a man, by the tail. The other sorts don't show."

"Another woman could have done it?"

"Certainly. Christelle here, for instance."

"But spare my blushes."

Mustn't let them start joking.

"No drugs or anything?"

"Mm mm," shuffling notes. "Still in good physical shape, didn't smoke. Alcohol, if she'd gone on drinking like that she'd have been in trouble. No needle marks, mucous membranes where are we? Bit of sniffing. Not an advanced habit." But interesting to know where she got that from. Memo, VV, cocaine. "No poisons, that's no further poisons. Bar the arrow-poison-that-leaves-no-trace." Castang was used to this well-worn gag.

"So nothing more to help me?"

"Not really. Well-muscled, took exercise. Good legs. Good feet. Don't notice feet much as a rule. But good ones are rare. Good teeth. Christelle?"

"Just that she came to a sticky end. But I'm not a cop. I only write from dictation."

Building up the portrait is a classic approach to an enquiry, be it into the living or the late. Feet are not a bad starting point. Monsieur Lecat would be the obvious person to continue. But he was in Paris again, if indeed it wasn't New Zealand by now. So – the family? General Laurens being indiscreet about his sister-in-law . . . That was not the right word. But he had not been reticent.

There are two sorts of witness. The reticent, not to say recalcitrant, who think that even talking about the weather might be compromising. And the garrulous, who appear helpful and are even more misleading.

It was an easy approach; speaking of 'the servants', engaged on his recommendation. Understandable that they spoke well of him, when he was so loud in their praise. 'Best I ever had': 'best I ever knew'.

"D'ye know, I've known very few really bad people. I dare say I wouldn't have got on very well with Herr Hitler."

He had come back from riding and was getting his boots off.

"After being accustomed yourself to a lot of servants d'you find – ?"

"No no, my dear boy, we were brought up to do things for ourselves. And unless you're as rich as Félix – but he's modern, sees them as tools, like his aeroplane, depersonalised; no, that's not fair to him. He works hard himself and expects a lot of them. Extremely demanding but I think he does understand that one mustn't treat human beings as machines. He's an excellent chap, I get on very well with him."

"He comes from a different world to yours."

"True, true, we live a good deal under his wing. One didn't speak of money in the old days, money was vulgar, but one must move with the times. Now I'm comfortable enough, not hurting we'll call it, but with costs higher every day, tax people lurking about with skinning-knives – the cost of grain for horses! – Félix gets us all sorts of things cheap. I've only a paddock here of course, couple of oldies out to grass I'd never let go to the knackers, look at that old mare out there, nineteen years old and awkward as sin but a wonderful old girl."

The general did go off at tangents.

"It's been confirmed that your sister-in-law was killed."

The general had apparently plenty of time, and lit his pipe.

"Well my dear chap, not going to teach my grandmother to suck eggs but eliminate the improbable and it must be the impossible, suthin like that, whosit, Sherlock. Old Georges swears by his electronic defences, and Félix too of course. As an old army man, I know there is always a weak point in a perimeter and the thing is to spot it. Skorzeny – now there's a chap I should like to have known –"

"There's no sign of it," said Castang hurriedly.

"Maybe. These modern criminals, they're very ingenious. Marguerite had some good jewellery. I know Félix says there's nothing missing, but the way I read it, Marguerite came back and surprised a chap. Nobody in the house, you know. Smothered her to stop her yelling, lost his nerve, took nothing to cover his traces. Find me foolish but I wouldn't write it off altogether."

"It's possible," said Castang. "I'd have to remain sceptical without direct evidence. Sort of story we'd tell the press," candidly.

76

"Don't like it I'll give you another." The general would yield to nobody in candour. "Marguerite might have brought somebody in." And since this was Castang's own notion it was interesting to hear it from another. Even if one must be careful not to fall in love with one's own theories.

"Don't get me wrong. Wouldn't mention it. But you're plainly an intelligent fellow, and discreet. Marguerite was well brought up – not married to her sister for nothing, doncher know – lovers and stuff, it's not on. But she had her wild side. A sort of silliness about people. Drank a lot. Kept her horse at the riding school, and some of that countryclub lot, nouveaux riches, don't want to sound snobbish, dare say we were brought up much too narrowly, but pretty rackety, and there are people who look on adultery and stealing as a sort of joke, see what you can get away with, what. She just might have brought somebody home" – embarrassed – "a joke no, more a sort of bet, dare d'ye follow me, horseplay really. But some young chap, drunk perhaps, offered her violence, she wouldn't have stood for that, there was a struggle, just worth bearing in mind perhaps, 'm I making any sense?"

"Maybe you are."

But it was at this moment of male confidences that Cécile came in, hot and lathered from a ride, still in her breeches and had been caught in a shower. The general started instantly to make a fuss about catching chills.

"I'm on my way to change," with a hint of irritation. She greeted Castang politely but looked distinctly cross-grained. He thought he had been around long enough. The general was looking guilty (caught gossiping with the social equivalent of a stable boy, and Madame Cécile would be touchy at the suspicion of her sister's reputation getting bandied about at the riding school). But when he murmured about must-be-getting-along, Madame Laurens took a sudden interest in him.

"Are you in a hurry, Commissaire? It's really coming down now; wait till the shower's over. Let me offer you a glass of sherry. No no, dear, I only caught a sprinkle. And I wish you'd see to the man about the logs: he's sawing them much too short." The general took the hint.

"Might one have a word, Commissaire?" And so did Castang.

Thus it was that he came to forget his umbrella, his 'Schirm', present from Vera on becoming middle-aged . . .

She roamed about and fiddled with china on the chimneypiece. Logs about a metre long would be right for that hearth. She was slim and good-looking in her shirt and breeches. Soldiers do not marry young: the general would have been a captain at least and a lot older. She would be in her early fifties.

"Your enquiry is not making rapid progress, Commissaire?"

"We've scarcely begun, Madame."

"Yes. My husband quite frequently sat on courts of enquiry. You know, peculation in the sergeants' mess, or mysterious damage to expensive machinery. I remember noticing that either one got at the truth quite quickly or the odds were one never got at it at all."

"Good deal of truth in that."

"I don't recall any murders . . . but it's a matter of hearing witnesses and establishing their credibility, I imagine?"

"Very largely."

"You won't take it amiss if I tell you something off the record and ask you to keep it that way?"

"Certainly not, but I'd have to warn you that though I have powers of discretion, I can't keep evidence from the instructing judge." Said cautious Clara.

"Come, Mr Castang, you people have confidential sources . . ."

"Certainly."

"I am asking you straight out whether in return for information you agree to keep it anonymous. I don't know the judge of instruction, don't particularly want to."

Castang made a tactful listener's face, like a doctor enquiring about bowel movements.

"You're being needlessly obtuse," she flung at him. "Surely you understand that honour keeps silence over family secrets."

"I'm to understand that you have knowledge of facts relevant to an enquiry, which if made public might be damaging to the reputation," feigning not to see her foot tapping, "of someone close to you."

"I'll say no more without a guarantee."

"We understand such circumstances. They occur frequently. They are made known to the judge but not to the press."

"How can I trust you?"

"It isn't just a civic duty. Nobody gives much more than lip service to that. Conscience is honour – you used the word."

She swung around and stared at him, a bright blue direct gaze.

"And what sense of honour have you?"

"What a damned silly, ignorant question!"

"I beg your pardon. But – people don't have much time for that kind of concept, nowadays. In the army – but the police . . ."

"Sorry, I don't see it as a caste sort of thing."

She stopped pacing about.

"Will you explain yourself?"

"As a police officer I take an oath of allegiance to the republic. Lot of rigmarole."

"Yes? Go on."

"I was going to say that outward show – flags in the school classroom or standing with your hand on your heart during the national anthem – it's a bit ludicrous, isn't it?"

"Flaunting it like that, yes. Sentimental vulgarity."

"So I prefer not to discuss my conscience in public."

"But this is between us."

"I have to remind you, Madame, that I am here in my capacity as a state official."

She looked at him for some moments before swinging away abruptly. Then she spoke over her shoulder, formal and wooden, keeping her back to him.

"If, Commissaire, you find the means – and," sarcastically, "the courage, to look more closely at Monsieur Lecat's activities, you will find a bad man. I suppose, oh I have no doubt, that you'll find plenty of people to say he was in San Francisco that night and I can tell you they'll be perjuring themselves blind because don't look for any sense of honour in that sort of milieu."

"And is that all you have to tell me?"

She swung round on him and planted her boots as though tensing to come at him with a bayonet.

"Isn't that enough? My own sister's husband!"

"That's mere hearsay, not evidence."

"Are you such a fool as to imagine that from my mouth an accusation is gossip?" She controlled herself. "It is to be presumed,

Commissaire, that you have intelligence as well as a conscience."
And walked quickly out of the room without looking back. Her
boots sounded a sharp military tattoo on the parquet. He observed
the parquet; beautiful, with inlaid patterns of some wood that kept a
pale gold colour. Nicely cared for too. Well, there was nothing but
to put his feet one in front of another.

The shower was over and the raindrops glittering on the foliage.
How good it did smell. He was rummaging pockets for the car keys
when hasty footsteps made him raise his head.

It was a young girl, a little flushed and tousled. Young meaning
eighteenish. A fresh open face. One would decide about calling it
pretty in another year or so.

"Oh, I'm glad I caught you. You forgot your brolly."

"Thank you. Stupid of me. And kind of you. You're the daughter
of the house?" Tall and solidly built, like her mamma.

"Yes, sorry, we weren't introduced," holding out a hot dry hand.
"I'm Miranda."

"Henry Castang," formally.

"You're the Police Commissaire. You're investigating. Because
you aren't happy about the death of my Aunt Marguerite."

"I wouldn't be happy about losing my brolly either and I'd have
had to investigate that, but for your help."

She grinned back, lowered her eyes suddenly as though
Reverend Mother had hers upon forward behaviour, raised them
again, said "Goodbye" politely, turned and ran. Coltish movements, hair tied back in a ribbon, cotton summer frock and
ballerina shoes. A pleasant sight.

He was glad he hadn't lost the umbrella. A joke of Vera's – he
had complained about the choice between getting wet hair and
losing more hats.

'Here. A present.'

'Oh I like presents.'

'Here, Italian men carry them. And Germans, the "Schirm".
And in England the dignity symbol, you aren't supposed to unfurl.'
French men are oddly allergic to them.

'And am I supposed to unfurl?' grinning.

'You can please yourself about that, Mister.' He'd whipped her
into bed smartish. 'Don't lose it though!'

**8** Vera, a compulsive reader, had had *Homage to Catalonia* as a present from Judith Richard and had much warmed to Mr Orwell: she'd gone digging up more. Such bad luck to have been a colonial policeman: fallen foul of dreadful colonial Brits. One reconciled the conscience to an awful lot of things, as a cop; and there were things that honesty forbade one. The never-ending dialogue, with the meanings of truth, and government, and freedoms, and responsibilities, with one's sense of irony and of humour, with those awful English schools and those shitty jobs, with punishing oneself and respecting oneself and living with it all. There aren't many journalists who've had to shoot elephants. Or be present at executions. Or get a bullet through the throat in Spain. She had felt, since, that she understood her own man better. Another member of the awkward squad even though his feet weren't as big. That special vision led you into errors and excesses, prejudices and dogmatisms: it also gave you an exceptional clarity. Much pride and much humility. And you were lucky maybe, to die of t.b. at fortysix. But that bullet, only five millimetres out, had given you nigh on twenty years extra, for free. One would always wonder whether one had deserved as much.

"You never told me there was a daughter." Castang to Inspector Varennes, slightly querulous.

"Didn't think it had any importance." VV unabashed.

"Everything's important."

"Platitude of the year. First prize, a visit to the White House."

"And Miss Varennes only second prize which is two visits to the White House. It's a beta minus, why wasn't I told?"

"She's just a schoolgirl. There was an elder brother, in the army. Parachutist or something, and was killed in one of those obscure situations, Africa or Syria – somebody threw a bomb at him." As vague about geography as Vera, who had said, 'Prospero's island, daughter of the good magician.'

'Where is this island?'

'In Shakespeare, stupe.' But of course Castang had his own collection of tedious facts of no possible interest to anybody.

81

"She's a Spanish verb." VV gave him a look, tapping her middle finger against her temple. "Mirar, to look at. Hence, she who observes. Or uses her eyes. From which derives mirador, a lookout post. Um, I wonder . . ."

"Fascinating." VV unimpressed by these pedantries. "Veronica, a holy lady. Also a Dutch commercial radio."

And right on cue Madame Metz announced "There's a young lady to see you" with that particular leer in her voice. This overweight personage, who had cultivated an unctuous manner in answering the telephone, regarded herself as the pivot upon which the whole office turned: it had proved impossible to get rid of her.

Nor was it any use asking 'Who is it?', since she constituted herself sole authority over who should be allowed in, so Castang merely said, "Introduce the young lady."

"I'm sorry," said Miranda. "I know I shouldn't have. She asked me 'on what subject?' and I couldn't think of an answer and said personal."

"Sit down then," said Castang kindly. It was no moment for jokes. The child looked very nice; not particularly pretty but the cleanest thing ever seen. Was it Jean Jaurès who had said that if you could only get the French to wash twice a week the battle would be won? Things are a bit better now though the Metro can still get pretty ripe, of a sultry June evening. VV had that look too of being just out from under the shower – so unlike Madame Metz – but was grimed by associating with the Polizei. Miranda appeared clean inside. Nuns have this occasionally but it isn't widespread.

"Well now, you've something to talk to me about." And the girl sat, straight and correct, knees together and hands in her lap, model of well-brought-up behaviour; and didn't utter. He tried again.

"There's something you wanted to say. You don't quite know how to describe it but 'personal' covers it . . . Take your time. I've plenty." He looked about, found one of his tiny cigars, lit it, put his elbows on the table, gave the big reassuring smile. This had precisely the opposite effect to that intended. Something in the face tightened up more.

Castang had papers on his desk that needed reading, initialling. He started on them, not looking at her.

"How old are you?" he asked a piece of paper while laying it aside. One had better know where one stood. Minors are a frequent and fertile source of traps.

"Seventeen," with enthusiasm: she wasn't lying. "But that's just it. They treat me like a child."

"Then I won't treat you like a child."

"When I had to run after you with your . . . I thought I'd . . . I made up my mind I'd . . ." It tightened up each time like a knot in wet rope, and paralysed her.

He wished he could find the key. A witness who will talk; fresh, unguarded, free; and will speak the truth! Great rarity in police acquaintance.

"It was, I imagine, about your Aunt Marguerite?" She shook her head but did not utter. "Then your Mother? . . . Your Father? . . ."

It didn't work. A child taken to the dentist will sometimes behave this way. It isn't frightened: there is nothing to be frightened of. The dentist is experienced, gentle, kind; joking just a little. The child sits there, clenches its jaw and will not budge. The dentist smiles then and says 'Well come again when you feel more like it' and when she scampers out, tells the parents 'It would do more harm to force her than neglect it a few months.'

Worried about her bad manners and ashamed of wasting an important official's time, Miranda looked unhappy and said, "I'm sorry."

"Give me a phonecall some time."

There are plenty of occasions, thought Castang, when the police are worse than useless. The child suddenly got up and scorched off, and he sat there and thought of Chantal.

A girl of just this age and background. She had fallen in love with a wretched, penniless boy without job or prospects, hampered in just about every way you can imagine: background, neighbourhood, school – even a record with the police; stealing from supermarkets or whatever (Castang could not recall the details). And there was absolutely nothing Chantal could do. The boy shot her. While they were clasped together under one overcoat. In the Trocadéro garden. To keep her purity. One could not expect that the Police Judiciaire would understand anything at all about that.

The really heartening feature of this had been that Chantal's parents showed they deserved a daughter like that. They weren't going to let her die wasted. They'd got a son, perhaps, to take her place – they'd fought for that boy like two tigers.

What happened afterwards? Castang did not know. Perhaps it worked. Perhaps not. But 'What else could we have done?' they said.

Miranda knew something. But there was no point in worrying about that. She would tell him or she wouldn't. Questioning her would be useless. Quite likely she would go and sit in some coffee shop with her head in her hands clenched into fists, longing to kick herself. Nothing he could do about that, either.

He didn't have anybody to do the job. Monsieur Bianchi, who washed seldom but possessed uncanny skills, would very likely have known how to open this oyster. But all he had was a Metz, who knew how to bully and who knew how to cajole, and would here be worse than useless. Or a Varennes, quite good at an elder-sister act but too coarse, too cop. One could wheedle and one could intimidate, but come up against a young girl's obstinacy: 'she'd rather die'. Like Chantal, who did.

Monsieur Metz lumbered into his office, armed with paper and a great deal of information about Lecat affairs. Castang sighed, and got down to work.

He didn't even get home for lunch and sat staring into vacancy biting on a hamburger revoltingly warm and squdgy and bland, not even noticing it, this assemblage of American molecules so carefully designed to be the very perfection of tastelessness. How could you possibly use the word design? Di-seg-no; three Italian syllables like rifle shots, something as tough and alive as the town of Florence, meaning a drawing by Giotto and strictly inapplicable to plastic bottles. He'd got home the evening before, feeling fairly weary, passably dispirited, and sat for some twenty minutes staring at Vera's half-finished picture. Some disegno there. He didn't know whether it was good or bad. Most of her drawings he thought good, but was he any judge? An unsentimental woman but who put a high value on emotion. An italianate simplicity about this and no simpering. The naked body was full of muscle and movement. The face was hardly begun but the beginnings showed vitality, something direct and ordinary, but real, alive.

84

This tiresome Miranda. Half-finished, but already full of complications.

These old towns knew the value of a hill. Today is the first breathing-space in two thousand years from the fear of the invading army. The ridge at Vimy – say, or Messines – already small enough, is flattened into further insignificance by the rolling weight of the statistic (so many zeros crushing one flat) of the lives spent there. Like today's unwanted oranges or cucumbers: how many thousand can you pack on to a thirty-ton truck, but who would bother to count them? Tip them out in a heap and let them rot. We have forgotten the basic survival principle: live on a hill. That way you see them coming.

The old towns thus have citadels at their centre. And the sightseer or even the police bureaucrat with an errand at the Town Hall finds himself scrambling up steep cobbled streets, greasy and slidy in wet weather.

But Castang likes these old streets. The town of Etablissements Barthélémy is fortunate, also, in what too many find matter for regret; old shops with belle époque signpainting and artisanal fittings. These were knocked down wholesale in France during the great modernisation frenzy of the sixties, when ministers were eager to make Paris look as much like South Bend as they could. It has since been belatedly realised that they had character. So that now there is a ludicrous rush to have the quarter's last remaining sweet-shop classified as a Monument Historique, which is the only way to keep the promoters from knocking it down. Thus the corner fishmonger becomes haughty and selfconscious and adopts fancy labels and ridiculous prices, exactly like that other of today's rarities, the honestly made local plonk, which is now classed as a Grand Vin and swanks about, an absolutely ordinary Savigny, at the price you'd have paid for La Romanée a handspan back. What a lot of Castles we find in the Bordelais now.

Castang considers himself fortunate. Since coal and iron became a drag on the market these towns, his towns, are poor and backward. In the Lecat caves behind the great brick arches are ten thousand thousand bottles of Château Municipal Abattoir and Clos Public Lavatory contributing to the Lecat millions. But

Monsieur le Commissaire, a civil servant whose monthly screw is substantial, drinks Rioja for supper. He has been working all day, had only had an indecent hamburger for lunch, and has found a pub with 1900 furniture and on it a visible, tangible patina formed by a century of smells.

An hour of road to cover, before getting home. Much longer, at rush-hour. No question of even trying. Is this a place where he can get some small thing to eat, to stave off pangs before the haul back to the bosom and cooker of Wifey? Yes, among the good smells is that of vegetable soup. Every cook's a chef now, and is doing tricky things with the foie gras, and nobody can make soup. The place swarms with pretentious and mediocre restaurants. But the 'little place', 'nothing to look at' (qui ne paye pas de mine) and where you eat well 'for half a crown' (pour deux fois deux sous) which is so dear to French myth – myth is what it mostly is.

Has he found one? May be. There's stew on the menu. But Vera will have supper for him at home and soup's what he wants. Fresh and hot and lots of it. And he gets it. With bread, and butter – butter! – and a pot of grated parmesan. Very tolerable. There aren't many people at this hour. One other chap eating: he's got a big slice of a fresh-looking terrine. As well as bread-and-butter some salad goes with it, and an earthenware pot of home-made pickles. It's an address to write in the little book. He tastes his quarter-of-red, house wine in the jug: it's nice. Where do you get it from?, he asks the waiter, and is told 'Barthélémy'. Not surprising since the Caves are practically next door, but it's a good mark for Lecat.

There are no tourists, unless he counts himself. But workmen come every day and sit at the same table, poker dice rattle at the bar and chessboards appear in the afternoons. The brass is polished, the ashtrays clean, and the plants healthy.

None of this, it has to be said, is special observation. Just a cop keeping in trim. Trivial details like a card pinned by a bellpush, a car registration, or when the paper-basket was last emptied. He is detached: it is not a strongly French characteristic. He is unpatriotic and sniggers at shibboleths, and is often accused of being no true Frenchman. He doesn't much care.

He has always been like this, from childhood. In the thirteenth arrondissement, where artists came to buy materials from his auntie. French or Dutch or Mexican, they were mostly weirdos and he liked weirdos. What took him into the police? Certainly not the idea of an administrative job with a pension tacked on. He liked to say it was the result of seeing Louis Jouvet in *Quai des Orfèvres*.

There is, too, 'a technique'.

The Frenchman walking in here, anywhere, sees nothing much out of the ordinary. The patterns are familiar; be he from the west or the south he's still in France and knows the passwords. Castang tries to ask himself 'And if I were a stranger?' Especially as regards the more ingrown, deeply-rutted convictions held by the French. That there are beaches on the Côte d'Azur. That the really important thing about a car is its acceleration from a standing start. That the Louvre is the world's finest. Now how do these fixations strike the spectator from Finland? It's really no more than the effort to keep sharp, to be that little distance ahead that makes a cop.

'I love you,' said Vera one day in bed with him; 'you listen for sounds.'

'Oh?' puzzled. 'What sounds?' She found that difficult to answer without sounding pretentious, at which she giggled. Distant drummers? The axes chopping down the cherry orchard? She does the same and much of it she has taught him. Looking more carefully one sees more: seeing a lot one is older than one's age. What does age mean, anyhow? Some imbecile asked Nappy Lamarr, one of the jazz 'living legends', how old he really was. 'I'll tell ya,' said Nappy. 'I was a waiter at the Last Supper.'

Castang is looking now at the waiter. It should be a waitress: the brushing crumbs off tables and covering winestains, watering plants and dealing out clean ashtrays, the little foibles – they are women's skills. Hell, a boy can have women's skills, without being on that account gayboy, no? This was a dark, sturdy young man, nothing languid. What appeared a bit pansified was the extra touch of servility. 'Would you like some mustard?' where a woman would bring it without asking.

The soup had given Castang an appetite.

"Is there any cheese?" He has been tempted by the terrine, but that would be too much. Looks good and much unlike the industrialised product of France that says it's baby wild boar. My ass, yes: those nubbly old pigs' leftovers. He has had sharp eyes for the

crinkly pink and green batavia instead of the limp lettuce-leaf and
sloshy quarter of tasteless dutch tomato. He has peered greedily
into the little grey-blue pots: silver onions, crisp little gherkins,
mustard pickles (which he dislikes) and green tomato pickles which
he loves (but Vera being Slav will put in too much cinnamon). It has
all engendered an insane longing for cheese.

"Cheese, sir," interrupts these gluttonous reveries. Lo, one had
only to ask. But —

"Wow." The trolley has floated up to his elbow. He is startled
because there are twenty different sorts. The boss stands there
to serve it, with a knife and a jar of boiling water; a fat fellow,
buttery, butlery. Stage-managing his effect because the cheese is
sensational.

"Yes, we're rather proud of it. House speciality." The insane
longing had only been for Roquefort and twenty is nineteen too
many but he allows himself weakly to be cajoled.

"We charge a high price because we only take the best and some
comes a long way: inevitably there's heavy wastage. This and this?
And a little of that? But I only charge for what you take. And with
that a glass of the special sauterne? Some port perhaps?" Beside
standard classics are a number of foreign-looking things and
Castang suddenly yaps "What's that?" Behind greed lurks cop-
curiosity.

"Leiden from Holland. We cast our net wide — that is Belgian
and this is English. I can see that you're a connoisseur, Commissaire. You'll get to know us better, I hope. Your predecessor used to
come, for our cheese. You'd like to try?"

"A little piece to taste."

"Véronique, I've a job for you."

"What, again?"

"The thing is to get those path people interested. A bit of cheese
to bait a mousetrap," unwrapping a paper hanky. "Give me one of
those glass tubes."

"Caraway seeds."

"That's right. They can simulate digestion, enzymes or something. If that were to match what they found inside the woman we'd
be a step further."

88

"Oh yes?"

"Come come, where's the wellknown charm? Because supposing it is, this is Dutch, and there's not likely to be a lot of places where you find it. I got it in a pub where they specialise. Near Lecat's office. Now with the photos to refresh their memory –"

"You mean the Fox and Geese?"

"I gathered that it's quite well known. Reference to my distinguished predecessor."

"It is, and I'd prefer you didn't ask me. That's Campbell country, mate."

"Is it? Is it now? Very well, just get the lab test run and tell me if it matches."

There are two special sorts of wasps' nest not to step into, in cop country. And one he'd already stepped into. The highspeed local notable has invisible threads to everyone from the Procureur to the Ministry. A false move, and it's down the oubliette. So you go very fairy-footstep indeed.

Like this country-club place where Madame kept her horse, played some tennis, used the pool – and the bar. Tight-lipped people there and with good reason. A couple of doctors with lucrative specialities and an appeal court judge on the membership list, and an extremely dim view taken of policemen hanging about. What was he to do? – construct a hide to watch the rare birds nesting? Still like a mouse behind the good Nikon with the telephoto lens? In that neighbourhood the mouse would get picked off by a hawk, smartish.

The other can be painful too. If while pursuing one police enquiry you come across traces of another police enquiry, you are well advised to take a hint that it's nowt to do with you.

A Principal Commissaire, Castang is the wrong rank. Higher up, you may get to know. Lower down, you keep your nose clean. The specialised squads are jealous of intrusions. The gangster brigade, who are quicker on the draw than their own shadow, can take weeks sitting on a bank holdup they have got to hear of. They will even allow it to take place, because without 'commencement of execution' they won't get a good conviction. You might stumble on it without knowing. Withdraw the hem of your garment quick. The vice squad too can be very waspish if inadvertently stood upon.

Within the small group where Castang found himself this can be going on in small personal compartments. One knows about some of it. The new young Commissaire knows that a foxy old Inspector like Paddy Campbell is extremely secretive about undercover deals. Brief, don't let the right hand get over-curious as to what the left is up to . . . One fox is enough, especially when dressed up as goose.

Glue everywhere; sticky and he was stuck in it. Gloomy he went home.

When he is sullensilent Vera tries to leave him alone – except when propelled, by some demon of her own, to make a scene, which always ends badly. But today she was in a relaxed state of mind. The painting was meeting numerous glitches, some technical, but she was working well, was satisfyingly tired, had done the dinner; went and got two drinks. He got through half his in the sullens before it trickled through and he suddenly said "Velitchko", drank the rest, held out the glass for more. Feeling better.

They have to talk, at these moments. It tends to be dull and Vera does not always listen. But the floodgates must open, and faces of intelligent interest must be made. Vera lifts her bottom off the sofa, arranges her skirt to be comfortable, makes the face and says, "Who?"

"It was one of Richard's witchwords. Used when counselling patience, the clear head, keeping cool, all that bullshit. He used to tell the story. I know it by heart."

"So tell," said Vera.

"In nineteen thirty-four –"

"Richard wasn't around then, surely."

"No, but as a young subinspector he was trained by an old stinker down in Marseilles, who was. Don't interrupt. I'll start again.

"In 1934 King Alexander of Jugoslavia came on a state visit. Disembarked on the quay in Marseilles, met by the Foreign Minister, Louis Barthou. A terrorist called Velitchko assassinated the king. Barthou died on the way to hospital. There were two spectators killed and four wounded. Pretty good going for one terrorist, would you say? You'd be right. Strangely like Sarajevo, would you say, poor Franz Ferdinand and his nice, pretty wife. An open carriage and a cavalry escort. Or poor Sissi of Austria. They still hadn't learned.

"Big deal. The cavalry officer, carrying his drawn sabre in salute, cut Velitchko down. Grand job. Rather belated." The old story has taken possession of Castang. His eyes gleam. It is, actually, a socking malt whisky that makes his eyes gleam, but no matter.

"An enquiry was held by the Inspector General of the police. The report was never published and we will now learn why." It is no longer Castang speaking, but Commissaire Richard.

Unconsciously he was copying Richard's quiet controlled voice.

"Velitchko was carrying two guns, both of seven-sixtyfive calibre. One, a Walther, was found unused. Of the other, a Mauser, one full magazine of ten cartridges was used and afterward accounted for.

"Louis Barthou died of a wound from a copper-jacketed bullet of eight-millimetre calibre. A police weapon. They lost their heads entirely. There was a milling mob and they fired into it. A terrorist carrying two guns provided them with a smokescreen. The Forces of Order are to be sure rather better disciplined than in 1934. They remain poorly trained and highly irresponsible in the use of firearms." Castang's voice trailed off. Vera tried to think of a comment that might sound like taking intelligent interest.

"But it was an awful time. Wasn't Goering Police President around then?"

"It's only an anecdote," said Castang. "But it doesn't help much saying that it was a long time ago or that other people's police forces were still worse. They still are. Before my time but in Richard's it was a rabble down there, a fascist private army run by the Action Service gang. It still happens all the time.

"Oh we make efforts. We do try not to cover up automatically every single time. There are suspensions and enquiries, even if they aren't independent or judicial; you'll get charges made, and pressed, so they get brought to trial. Nothing very dreadful as a rule. Something like culpable negligence, enough to get them a suspended sentence, which is enough to get them sacked, instead of just a cosmetic change of scenery."

She went away and left him because what was there to say? The men get these moments of extreme discouragement and you won't help by pointing out how much of it is selfpity.

Music is the better therapy. There is a woman – from Berlin as it happens – with a purity of voice . . . There is a Schubert cycle from Sir Walter Scott. Ellen sings. 'Raste, Krieger; Krieg ist aus.' Let us have no more Mirandas. Let us have Gundula. We will not then say 'Better' but after the Spanish manner we will perhaps say 'Less bad.' The war is not over, and quite certainly never will be, but . . . 'Warrior, rest' . . . Janowitz tells you. Believe her.

Because tomorrow morning Alice Jimenez will be asking tetchily on the telephone whether he is playing about or what, and would he like to fetch his ass over to her office with no further loss of time. Worse is going to happen. Sooner still.

The home in France is terribly private. Neighbours do not drop in. Friends will not appear unannounced. A ring at the doorbell is likely to be the man come to read the meter. But not in the late evening. Then it's a drama. What are you to do, throw them out? Say they must come to the office in office hours, because even cops have a right to their family life?

The doorbell rang and he had just gone on sitting, until Vera came standing wooden-faced, her arms folded, saying "Madame Laurens" in a voice without expression. And he said "oh fuck" but only in a whisper because she was just outside. Cécile in trousers and a pullover, long legs and a lean figure, with a well-bred expression of refusing to notice the squalor in which other people live. Tightly strung, but socially impeccable.

"Madame Castang understood the motive for my being so extremely rude."

"Do you want me to go away?" asks Vera simply.

"I couldn't mention the matter in front of my own husband."

It's not easy. The woman is begging for a confidential word, which he cannot refuse her. At the same time, he is not having Vera turned out of her own livingroom.

"In here," trying to overcome his awkward stiffness. The new flat is quite large but there are not that many rooms. The big all-purpose livingroom has a good light and is full of painting materials, toys, children's clothes; junk. Castang has nagged about a place-of-his-own, where tools will not be fiddled with by brats, where pieces of wood both old and new hang about in a mess that Castang would never allow in his office. There is a commode, nice wood that had a frightful phony-antique patina which he is sandpapering. A pine cupboard which he has stripped: it is waiting for Vera to paint it in the Chagally style of Czech peasantry, for children's clothes. There are linseed-oily smells, but those are in the livingroom too. And his workman's overall.

"Sit down," clearing a screwdriver off the chair.

"I'm sorry. I had to screw myself right up to this." He did think of offering the – he had it in his hand, could just say here, try this . . .

"Would you like a drink?" he offers.

"No. Thank you." Her hands are clasped together; she strains at them, her eyes fixed on the whitening knuckles. Strong well-kept hands, used to rein and bridle. "I must come to the point quickly. I must not disturb you for longer than I have to. But I can't be seen in your office." Castang cannot stop himself fiddling with a steel measuring tape which lives in a small plastic box. It pops out at one edge, winds back in on itself. He realises how irritating this is; says "I'm sorry" and puts it down. The fine bluish grey eyes stare at him, hard and determined, blink dottily and steady themselves.

"Nobody knows I am here. I don't intend that anybody should know." She is asking to be pushed over the last obstacle towards talking freely.

"Lecat?"

"Has been trying to seduce me. He has used every trick, every possible approach to persuade or trap me into going to bed with him." To Castang maybe an anticlimax? But not to her.

"And you haven't spoken of this to your husband?"

"I wouldn't speak of such things to anyone. Anyway, he'd never believe it. He'd say 'Preposterous!' " The imitation of General Laurens was recognisable.

"And you wouldn't have mentioned it to your sister."

"The very last – oh, I see what you're getting at. That she might have taxed him with his behaviour and he determined to silence her." Castang had not been getting at anything at all but kept his mouth shut. "Sisters have ways of telling. We were close, always. She may have noticed in me . . . even seen. Not long ago – and she was in the room. I was pouring out coffee, he came up behind me, put his hands on my breasts . . . This is very painful to me. Surely you can see what it costs me to speak of this. Contrary to every belief and instinct, undignified and humiliating, vile. To you it no doubt appears trivial." She pulled herself together and sketched a papery smile.

"But coming to see me, telling me like this, gives it importance."

"These philanderings – there must be others. It's at the bottom of this. I'm convinced. My sister must have found herself forced to face him with it. Threatened to make it public. Something he couldn't risk coming out, that would damage a business interest. The only thing that would hurt him no doubt, that he'd be capable of feeling. This is disgusting, but he's a disgusting man."

"See here, Madame –" No. Exasperation made the voice too loud, the tone a blare. A chisel had fallen on the floor: he felt the edge tenderly with his thumb, for damage. "This won't do. Accusations made with nods and winks and veiled hints are evidentially worthless. It isn't a case of divorce but of homicide. Respecting your finer feelings might do credit to my own. I appreciate your natural modesty, your social status, your very understandable reluctance to wash dirty clothes in public, but I can't make bargains. Behind me there is a judge. You'd have to be prepared for the intimate details of your life to be searched with hard questions. It is all done in private and remains confidential. But look ahead. If the instructing magistrate decides that anybody has a case to answer the papers go to the Chamber of Accusation, and if they agree, to the tribunal of the Assize Court. The President there has discretion and would doubtless use it to exclude the public from aspects of private life and forbid press reporting, but d'you realise that it's basic, it's constitutional that the debates in a criminal case should be oral and contradictory? You'd be cross-examined. You seem to think that you could tell me your story and that I'd agree to suppress it, while using it as leverage in an enquiry. I can't do that. You can make a bargain with the judge, through lawyers, it's done all the time, but you can't with me." And I don't know whether that's fury or fear, or even respect, in the way you look at me.

"What are you using the wood for?" abruptly.

"It was an old sideboard. Dirty and hideous. I'm hoping to make a cupboard thing for children's toys. I've two small daughters," wondering whether to go on pretending he didn't know Miranda existed.

"I'm in no position to impose bargains on you," slowly. "I can only hope that you will respect my confidence. I would refuse to speak of this in a court. I'd deny it. I can only beg you not to try and force me further into this. Making up my mind to come here was agony. Please do not speak of it to the judge. And let me go now."

"You leave me with no choice." And the ambiguity of that only struck him after she was gone.

"But what kind of world are these people living in?" exasperation screwing his voice into a weird countertenor register. "The Pope won't talk to women and upon my word I can sometimes sympathise – I could almost wish I lived in the Vatican." Vera burst out laughing.

"I'll make you some cocoa! You can tell me. It'll make better listening than tedious old Velitchko."

9 In the office next morning he was scowling at a hideous small object. A twentytwo-calibre brass cartridge.

"Yaysusmaria," said Castang resignedly. One had a homicide one needed like the cholera, but these things were like dead rats found in the street: they announced the plague. Arms of any sort he hated. Do not let us speak of hatred because that only brings us back to violence. But detestation ... these things are sold across the counter like sausage. Pistols are forbidden, meaning there is a flourishing black market. But parliaments (the hunting lobby is as vociferous in France as in the States) have decreed that the pleasure of shooting virtually anything anywhere is not to be denied to simple folk. All the Indians here have rifles, especially those who live in apartment tower-blocks. There are fewer bigger calibres since these are more expensive: only this consideration stops Suburban-Dupont from making with the Winchester like a western sheriff.

But cheap twentytwos, with an automatic action and a tenshot magazine, flourish like dandelions. Hence yaysusmaria.

What Castang was looking at was ammunition from the good old USA. An ingenious people. Only a twentytwo, but with a copper-jacketed bullet and a hollow point will make a hole in you like any lion calibre.

Several had been fired from the back seat of a car. At, to be sure, an Arab grocer's shop. A number of ejected shells were found and one cartridge intact – this one.

"Fell out while reloading," said Mr Steelpath who was investigating this happening.

"Well, perhaps for once in a million years the lab will find a print on it," and the telephone rang, and wouldn't you just know it. He waved his hand drearily at the little plastic box. Take it away with the beastly thing inside it.

"I was wondering whether, er, anywhere," said Miranda's voice, "I mean something private, could I talk to you, er, perhaps I could meet you, somewhere like a coffeeshop perhaps."

"Hold the line." He put the phone down, took a long breath,

held it, let it out again, took another and picked the phone up. There was a cake shop on the marketplace. Nice and public. No hole and corner meetings.

"Very well. Upstairs in Galand's – you know where that is? – in half an hour." Would there be bourgeois biddies gimlet-eyed, wondering what the little Laurens girl was doing with that rather peculiar-looking man? It would get back to Cécile. He didn't care. This time he was taking precautions.

You don't scowl at young ladies in cake shops as though they were rifle bullets. You make your face a polite blank. Everybody comes and tells the family lawyer secrets. Kind fatherly type: daughters of his own. You fold your hands, elbows on table, thumbnails against the lip, to ensure that the dracula-fangs do not pop out. You don't want any cake. You don't worry about the young girl being over-heard: she has a well-brought-up thread of a voice just above whisper level. But you do worry whether if inaudible to neighbours it would pick up on the pocket recorder. There is a background racket of cups and saucers and chairs and conversations. But Japanese electronics are wonderful and he has the microphone in his sleeve just the right distance from her mouth. As long as the cassette doesn't run out. As long as the little silicon thingies do not overheat and burst from these enormities.

Well, there's no turning back now. He has explained to Alice Jimenez and put her off till after lunch. Now let her bite on it. The women of the Laurens family – holy cow, holy mackerel. Are they in it together? First, Vera, because our sophisticated commissaire of police is feeling more like the Pope than ever. When in the confessional, Holy Father, stick to Turkish assassins. Don't let in any young girls.

He hadn't had much faith in the cassette, and lo, he had the volume just right. There wasn't even much distortion – technically, that is. Extraordinary people the Japanese. Just as well because he'd rather play it back than tell it.

"Cécile refuses to utter, but boy, does this child make up for her!"

Vera listened with a face that got longer and longer. It was almost all monologue. Castang had not wished to interrupt the flow, deciding that questions would be better when framed in more suitable surroundings than a cake shop. Alice Jimenez' office, for example.

"Where does she get this stuff?" asked Vera at the end, disbelievingly. "It has that glib, ghost-written sound like something out of a true confessions magazine. Does pornography circulate in the convent? – not that I'd be greatly surprised."

"Is there any truth in it at all? She's legally major, and Jimenez could order a gynae examination even over the objections of the parents."

"No no, pure fantasy."

"Pure's not the word."

"Just say overheated."

"It's highly circumstantial."

"My dear boy, you must recall numerous classic cases of young girls who were very circumstantial indeed. No, the amnesia switches on and off too handily, and she's much too complacent. Jimenez will agree. Is it even technically convincing?"

"Yes, that's commonplace and she could have heard about it. Any number of psychotrope medicaments in combination with quite a small amount of alcohol will produce amnesia. I'd have to get an expert opinion – I'd have thought either you have amnesia or you don't. If the dosage was just right you might get this dream state and blurry passivity with that amount of vague recollection afterwards – moot point."

Boiled down, the family had guests who liked a drink they'd run out of, and Miranda had been sent on her scooter to pick some up at the Barthélémy depot. After hours but Lecat had stayed to let her in. As a joke he'd given her 'something strong and orangey' – cointreau perhaps or curaçao? – and almost immediately she'd 'gone all swimmy'. Anyhow limp and 'like a double personality: like it was somebody else and I was watching' . . . Followed, highly explicit, a lot of heavy-breathing stuff involving a series of photographs with progressively fewer clothes on 'just like a zombie; I mean feeling simply awful but not able to stop.' He'd given her then another little glass and she couldn't remember anything at all after that . . .

"How did she get home and wasn't her absence noticed?" sceptical.

98

"People have done some odd things in these states: there's a wellknown case of a pilot flying the Atlantic. And it's conceivable that if the parents had guests they might not have noticed her getting home late."

"But didn't you ask whether next day she noticed a soreness or whatever?"

"Thanks very much, in a coffeeshop, I have to ask about her tedious vagina? Thanks, I'll leave that for Jimenez."

"I don't believe a syllable of it," said Vera flatly.

"Quite, but why do both Cécile and her daughter, inside a day, produce these tales? No coincidence, but is there collusion? Tricky ground. So Mum belongs to a class that is highly inhibited, does not talk about sex, and would rather it didn't exist. Conveys all sorts of enormities in a glancing mention of Lecat feeling her tits up, which she finds intensely shocking. So it would be, if it ever happened.

"Whereas the girl, convent or no it's a different generation, she's seen and heard a few things. I mean can you imagine General Laurens bringing *Penthouse* home and Cécile finding it a good read? While the daughter can bring it out tuppence-coloured. But isn't it the same accusation, the same fantasy? Surely Lecat who is pretty damn bright is not very likely to play knickers-down games with his schoolgirl niece or his tightass sister-in-law. Or maybe he is: I'm damned if I know."

"So okay," said Vera. "They both hate his guts and accuse him of vices because they've no grounds to accuse him of killing her."

"Why?"

"How should I know? Why don't you ask him?"

"I will."

Monsieur Lecat was not at the office: 'preferred to go home for lunch as a rule' said the delicious Aurélie when telephoned, and there Castang found him.

"Quite right; it's more comfortable and one eats better. I like a good lunch but I don't drink then. And to let you into a family secret it's easier at home to get them pissed while feeling flattered and that's good for business. Now what can I do for you?"

"Well, to let you into another family secret" . . . And Lecat fell about laughing.

"Glorious!" when he could stop a real laugh, and real tears. "So I did, I did feel her tits up one day, bored stiff and I'd had about five glasses of champagne. Wickedly irresponsible notion of wondering what she'd tell the Jesuits in the confessional; she's a very proper soul – and lo, you're the jesuit. Good for you. The child of course is out of her mind but there, you're an experienced man.

"And why both together – that was what worried you, huh? Come into the study and I'll show you something, because I'm pretty sure I know the answer." He rummaged about in a rolltop desk full of papers in disorder – but this wasn't the office. "Now where the hell – these never got stuck in any album – oh here we are. Ach," taking a bunch of photos from an envelope, "it's saddening to look at these now. Poor Marguerite . . ." And again there was something genuine in his voice. "I wouldn't have shown you these while she was alive, and I wouldn't with her dead. I have to, though: they're all the evidence I've got. She was almighty pissed and I was pretty far on. Here. Just about as the child describes." Castang looks and feels shame because Marguerite had not deserved his eyes on her, and they do not have the anaphrodisiac vulgarity of the ones in magazines.

"Who could have got hold of these?"

"A blackmail angle? No, I took these. And I keep this locked as you saw, because servants will snoop anywhere. But Marguerite had a key. I don't keep business papers here. She wouldn't have shown them to anyone, that's for sure. In fact if she'd found them she'd have burned them in a hurry. Proof to my eyes that it wasn't her snooping about."

"And why did you keep them?" asked Castang, not quite blandly. Lecat shrugged.

"I liked looking at them."

"How old are they?"

"I don't know, a year maybe. No, I think sweet Cécile's been in my drawers – forgive the pun, imposes itself – sure as hell haven't been in hers. Maybe I should have, sounds a bit crook, but the child must have got the idea from Mum."

And Castang has to admit to himself that it is more convincing than the stories he's been hearing. He himself had seen Cécile rummaging about, and Marguerite's keys would be in her bag.

"While we're playing truth, what exactly was your business in Brussels that night?" Lecat smiled, just sarcastic enough to show he appreciates rude questions asked politely.

"I was in the Golden Pheasant, teaching Japanese to eat with a knife and fork. Thereafter eating girls with knife and fork and I was along to make them feel cosy. The Japanese have gone back to the native habitat but I should imagine it can all easily be vouched for."

"Your driver waited?"

"My dear chap, keeping the driver out late is frowned upon. I drove myself, the autoroute from Brussels is under an hour but I'm afraid I paid no attention to the exact time. Not later than two; the Japanese athletics palled fairly rapidly and I'd done all I should to be hospitable." He made no hesitation over the address of the bordel – "highly thought of in Nato circles."

"Where have you been then?" asked the Judge of Instruction in querulous accents. It is not easy for a young woman to find herself the legal superior of a police commissaire who might well be double her age and have experience to match. Think about this and one will see that it is a severe test of character. Umbrage again, Richard was fond of saying.

"In Brussels for a quick blow job." She laughed rather harder than this simple joke merited, but it stopped ice forming round the edges.

"I deserved that. Worrying affair though, and I do believe in keeping close touch. Your predecessor was a devious person. Trusting nobody is a sign of mediocrity, would you agree?"

"People who think only of protecting themselves . . ."

"When people only see collaboration in terms of collusion. Where candour is regarded as naïveté and trust jeered at for innocence. Angelism as they call it here. While slyness is prized and too often rewarded."

"An atmosphere in which an assumed candour can be a clever tactic," said Castang.

"You talk and I'll listen."

"It struck me at the outset that Lecat phoned himself and to the PJ direct. Local notables as a rule don't get involved with cops, do they? They like to keep things in the family, meaning the Proc and a nice well-mannered instruction that knows what not to instruct. Lecat seems to invite trouble, with total confidence in handling it. Is that candour? He's an able and intelligent man. Does that mean much? I've known one or two highly distinguished men, impeccable in their professional world, who went all to pieces when faced with a domestic catastrophe. His alibi isn't worth much. The autoroute late at night, in a Ferrari . . . if the estimated time of death is wrong by even half an hour, which the pathologist agrees it might well be, then he fits in nicely."

"When we speak of keeping things in the family . . ."

"Yes, it's a closely knit group. I may say we've found no sign whatever of the hypothetical intruder. So – general heading; people who had a right to be there, the servants: those who are always in and out, whose entrance or exit cause no comment or pass unnoticed, the family and some of the business staff: lastly some unknown person deliberately introduced by one or the other."

Jimenez lit a cigarette. Pale lips and strong white teeth; brown bread and goats' cheese.

"The servants show an extraordinary coherence. Anachronism like the old-family-retainer. In the army with General Laurens. Works systematically: give total loyalty to the men and they give it back."

"Enviable relationship."

"Yes, and this confidence admits of candour. One admires the General; he speaks well of everybody because he refuses to hear ill of anybody. Speaks highly of Lecat, 'splendid chap'."

"Is that genuine, or is it a system?"

"Isn't it both? Old Army, not like the technocrats nowadays. Caste. The world is crooks and thieves, jews and freemasons: we are catholic, monarchist, and live by our sword." She nodded; the 'same in Spain'.

"Clearcut and no grey areas. In combat you know who'll come out for you under fire, and who stays in the dugout with his steel helmet on, counting the soap ration. I suppose it's laughable?"

"One can laugh, and still have respect."

"Yes. Physical courage is two a penny but who's got moral courage? Am I to call him a wooden-head because he finds it not the thing to beat the wife or cheat at cards? See the men fed and look after their socks before you go to your own dinner. No, I don't think the General a contemptible witness. Speaks well of Lecat and I give it weight. Vouches for the servants and I incline to pass them. The office crowd? Attract no attention during the day, but what would they be doing there at night. Remains the family. And who can tell, about that?"

"Mr Castang, I'm only an ignorant young woman but people have their concealed side and can often keep it well concealed."

"Sure. Hit people at the right angle and they'll splinter apart. Everybody has a weak patch; you, me, the Pope and the Brothers Karamazov. I'm hoping that you've confidence enough to let me go on tapping quietly from all angles, while the press and the public and the Proc are all screaming for results: arrest somebody."

"You're tired," said Miss Jimenez. "You are emotional, garrulous, and highly unsure of yourself." It sounded so like Richard talking that he burst out laughing.

"I am anxious. God forfend I should ever be sure of myself."

"A relief to listen to a man who doesn't feel obliged to keep his defences up the whole day in front of a woman." She was laughing too.

"Maybe I'm falsely candid, like Lecat: one sly schwein deserves another. Seriously, I've found a flaw and I don't know what to make of it. Madame Laurens, openly and emphatically and without any evidence, accuses Lecat of making away with her sister. In case I'm not convinced which I plainly am not, she adds accusations of lecherous behaviour. Within a few hours her teenaged daughter comes up with a similar highly-coloured tale, begging me to keep it dark. I must add that when I put this straight up to Lecat he provided a spontaneous and convincing explanation. Thought it very funny . . ."

"Young girls," said Alice in a tone resembling Vera's. "Leave that aside; what kind of woman is this?"

"Army-wife caste to match Laurens. Traditions respected, appearances safeguarded, honour maintained, and no cracks must show in front of the servants. So I'm a servant: why let me see cracks? Why be so eager to accuse Lecat? A lot of strain there: something nasty in the woodshed."

"Oh dear. And the child? Says Uncle Harry was romping

with her in her pyjamas and touching her where he shouldn't, is that it?"

"Lecat explains it as a put-up job inspired by the mother. I'd think it needed more than just malevolence. It worries me a bit."

"And it worried you further that Jimenez would get excited about it? All female and socialist, and anxious to bash these reactionaries with their inherited incomes – right? You may as well admit it; you were reluctant to mention it."

"Some truth in that," said Castang ruefully.

"Very well. I'll restrain my prurient and indecent interrogations for as long as I can. I'll tell the Proc that cracking the servants' alibis is a delicate piece of dentistry, and that you must be left to your devices for a day or so."

"This is appreciated."

"And, Castang –"

"Yes?"

"You don't have an awful lot of time. Tick tock, tick tock."

"I don't have an awful lot of anything. Shit shot shit shot."

"Cat shat mat," said Miss Jimenez, not laughing.

"Preposterous!" said General Laurens.

"I quite agree, sir, but is that the point? What people say is one thing and why is another. It doesn't have to be the truth; it very seldom is. You must have met the situation often."

"You find me ossified, isn't that it? Arguing about the guilt of Dreyfus. Preaching the merits of an offensive in Champagne. Replying to you haughtily that the opinions of some junior functionary in the intendancy were of no interest to me. Don't stand there looking embarrassed!"

"I am embarrassed. A homicide enquiry leads me to meddle in private lives. All this is quicksand. The press tries to winkle out confidential details. If I resist, any innuendo will do – that I'm incompetent, that I'm in Lecat's pay, that I'm subject to political pressure."

"The English won't have it," said Laurens filling his pipe. "Contempt of court. But that's our country for you. Ever since censorship was abolished and that's eighteen-seventy, the freedom of the press has been abused. There's no proper sub judice rule."

104

"I'm grateful to you. Because the suggestion of tampering . . ."

"Sit down," shaking out one match and striking another. "Tell me," puffing, "if you can – whether you seriously believe – that Lecat is in some way – responsible for my sister-in-law's death."

"I'd have to answer that any such allegation is unsupported, resting upon vague hints and suggestions."

"Originating with my wife. Quite. Can't help you there. She wouldn't mention them to the press. Can assure you of that."

Castang did not feel that any mention of Miranda would help matters.

"My position is that I must verify suggestions. That is no indication that I give them credence."

"And my position," said Laurens mildly, "is that I can do nothing to block or object to a line of questions bearing upon my wife's private affairs."

"Oh yes," said Castang, "you could complain that I was being unwarrantably intrusive."

"And what would be the result of that?"

"Probably that I would be instructed to direct my enquiries towards more fruitful areas. If you were to press the point it's likely that my superior in Lille would find other outlets for my talents."

"You are candid."

"Just pragmatic."

"It is honourable to warn me."

"If you feel able to confide in me, sir, I can perhaps establish, uh, that these allegations . . ."

Laurens tapped his pipe, struck another match.

"The two sisters have always been much attached. That my wife was greatly shaken goes without saying. There was also a tale . . . I don't know how much weight to give this. I don't even know whether strictly speaking it is true. That in their youth, perhaps childhood, some older man, some relative, was said to have taken advantage of their innocence. I should hope you could agree that fact or fiction it lay outside the what d'you call it, frame of reference, of your enquiry?"

"I'll respect that. I'm grateful and relieved. Something of the sort had occurred to me."

"One sister tended to be rackety. I can't deny a certain reliance on alcohol. The other does take up a rigid, you might call it puritanical attitude, towards some subjects."

"We're trying," said Castang, "to clear away all the irrelevancies. While we're at it, for the record, do you mind telling me what your own family activities were, that evening?"

"Not at all. The question was due, and I'd given it thought. Won't be much help, I fear. Cécile was at a concert, charity I think, don't know where but it would be easy to look up. Music doesn't mean much to me, I'm afraid: chap for me might as well be winding a clock. And I was right here in this room. Quiet evening, reading a book, playing patience, knitting socks. This woman who calls herself Yourcenar – she's good!" It lay on the table beside him, the place neatly marked with a trombone paperclip. "Cleenewerck de Crayencour, that's a splendid old Flamand name. I recommend it!"

"And your daughter?" slipping it in where it might not be noticed.

"Miranda? Don't recall seeing her but I do remember the noise. They shut themselves in the bedroom to play their pop records, there seems no way of putting a stop to it."

"I'm really grateful," said Castang.

He was less grateful outside the door because there were press men as usual. He uttered the usual prim formulae about gathering information that might aid in shedding light upon the movements of certain persons but they hung on, dogs baiting a bear. Unless something startling happened and, he fervently hoped, a long way away, let's say Perpignan, they would keep on. Alice Jimenez was patient, but how long could she – could he – keep it up?

"They do know," said Lecat, putting his foot on the office desk and swinging the black leather chair idly about, "that I'm notoriously quick to sue, at even a whisper of defamation; and they've rather changed their minds about thinking it pays off in increased circulation; I took one to the cleaners not long ago, and whatever dear Cécile says about me they aren't going to print it. But any suggestions from you," laughing heartily, "about my private life would result in your going to the cleaners too. Make no mistake about that, one-way trip." The press had been insufferable and Castang

106

could sympathise with some shortness of temper. Lecat's nerve was solid: was that wearing thin? But stand up to anything that sounds like a threat.

"You hesitated, didn't you, before calling me? Maybe Lille. Maybe nobody, but that would be a bit much, even for you. You settled on me. Handy, close by, easy to control. Fairly junior and new in the post. Vulnerable on all counts." Sleepy smile from Lecat . . . "You've learned that you can count on me to do my work, and also that I don't leak to the press."

"That's true. But what is all this shit?"

"It'll take a few days, no doubt, but I'll find out who killed your wife. It's a narrowing field."

"Wasn't me. That's all I can tell you."

Many a true word: that indeed was all that he told.

**10** In his early days, as 'pupil officer' and trainee, Castang had beside gymnastics done a bit of boxing. He had never been classed more than Fair. Interdepartmental semifinalist; thereabout. Good footwork but not enough reach and not enough punch; remarks that were still being made. He remembered little, but when you took a big one, jaw or temple, you went woolly for a space. You covered up and dodged about, and until you got clear again you took several more heavy ones and hoped they were in fairly harmless places. So hold on for clarity of mind, boy.

Ah, the famous French clarity of mind. Monsieur Richard, snarling at the extreme woolliness of minds surrounding his own, used to threaten his staff with lessons in elementary grammar and basic spelling, to be conducted by Fausta.

Belt tight, thus, lip tight; hold on tight too to fundamentals, a polite word for asshole. Vera had long ago found a slogan to suit these circumstances, in the instructions given by an English gentleman to his soldier son, setting out for the trenches in Flanders.

'In case of a bombardment, retire at once to the undercroft.' And there Castang remained, under heavy fire from journalists and Monsieur Sabatier in Lille.

'Rebondissement Spectaculaire' said the newspaper headlines. A spectacular rebound: youse can say that again, boys, relishing your venerable cliché reminted with for once strict and perfect accuracy. Castang recalled Félix Lecat's last words to himself, which weren't far from being the last words he'd addressed to anyone. Because Lecat had been found by a badly upset Perrine when she came to work – good God, still this morning . . . Felled, stretched; and quite dead.

Alice Jimenez had only looked with a cold eye, saying nothing beyond 'This shouldn't have happened, Commissaire, should it?' The Proc had had a mask like Castlereagh – 'Very smooth he looked, and grim. Seven bloodhounds followed him.'

Four times seven, counting the television crew.

'Start running,' advised VV. 'Don't stop before reaching Amiens. Don't stop there, either.' He had been saved from the television crew only by old Georges saying 'Any journalists, I'll shoot on sight.' But from Procs and Sabatiers he had been saved only by General Laurens, who had appeared to take charge, and had not lost the habit of command.

"I fail entirely to see," in a highly military tone, "that anyone should withdraw their confidence from Monsieur Castang simply because things have taken a nasty turn." Initial, and fatal, hesitancy of the enemy. "Puts a panicky complexion on things. Press won't fail to jump on that. In on your flank in a flash." Withdrawal of enemy disguised as prudish wraparound of long prim skirts. Castang was not to know whether it was 'In this region the General is much respected.' Maybe too it was the riding school connection.

"Well General, since you feel your responsibility engaged . . ."

"Accustomed to it, dear man." These bland tones completed the withdrawal: the Proc left on heavy feet.

"Doesn't do," said Laurens returning from 'having a word to console that poor Perrine', "to flap."

"I owe you a debt," said Castang.

"Have a cup of tisane. All that coffee's not doing you any good."

"This has shaken me."

"That's natural. A surprise river-crossing. No reason why you should not continue. But I must apologise for everything being moved before you got here."

Yes indeed. Why had he been called at all? (Why indeed? Because the General had done so himself.)

He hadn't needed the camera, nor any of the other junk in the doggy-bag. Everything had been mopped and tidied before he'd got here. If he'd seen a dead body it was something laid out as though for a wake, on a stretcher ready to be carted. Nothing for him to do but listen to a lot of talk. Hear Say . . .

He said. She said. They said, or that's what they said they said at the time.

Perrine, one could hardly blame her, had gone completely off her trolley. Found him on the terrace by the pool. A horrible sight, and she was alone in a house with assassins lurking in every shadowed corner, and she'd gone running, yelling, to Violette.

Next to arrive – or so he said – had been Rémy-the-baker, who'd claimed he'd never have touched anything himself, meaning to say

109

he knew better. But talk to old Georges, obstinate old bugger that he was.

Old Georges said nothing save – at considerable length – that he wasn't going to talk to a lot of useless cops.

And if Mos-sieu Castang didn't like that he could go take a good crap in the corner because he, Georges, didn't give a monkey's bollock for what cops said or thought.

"I must apologise for that, too," said General Laurens.

Georges said he'd done what he should, which was phone for his commanding officer. Meantime, as senior rank present, take charge of matters. Tell that fool Perrine to take hold of herself, and if she couldn't then Violette would, and get this mess cleared up. Blood, blood, there hadn't been any blood to speak of, women exaggerated. The Commander had been taken out by some ruffians with a gun butt or something of the sort, depressed skull fracture. Think he'd never seen one before? Get him to reanimation quick and there might be some chance but not a hope, his view, and he'd died before the ambulance arrived.

Castang had been notified by the hospital, perfectly correctly, even before he'd had Laurens' phone call. Standing orders. The doctor on the reanimation team has a death in suspect circumstances, query violence. In accordance with which he has left the body in situ and we hereby inform the judicial authorities, thereby degaging our legal responsibilities, Commissaire, and take that as read.

Very well. Who is in a state now to give coherent answers to elementary questions? Rémy for a start.

No use asking me, I haven't stirred from here and I know damn all, my job is to keep this household fed and right now I have to rethink my whole marketing, okay? Confirmed, for what that's worth, by old Georges.

Disbelieve one, you disbelieve the lot. That's not Richard, or maxims-of-my-grandfather, that's just elementary procedure; take all the statements on their face and match up afterwards.

So Jean-Baptiste. Laconic as ever. Was sitting there having breakfast when Perrine came tumbling in. Called by the old boy to bear a hand, so bore a hand. Being of no further use, went to work. What else did you expect? Confirmed by Violette.

110

Caroline had got out of bed and gone to have a shower. In this house the women washed in the morning. The men came in at the end of the day dirty from work and liked to have the bathroom to themselves. She'd heard voices and understood Perrine to be in a state about something but hadn't the curiosity, thanks, to come running with just a towel round her. Confirmed by Violette, who'd had her own shower first and was making the men's breakfast.

Their nerves were on edge. The idea that a few people, sticking to a simple fabricated tale and giving one another alibis, can diddle professional questioners; that is cardboard. When interrogated people tell their little grievances. Petty emotions show in the fabric. Old Georges, indignant about his precious perimeter, said the gate was the weak point. He'd always said so. That louse Frédo, thinking himself privileged because he was the driver with opportunities for gossip. Wouldn't put it past him to fall asleep leaving the gate open.

The interrogator loves repeating gossip.

"Perfect, utter, total bullshit," said Frédo. "Old cunts who know everything. Do better to have left their frigging bones in Indochina."

"When did the boss get in?"

"Early. Nine, halfpast? I had to put the car away, lock up. I watched the television a while. No need to be stroppy, it's easily verified. Guillaume was with me, and Belle-Gueule and Aurélie."

Lecat could have been several hours in coma. Would there be any way, perhaps from the manner or the quantity of internal bleeding, to tell even approximately when he had been hit? The pathologists wouldn't like the question much, thought Castang.

Guillaume was in the office; a worried man.

"Thought you'd be around. About last night? There was a plan for restructuring – all right, all right, fancy word. Reorganising."

"Jobs going to get lost?"

"No jobs getting lost. But he was a pretty tricky man, Mr Castang, pretty devious. What he said was he wanted to spend less time on the operation. Simplified accounting procedures, internal audit. Jobs weren't at risk. At least I don't think so. Better say, way things stand now, I hope not. Lawyers no doubt will come sticking their fingers in everything. But he'd have said, behave as though nothing happened. That's what we're doing."

"So last night?"

"We worked here till I don't know. Sevenish. We had a bite in the pub."

"The Fox and Geese?"

"That's right, the grub's good there, we use it often. We went back to the house, there were some papers there. He gave us a drink, we left around – well I was home before eleven. Nothing abnormal. He was in a good mood. Said he was going to bed."

"You left together?"

"Yes of course, he had to open the gate for us."

"Where's Cesari?"

"Paris. Standing off journalists. Reassuring suppliers. Smoothing out customers. Or so I should hope, it's his bloody job."

"I'd like to see Mademoiselle Aurélie."

"I'll send her in."

Castang had thought nothing much about her, beyond 'pretty girl'. There would be more to her than that but what are we to do about it? Insist upon having homosexual policemen to interrogate girls?

She's the hostess, there to put a bit of charm into operations. So she's corn-ripe, cherry-ripe. Character, too?

He said nothing, lit a cigarette while pointing at the chair, on which she sat herself. She was not disconcerted. She took one of his cigarettes and lit it with his lighter, blew a plume of smoke and stared over his shoulder, letting the silence go on, so that he had to break it. It is an obvious ploy for putting people off balance and hadn't worked. Poise; well, you'd expect that.

"What's your real name?"

She smiled a little.

"Marie. Not Jeanne-Marie or Marie-Rose. Just penny plain."

"Which is as good as tuppence coloured so why call yourself Aurélie?"

"There was an argument I didn't win. It was said that customers like something gaudy."

"What does your father do?"

"He reads meters for the electricity board. It's extraordinary what people get up to, inside their four walls, he says."

112

"You live at home?"

"No. I have a flat here and my parents live in Lens."

"Your own flat, or somebody else's?" She smiled again, to show him that she understood; cops ask needling questions.

"My own. I have quite a good salary. More on commission."

"Independent, then."

"Just so that you don't get wrong ideas. Selling the Bordeaux that is ready-to-lay-down doesn't imply my laying down with it."

"Neatly put."

"I've had practice with the idea."

"Yes. These are rude questions, but they have to be put."

"The police have this reputation. Or so I'm told." She was intelligent, well controlled. The poise was professional. Plainly she had expected to be questioned, and had prepared for it. Her attitude, careful and alert, was natural in the circumstances.

"The police does not try to be horrible," said Castang. "It just is. But facts have to come to light. We had one homicide, now we've two. There can be little things that might look awkward, and that one prefers to keep secret; and I have to have them. I have no wish to embarrass or humiliate people. People sometimes fail to realise that when one is frank with a police officer he's readier, and finds it easier, to respect the confidence given."

"I've nothing to hide."

"Like Monsieur Lecat. I found him very frank about his relations with girls."

"Did he claim that they included me?"

"His being dead needn't make you afraid of saying so, if it's true."

"His being dead wouldn't make me afraid of calling him a liar either: it isn't true." The eyes had flashed. Nice eyes, dappled between brown and green, striking with that fair hair.

"He made no such claim and I'm not pretending he did. But others might."

"If you have names," now tight and hard, "name them."

"Cesari possibly?" She laughed then, relieved. A soft laugh without malice.

"Le beau Roland. It suits his vanity to let people suppose that. You should know that the bigger the puff made the bigger the discount they're ready to knock off. Roland's act of the world's greatest lover I don't set much store by."

"Or Guillaume then?" She was frowning now.

"You're thinking, then, the woman in a man's world, has to screw with the manager or she won't keep the job? I'd answer that it depends on the value she puts on herself."

"Just that it's been known."

"I can't quite make you out. You seem reasonable, for a cop, but you seem to have a conventional sort of mind."

"Most people are conventional, or what's the meaning of the word?"

She thought about that and nodded to show she had taken the point.

"Any girl has trouble with conventional minds on the let's-do-it question. They want to believe she adores it and rushes to it on every possible occasion because they like to believe in Irresistible Me."

"That's me all right, looking pathetic, like the child that didn't get enough porridge."

"Glad to hear it," tartly. "I was beginning to wonder if you'd been watching too many porno films lately."

"My mind is now clearer on the subject," said Castang stolidly, "so I'll thank you, for now." She got up, and turned back to him.

"This is a good job. I enjoy doing it. Félix gave me an area of responsibility, and the liberty to organise it. He was a –" she looked for the right word – "multifaceted personality. This could be startling, even frightening. He'd be utterly inhuman and then suddenly come out with a kind and sensitive remark. That's rare I should think in these highly structured computerised operations. I suppose it's awfully banal to suggest that this variety was a factor in his becoming so successful, and rich. It's only fair to say that he did have his nice side, and you ought to know that." She does have a convincing ring, thought Castang. I'd like to believe her. Maybe she can be believed, at that. I do of course have an evil disposition.

That pathology department – looking at him with dislike: too many dead bodies were coming in with him at the door. He could see their point. Out there, if so disposed, you can rhapsodise about

114

Eloquent, Just, and Mighty Death, making it sound pretty fervent. Inside here it isn't even a body. More likely to be a sense of aggravation about overtime. So this is the late Monsieur Lecat, is it? Fortunate in the possession of many millions. What are we supposed to do, turn his pockets out? There might be a few hundred-dollar bills tucked away? To us he's just late.

Outside the big cities with their own Medico-Legal department, hospitals loathe forensic work. Lot of extra labour the indemnities for which are meagre, and you might find yourself in court with some evil lawyer nagging at you.

Still, they were patient, in a fairly short-suffering way. Naturally the head had gone to radiology: head wounds are . . .

Stubby fingers slammed photos into the show-up screen, pointed at obscure shadows. There and there, bloodclots. No no, impossible to say how long the coma had lasted.

"It's possible to theorise," with the limited tolerance of those who did so. "If they'd found him straightaway, helicopter, specialised cranial unit, if, if, if. Wound like that, death pretty well irreversible. Don't take my word, ask five experts, you'll get five different expert opinions."

"Could he have got up and walked at all?"

"Now that at last is an interesting question. You mean was he necessarily hit where you found him? Unlikely. Might have tottered a few steps. It does happen; the literature is full of examples. That sort of wound makes it dubious. Quite deep. Fellow was sabred."

"Can I have photos and the calibrated measurements?"

"You can," generous.


In the office he propped photos on shelves, gazed at them; put them on his desk and stared through the magnifier, muttering. He became aware that VV was imitating the muttering sotto voce, taking the piss again, the evil cow: he stopped it. He was no longer feeling hemmed-in, drowning in selfpity. A stoic, stubborn feeling had replaced this. He still wished he were Marlowe and had an office bottle of whisky because he needed a big one. But that would only lead to another. And another. By-our-lady of unanswered questions . . . As Mr Ricardo says so sagely after another homicide, 'There are things that must be borne in mind.'

'How true, how very true that is!' remarks Hanaud with un-bounded admiration.

Sabred, was the word used by the pathologist. Now cutlasses, sabres, yataghans and the like, are rarities round here, are they not? The description isn't right. The wound was not a slash. Shorter, deeper, with a corner to it. More like, like –

"An axe surely," said VV patiently. But swing an axe at some-body, wouldn't the wound be deeper, more crushing? Still, with that for a start, let's go look for weapons. A concrete item of evidence concentrates the mind.

Rémi-the-baker was every synonym you could think of for edgy, touchy, wary. One is the more so, Castang told him, for imaginary horrors and portents. No fear as bad as the one the girl gets in the Hitchcock film. Rémy agreed that this was so.

For Castang had had an idea. He walked about the kitchen opening drawers. A professional cook amasses a collection of knives. Some five or six are in constant use. From thin and flexible to stiff and stubby, from the long narrow carver to the little onion-peeling 'économe'. A professional chopping-knife makes a fair cutlass. Castang put it on the table on a clean sheet of kitchen paper, holding it by the tip.

Quite a weapon. Fortyfive centimetres (among much rubbish cops carry pocket tapemeasures) end to end. Blade at base seven centimetres. The cutting edge tapers from a butt one centimetre broad of tempered steel. The massive wooden handle gives a good grip.

He put it on the scale. Five hundred and twenty gram. A well-worn knife that had been much sharpened and lost a lot of metal. He looked along the edge. Wavy near the base, as though notched and ground down, but along the whole length sharp enough to shave with. Rémy watched these manoeuvres with an indulgent, unfrightened eye.

"Pretty efficient tool." The answering nod was casual.

"You could kill somebody with that."

"And very easily. As it happens I didn't. I'm pretty sure I could prove that, fairly easily."

"Tell me," said Castang, sitting down to be comfortable.

"It's used every day but not yet this morning. I clean my tools every night before I put them away, but I reckon with a really good microscope you'd find traces of everything I've done with it for a week. I mean, a rinse under the hot tap, a wipe with a rag . . . There'd be blood, sure, bone. Show up like a landrover in the Sahara. But human blood, human bone – still, I'm not a cop, I'm only a suspect."

"But somebody else could have taken it? The drawer isn't locked? Anyone who'd ever been here and seen you work?"

"They could, I suppose."

"We won't worry about taking it to the lab. It won't fit the wound. For a start, it's much too sharp."

"You were having me on?"

"A bit. And I did think it might have worked, until I looked."

"If I wanted to kill somebody with one of my own knives," said Rémy, "I wouldn't take that; I'd take this." A longer, slimmer steak knife. "Quicker – you know what I mean?"

"Yes." Point is a lot more efficient than blade. Gets there quicker. A chopper is a loony's weapon. Or maybe a woman's.

Before the court is also the important question of impulse. If you have for some time meditated assassination, then you can choose your weapon. Getting unexpectedly into a fight, you pick up whatever's handy. The choice, whether instinctive or deliberate, sheds light on the person making it. As Rémy had just noticed.

"Haven't you a meat-axe?" asked Castang with visions of butchers chunking off pork chops. Mathieu shook his head.

"Some cooks use them. Not me – clumsy."

"What we're looking for, maybe, is a sharp edge that's gone blunt – I can't find anything that fits."

"If it's an axe you're looking for, there's one in the woodshed."

Woodshed! Castang, where are your wits?

"Show me." As is the way of woodsheds, a dilapidated affair hidden among shrubberies; a door with a broken hinge; a lot of junk and broken flowerpots lying about. "Who comes here?"

"The gardeners; they saw wood and bring it up in a barrow." There were the remains of a beech trunk and some sawn branches. A sledgehammer and wedges lay about. A cross-cut saw and the axe hung on rusty nails in the wall. The axe was much too heavy, but a hatchet lay on a block surrounded by kindling chips.

"Hasn't been anybody here since winter: look at all those cobwebs," said Rémy cheerfully. "Lazy old bugger, Georges." Dust and sawdust lay thick. One needed no microscope to prove Mathieu right. Nobody could have come here without visible disturbance. Castang dropped to his hunkers to get the light behind the kindling axe, but the blade had not been wiped.

VV had taken Lecat's shoes for lab analysis. Inconclusive and likely to remain so. Dryish weather; plenty of people crossed the terrace and a flagged path led to it from outside. Perrine mopped the tiles daily. When she came, finding Lecat, it was to mop again The footmarks were all still there – but there were too many. The gardeners had come and the ambulance men – and the legal authorities – a suspect print would turn out to be the Proc's! His own . . . or those of General Laurens.

Nothing had changed about the basic problem; had it? As with the death of the wife, so with the death of the husband. There were the three groups, who had or could have had easy access. The servants: easiest opportunity but what could be the motive? Who among them would go about tomahawking the boss? Was it any more likely than asphyxiating his wife? There was no inconsistency in their behaviour, none of the little awkwardnesses and reticence which point to lying: it made no sense.

The group of office staff. They'd been in the library, where the litter of ashtrays and glasses was consistent with the tale told by Guillaume, and Marie. Had they all left together? VV had been sent to enquire into the living habits of Monsieur Cesari . . . she would be good at disentangling whatever might lie behind the stud and clothes-horse façade.

And there was Lecat himself. Monsieur Metz, the Enforcer, sent to rout about in all the dusty corners, had come up with nothing but the usual gossip.

Plenty of things were possible there. Those three might easily have agreed to put a lid on some damaging little affair capable of jeopardising the three of them. If for instance there had been crookery in the internal auditing of the Barthélémy business, and Lecat had found a trace of it, and called them to account . . . Speculation of this sort was worthless as Castang knew well, until the legal and actuarial gentlemen, whose task it would now be to sort out Lecat's affairs, had done their sums. And if Lecat had uncovered some fiddle going on, wouldn't he have included the accountant in the conference?

Marginally in consideration remained a deus – or a dea – ex machina: Laurens' theory that Marguerite had been visited by some boyfriend. Alternatively some girlfriend of her husband's. Who had settled the one with a handy pillow and the other – well, bring your own kindling axe along in a plastic bag . . . this one was so full of far-fetched fabrications that he couldn't, however hard he tried, bring himself to give it much weight. It presupposed both husband and wife letting in the mystery cloaked figure late at night, both blissfully unaware of sinister projects afoot.

One was left with the last group; the family. Especially the sister-in-law and the teenage niece, who'd both made weird accusations and might be tempted – who knew? – to come calling with a harpoon and a wish for personal vengeance. These family relationships . . . which a cop dreads. No means of delegating that: the area was the special old Castang reserve.

A pity, a great pity, that Lecat who had laughed the tales off as the fantasies of foolish women should have been prevented from any challenge to tell a bit more. One would be curious about that. Altogether it had seemed the most promising line of enquiry open.

Unhappily there was no way of seeing either Cécile or Miranda bursting in brandishing the harpoon: 'Buck, your time has come.'

Lecat, by two accounts at least, had let the members of his office staff out (operating the gate which they could not open without waking either Frédo or Violette) around elevenish: Guillaume who lived some twenty minutes off had said 'by eleven' but said he hadn't really looked and it could have been a quarter of an hour out. His wife said 'she'd looked vaguely' and thought it was about ten past when she heard the garage door go up. Lecat, according to this reasonable story, had been 'in a good mood' and had said he was going to bed. Fair enough; why would he do anything else? Would he have sat up listening to music or playing with his stamp collection? Nothing pointed to anything of the sort. He had been found in his clothes, those of the evening before. He hadn't changed or undressed: there was no sign that he'd been upstairs:

his bed was not slept in nor even sat on: everything, said Perrine, was as she had left it.

Assuming then that he had let someone in by arrangement, or been surprised by someone, at maybe two or three in the morning – what had he been doing in the interval? There were no papers out, no half-written letters (the 'papers' Guillaume had referred to, sales-chart stuff on graph paper, had been found in the yellow folder named, stuffed casually back inside Lecat's desk). He hadn't just sat there playing patience! It made no sense to suggest that he had been clonked later than midnight, even if the medical evidence was inconclusive: nothing in the post-mortem findings was inconsistent with his having lain in coma for six or seven hours. Digestion was consistent with his having eaten a piece of bread and butter and a hunk of terrine out of the fridge: Rémy confirmed finding crumbs and a smeared knife on the kitchen table. Just the sort of bite a man fancies before going to bed.

But at General Laurens' house, half an hour away by car, there'd been an evening party.

The good old tradition in provincial society: So-and-so's Thursdays. At Home: there was a regular occasion, second in the month or whatever, for these parties. Nothing formal, nothing grand, but a select dozen people, and the invitations prized by the local gentry. A catering firm in the town, well thought of since the seventeen-fifties, sent out its celebrated duck patty. A half-dozen needing no invitation would be reminded by telephone; as many more got a card.

A sobersides entertainment with an old military crony or two and a couple of legal luminaries from Douai or Béthune. Add a selected lion; perhaps a professor from the medical faculty or the chef de cabinet of the Préfecture.

And as Castang knows well, remarkably powerful, of immense influence throughout the department. In principle, nothing political is ever mentioned, nothing cultural, nothing controversial. The conversation an exchange of well-worn views, some family news and general gossip. The wine is good (Barthélémy) and the recipe for the duck patty dates from 1722. After supper there is a move towards some three bridge tables, armchairs in that pretty country salon, good cigars . . . An invitation to General Laurens' house is much appreciated.

And as an alibi it couldn't very well be bettered.

Commissaires of police do not belong, unless of divisional grade and godfathered by a substantial guarantor. Castang knew about these parties from Richard, who had gone occasionally, and without Judith.

'Disregard at your peril,' he had said simply. It was the plain reason why he had never got that controller's job in Paris. 'The word "establishment" in the provinces attaches a great deal more weight to the wife you marry than the abilities you show. It is as it always was – say your prayers to Madame Verdurin.'

Oh yes, General and Madame Laurens were provided for till well after midnight. But Miranda? On these social occasions schoolgirls are not a great draw (the rather special kind of party known as 'ballets roses' is an exception) but the daughter of the house is expected to be seen and to make herself useful. Good training in the hostess arts: we aren't talking about the kind of hostess that wears a uniform. Nice old gentlemen will notice these daughters, and say a kind word. But after nine, say, or half past, call it after supper, she would vanish and nobody would even notice, let alone think it worth comment. It was not, thought Castang, in the least degree a reassuring thought that his most promising homicide suspect should be a schoolgirl. The idea gives him the cold creebles down his back.

He had verified his ideas about narcotics with a young doctor from the Reanimation unit.

"What does the girl say she was given – a cointreau? Quite enough. Tell your daughters to accept no drinks from strangers. Valium mixed with whisky is the downhill run, Castang: that's the Streif at Kitzbuhel. Get your feet crossed there and you wake up with us in Reanimation extremely hard put to it to tell what has happened."

But suggesting that darling daughter would find it technically possible to take her moped, around ten at night, arrive at the Lecat palace about eleven, make an unnoticed entrance – to nobody would such a suggestion be welcome. That it was psychologically feasible for a young girl who has been (or imagined she has been) doped and sexually abused to get harpoons on her mind as a consequence . . . That, Castang, is the Hahnenkamm at Kitzbuhel right enough, with all the safety nets taken away and replaced by Dannert coils, specially for you to fall into at a hundred and twenty kilometres an hour.

Thus ruminating Castang reached the office. The word, he thought, applies to cows, oxen, bullocks; presumably bulls. He wasn't sure at all how much of a bull he still was: that might be an optical illusion down there.

He found Mr Campbell on duty.

"I've been meaning to ask you, Paddy, this Fox place. Lecat was there the evening before: the Barthélémy crowd use it quite a lot. And I've a notion in my mind about cheese. But since you're our resident expert –"

"Who told you that?"

"I forget – I don't want to take a closer interest without a clear understanding of its nature."

Mr Campbell made a noise, that might be yes, no, or maybe as the circumstances warranted.

"Your interests are strictly Lecat – and his frau? That right?"

"I'm keeping a very low profile, especially as regards the Press."

"Then you'll do better to leave it to me."

The door opened upon the secretarial Madame Metz, mincing, with a hideous smirk.

"Where's that animal of a man of yours?" enquired Castang pleasantly. With glee she held out a telex. "Well thank you," reading it, "and heartfelt blessings all around. I'll take the midday train, and confirm that with Paris, would you?" That was all that was needed!

The message, laconic, read 'Expect you soonest in personal conference inre delicate matter' and was undersigned 'Souschef Operations Criminal Affairs Division'. And that is a Controller: a rank higher than a divisional commissaire. The Direction of the Police Judiciaire – that's right, it's the Quai des Orfèvres.

The Souschef is sparing of words on the telex machine. In his office he might not be quite as quite.

"Very good, Madame, I'll be going home to change my shirt. If you'll get your little shorthand pad I'll let you have the outline of activities for your good man, for when he gets the toothpick stowed

122

away. You might then give the judge of instruction a ring, to say I've been summoned to Paris and would she expect me tomorrow morning instead? And while you're out there for the pencil you might just raise my wife?

"There you are, Paddy, I'm going to get this sales talk about Delicacy. So I'll ask you to brief me about foxes tomorrow morning – delicately." Mr Campbell smiled from time to time; did so now. The phone rinkled.

"Vera? I'll pop in, around a quarter of an hour, the clean shirt and the nailfile, I have to catch the train for Paris. If you can manage a sandwich I won't find myself in disgrace with railway food."

Farting in the souschef's office wouldn't do at all.

Inspector Campbell was extracting enjoyment from these proceedings, drop by drop as though watching whisky through a still. The new commissaire was at times a whippersnapper, upstart, a little bossyboots and a right prick. But only at times.

Vera knows the routine. Some years ago the Birthday Present had been the executive despatch-case. Not Cartier nor even Taiwan-Cartier, though very expensive. It held the shirt and the socks and the private necessities, and the sandwiches, and room over for Documents. She has everything packed. In fact she is like the legendary parrot which posted at the door of a famous French restaurant used to ask all the customers on their way to the lavatory 'Z'avez-vous du papier?' She is not worried by a summons to Paris: that is a commonplace.

**11** Vera sits at her kitchen table: it is a moment of great desolation but potatoes have to be peeled (she is no more than an average cook. Most of her meals are eatable but few are better than that. She is best at the simple dishes of frugal Central European forebears). How foolish to feel desolate, as though waving her hanky after a train leaving for Kamchatka. Her man has gone to Paris on a piece of simple office routine: this meal is to be prepared against his return and must 'warm up well'. She had long ago learned to live with the fear: the gun, the knife, the fear that waits at the street corner; the mindless, Assyrian bomb filling a marketplace with the decapitated, the impaled, the disembowelled.

The job? Like all policemen's wives she takes it as it comes: homicides are no worse than all the rest. She has read her way stolidly through the literature of psychopathology; knows all about criminal egoism that disregards all but the need for instant satisfaction. She is the Chorus. She can warn the city, bid Agamemnon beware; cannot check Clytemnestra's hideous course nor stay Cassandra from her fate. And at times too she is the mechanical smile and sequinned jockstrap of the jolly tit show, and that too, like Cassandra, she accepts.

If only I had been called Zsuzsa – not Vera – that plain-jane name, so I thought as a child. Then I might have been a dancer. Or with agile wrist and steel forearm a player of cimbalom or celeste. One becomes one's name? Alicia de Larrocha strikes fire from the great black piano, sets a still moonpath upon the serene sea. Though if I met her with her shopping bag in Marks and Spencers I would see only a fat comfy housewife in a headscarf, and I should need to be unusually alert to be struck by the nobility of her features.

You have done your job, Henri, all these years. At times well; mostly, perhaps, below your best. It is a truism to say that this job is not one where it is easy to give of one's best. What job is? The abiding symbol of this world is Sisyphus, rolling his boulder.

But you got a little complacent. You accepted the mediocrity, the routine, the comfortable umbrella of Richard's humour and authority. His leaving shook you. Foreseen, but when it came you blinked, and had to set your teeth. I liked you there: you showed readiness.

It was easier to stay dug in, in the cosy staff job found for you after your arm got smashed. Seniority would have led you to Lyon, to Paris. You threw out the comfort. You did not allow the mean little trickeries of politics to serve as pretext, for taking the easy way.

To think of all cops as crooked bastards is as sentimental as the notion of pipe-smoking scotland-yard daddies. Cops, like anyone else, would like to have ideals; aren't sure they can afford it.

Stendhal – of course – puts it simply. 'What fools men are with their ideas of honour – as though one needed to think of honour under an absolute government!' It is the Prime Minister speaking. 'Everyone here steals, and how should they not steal, in a country where recognition of the greatest services lasts for not quite a month? Nothing is real here, nothing survives disgrace, save money.'

We are born free, until we touch the cold iron. And that is never very long. It is in Mr Kipling's 'Rewards and Fairies'. The boy in the tale, symbol of the artist, sets out to seek his fortune; finds it – forged for him long before – a slave-ring. He accepts it: he himself snaps it shut around his neck. 'What else could I do?' he says. It is with folk in housen, and not with fairies, that his paths and his destiny lie. What else could I do, repeats the central character in each succeeding story. Cold iron is the master of us all. The slave-ring is the gun and handcuffs, that the cop carries.

Castang in the train cocks the ankle of one leg on the knee of the other, in the 'English' way he has that makes Vera laugh. Reads his notes, works on them, smokes, curls up and goes to sleep: what is the use of worrying? The train hurries on down through Compiègne and Creil. The louder, echoing note wakes him, telling him that this is Paris. He yawns and stretches and the monster slides ever so slow, ever so smooth into the clattering roar of the Gare du Nord, and everybody starts running. He took the métro, down to the Châtelet, the subway station where you find everything. You could live your whole life down there: there is an impression that a lot of people do. You can get born and die; you can even wash and change your shirt. Twenty minutes later Castang re-emerges on the banks of the Seine. Clean and fresh, smiling and confident – like a news broadcaster, as the music fades out and the camera tracks in upon this reassuring visage – into big smiling sunny touristy Paris.

And ten minutes after that – it is good to stretch one's legs upon these undear but familiar pavements – he is mounting the steps at Number Thirtysix.

The top brass have fine airy offices, overlooking the Seine and the Pont Saint-Michel and the huge hideous fountain that is so conspicuously not by Bernini, and the Quarter which is nowadays about as Latin as Fortysecond Street. The souschef has a lot of electronic aids on his desk. Aids to what? – not thought surely? Love, maybe: this is the Ministry of Love. Coarse, heavy humour, Castang tells himself sinking, asked to sit down, into a deep deep chair about two inches from the deck and needing a periscope to see out of it. Stop it! The souschef is said to be a decent man. It's his job to be bastardly but in his innermost heart . . . stop it. What is a souschef? Something deliberately vague, like a vice-president. How vice is vice?, and how sous is sous? Stop it. But I have to occupy my mind with something . . .

"Sorry, Castang. I know this is tedious. Won't be a sec." He is licking an envelope, banging it shut, writing an address. A missive, perhaps, to the Guardians of the Peace in uniform on the Place Saint-Michel, to tell them that picking their nose that way is not conducive to the Service of the Republic. He was a tall thin man with what used to be called an academic stoop, meaning he'd got roundshouldered in the service of the republic, the res publica, the public thing. A long clever face, grey shaved lips and chin surrounding a wide monkey's mouth. A civil-service rather than a police face. A lot of grey hair, unusual in France where baldness goes with political skills. Perhaps it was a wig, attached to the spectacles pushed up on a high broad forehead.

"Well now, Castang." Ringing for the 'planton' and pushing the envelope abruptly at him. "I know you better than you think. I was one of Richard's inspectors when he was still at Laval. So I know about that liberalising, humanising influence: I've felt it and am glad of it.

126

"He wouldn't have sat in this chair. He wouldn't have wanted to. You know the famous remark about politics being like a pistol shot at a concert; a loud and vulgar noise that has nothing to do with the work in hand but from which you cannot withhold attention?"

He should have smoked a pipe; a curvy one. Given it up: Castang loathed these strong-willed types.

"Richard liked to disregard pistol shots," the chef went on. "Probably too many of us make the contrary mistake, of never listening to the music."

"I used to wonder whether he was a bit too far ahead of his time."

"There's that . . . Naturally, I didn't call you here to listen to my reminiscences. You find yourself at odds with a sharp-edged piece of work, to which you are rightly giving your entire attention. Now you could have avoided a good deal of the responsibility for this. Calling in Lille would have been normal and understandable. I'd like to know why you didn't."

"Pride, I suppose, as much as anything."

"Furthermore you're answerable to a young and inexperienced judge."

"She hasn't been trying to put any undue pressure on me."

"Glad I am to hear it. Your answer interests me; I'll be as frank with you. Pride's no bad thing, except that it could isolate you and leave you vulnerable. You're getting a lot of flak from the press. You might be thinking that you've gone too far and can't shuffle out of it without losing face? Don't hesitate to take me into your confidence."

"If I get an order I'm bound to obey it, but I'd just as soon stay as I am." Rubicon, where is the Rubicon? I've never been able to find it on an atlas.

"Very well," said the chef, taking his time. "I'll give you a couple of confidences of my own. I've no reproaches to make you, nor has Lille. I've had a chat with Sabatier, I'll not deny it. If that's your choice he'll not be worrying you. It's our bad luck that the press hasn't anything to distract them.

"A word of advice; don't take it amiss. You'd naturally like to make an arrest: keep the press happy and transfer the heat to the judge. I'd like to suggest: don't do so hastily. Unless you've got it irrefutable, which doesn't often come our way.

127

"In confidence, Castang, the minister doesn't want to feel a draught, so don't open doors you can't shut. I needn't say this, but out of respect for you I will. The Army is a highly sensitive plant, very susceptible to draughts . . . Now this wife, who died. I gather that she was on the flighty side and may have been keeping odd company. But belonging to the caste. You probably know this already but General Laurens draws a lot of water.

"That's all, and rather too much. Put it this way: our minister always has plenty of sources of conflict with opposite numbers, and these he'd just as soon minimise. The chronic confrontation with Dear Colleague over at Justice – you know all about that; it's a permanent fact of life. So don't let's get Defence on our neck into the bargain."

"Has a complaint been received?" That didn't sound like General Laurens.

"No no no no no. But foresight, Castang. Let me just add a note for your comfort. Bring us out of this one well, without involving Lille, and your standing firm in a tight corner won't rebound to your discredit."

Castang walked on along the river: he had a call to pay.

There are a lot of the glories of France, gathered round here. Palaces and things. Viewed purely as architecture; that's one thing. What is to be found inside is another. Let's leave the Louvre aside: so much of a joke that even the French are beginning to notice. But the Mazarin Palace on the other side of the river, which houses the Institut: Castang doesn't believe there's one Parisien in a thousand – qué; one in ten thousand – who could tell you what it is or what it does. The Invalides – let's not complain, it is now again extremely beautiful, and even if it houses the grandest tomb in France, made for the one person who did France most harm after always dear Louis XIV, well that's France for you. The joke's a good one and it's on us. Or the Palais Bourbon and all those deputies: how can parliamentary government be anything but a joke?

But these monstrous monuments are 'les machins': there to support the Japanese camera industry. There are a great many others mercifully smaller and none the less beautiful, which tourists hardly notice and Parisiens don't notice at all. One such is the elegant home of the Legion of Honour, about which Castang is extremely vague: a lot of art, some highly decorative, Lancret and Boucher and the like, which the vulgar (like commissaires of police) would call a tit-show, and contrasting oddly with the military grandeur of improbably large cocked hats and sabres.

Well of course this is a joke too, and a bad one. As with the Order of the British Empire: the less there is about the more they hand out. Honour is a highly dilute solution.

A mere commissaire of police, walking in here, doesn't get to see the Chancellor, who is a good deal too Grand for the likes of Castang. But he'll find an intelligent influential official, very discreet and softspoken, urbane and immensely civilised. That's all right. You have enquiries to make about somebody high in the honours? You've come to the right shop.

They had the family (-ies) of the two girls. Distinguished. The Légion is good at looking after its widows and orphans and is hot on genealogies: as in the Polytechnique there are hereditary strains. And then General Laurens. In his dry light voice, the official spoke with unusual warmth. Chivalric orders are funny things. The English go in for them a lot. Being a knight impresses nobody: a God-calls-me-god is given to permanent secretaries the way we honour schoolmarms, village mayors or procurement officials. One would really rather like something impossible like the Thistle or a Knight of Saint Patrick – very nice, that. On a lower level, one wouldn't say no to being a Companion of the Star of India.

D'you recall that delicious comic scene in Dumas where Athos appears as an envoy-extraordinary from his britannic majesty King Charles II to Louis XIV, wearing the Golden Fleece, the Holy Ghost, and the Garter? And Mazarin rolls about intensely irritated and determined not to be impressed? Now you mustn't think of the Legion as something invented for Empire Marshals, the more ruffianly the marshal the keener on collecting other people's art. We too have our chivalric traditions. The tricolour flag does not exclude the white banner and the golden fleurs-de-lys, Monsieur Castang. Chivalry . . . look up the definition in the dictionary and you'll find hollow abstractions, as with Goodness, Integrity, and the like. Have you ever met with it in the concrete? – no, I didn't suppose that you had (dryly). So that I recommend you to cultivate any acquaintance you are so fortunate as to possess, with General Laurens.

"In other words a saint." He must have allowed some sarcasm to enter his voice because the official studied his face in a silence on the verge of becoming nasty.

"I make no claim to be a judge of sanctity. We have ecclesiastics for that. The men General Laurens commanded in the field, including no doubt numerous ruffians and poltroons, might if they thought about it have used some such term. You used it in a sceptical connotation, I must not insult you by terming it frivolous. No blame attaches to you for this: you are not a soldier and your experience perhaps predisposes you to seeing the worst in people. Might I hazard the opinion that it is salutary to take another view from time to time? I must beg your forgiveness: I have much to occupy me." As crisp a rap over the knuckles as Monsieur le Commissaire has had in a month of Sundays.

He felt, for no good reason, uplifted, and walked a stretch further. Paris in full tourist season had been brushed up and tidied: even the police, at least in the eighth arrondissement, chosen for uplift and saying 'Brush' instead of the sallow debility frequent elsewhere: these cheery smiles and smart salutes in face of the most cretinous query or querulous complaint designed to efface the fearful rudeness of the natives. He turned into a bar; the dimly lit and flossy kind mandatory about here, gone all anglophile with regimental badges and club ties and seventyfive sorts of whisky; asked for a quarter of champagne and the barman said there wasn't anything smaller than a half. Instead of uttering a furious imprecation Castang showed his badge and a very evil face. The barman retired in a dudgeon muttering about these revolting gorillas and when Castang went to pay said slimily that it was on the house: he had been laughing to himself the whole time and was thought to be flying on uppers.

Because it takes all sorts in the police and even the Sensitive Types like himself. As well as the security-detail horrors to be found wearing smartly cut suits and drinking Jack Daniels in the Rue de Ponthieu. As well as the psychotic puritans suffering from Dirty Harry syndromes. Or just plain yobbos.

A few months back a neighbour's daughter had approached him

with a view to joining the ranks. He had thought they'd be glad to have her: strapping big girl, intelligent and well-educated, mature and balanced. He'd call her a catch. A swimmer too, and had a judo belt. When she came back from her interview, indignant, she said she'd been turned down for scoring too high on 'emotivity'! Too inclined to be sorry for stray cats . . .

'And what about your emotional outpourings then?' had asked Vera.

'Oh me – there weren't any shrink tests then: only too happy to have someone who could read'n'write.' And had a law degree, which every streetsweeper now possesses. True, he'd had his arse kicked for emotivity. Trained on the street instead of in the classroom. And they were quite right! You be careful about these emotional judgments, Castang.

# 12

Castang had come into the office in fine form. A quick quarter of an hour, to initial reports and see that the Department (his three-men-and-a-boy) was on its toes, before going off all forceful to straighten out Miss Alice Jimenez: let her not start going all gloomy and Spanish with me or we'll post her ass to the County Clare . . .

"Mr Campbell," announced Madame Metz, "would like a word." Good; that's as arranged. But why so funereal? – looks like the Argyll coast on a wet day.

Mr Campbell is very slow and careful like an old woman paying the supermarket checkout in five-centime pieces.

"I have a source of information in that bistrot. Nothing grand. Like you thought, low-level trafficking in this and that, around the quarter. But I keep my ear to the ground. This near the border we get a traffic in papers. Common Market stuff, phony truck manifests and export licences."

Castang knows all this, but why is Paddy so forthcoming of a sudden about his little affairs?

"Truckload of pharmaceuticals, hundred thousand dollars worth, juice in that. Reward money gets paid." Bleak eye. It is a clear summer's day and Mr Campbell sits as though swathed in wet hairy smelly-dog scarves and overcoats; fog everywhere and frost on the stiff reddish eyebrows.

"Good boy. A waiter, likes to earn himself a bit of money. Maybe he hears something. Maybe notices something. Like a truck driver paying for a beer from a saddlebag full of dollars? Or a lady eating funny cheese? Maybe do you a good turn; do me no harm? All I know is, this young lad gets brought off in the dogsmeat cart. And now I'm a lamp-post, they're pissing on me. I don't like that. Just telling you." He is lugubrious as an old truck, grinding up a steep hill, burning a lot of oil.

"What happened?" Paddy had reached the summit: breathing heavily he lurched into a higher gear.

"My laddy told me he thought he'd something for me – you. He's off yesterday evening, got a flat out the Béthune Road, lives there

132

with a tart out the postoffice, nice girl. I go see him, no risk in that, big old house like a métro station. Real funny, I find my boy on the pavement outside, past tense, salut Anatole, nice to have known you. Police Secours running around blue-arsed; I fade into the wallpaper, not going to let them know I have an interest.

"It's so funny we're splitting ourselves laughing. Pissy old house, I told you that, so our boy improves the property. Busy with a window, frame rotten wood, knock it out and do a nice job."

"Defenestrated."

"Who's to say? Boy leaning out, wood gives way, second floor, hard pavement – hamburger. Isn't that just lovely!"

"Of course no witnesses or anything."

"Not a smell; how would there be? Other people beside me walk in and out like it's the Gare Saint-Lazare: I could have pushed him out myself. Municipal flattie does a door to door, none of those mothers are there: like me, they're sitting in the pub hearing the hot news, oh how sad. Any bloody one of them," glaring with the pale foxy eyes as though suspecting Castang who'd gone to Paris to create an alibi, "and now you tell me why!"

"Leave it accident," said Castang. "Can't afford a third unsolved homicide."

"Somebody's counting on that," nastily.

Castang played with things on the table. One cigarette packet, crumpled, so that one shook it several times without anything coming out. Two ten-cent plastic lighters. Two ten-cent plastic pens.

"Somebody. Mayhap, with an investment to protect. Valuable cargo of pills? I don't want to know about that; it's your business. And maybe, yes, there's a piece of cheese. Interests me, but who'd pay for it? The press might. There might be people too who'd pay to have news like that kept quiet. That could be a lot of things, from investments in the late Monsieur Lecat's business interests on up.

"But what we have is a fact. Boy pushed out of window. To stop a leak. Now we know it exists. So we do nothing for a day or two: officially it's an accident. But we'll make a pinch, I promise you that, and when we do you'll get the credit for it. Fair enough? Officially, no interest."

"Nothing proves it has anything to do with this stuff you're breaking your balls over," still nastily.

"Nobody says the maniac axe-murderer has suddenly changed his method," said Castang as nastily, "but if you believe in three different homicides with no link somewhere I can't stop you stargazing."

Be tough, Castang (putting all the rubbish back in his pockets). Be forceful. Buy yourself some smart clothes tailored not to show the gun. Get a Cartier lighter. Have a car that breathes fire, to show there's a tough executive inside. This poverty-stricken look of yours is pathetic.

Alice Jimenez was fed up.

"To put it mildly. And why put it mildly? What good will that do?"

"Yes, but do stop walking round the room." She needed a pile of thick black Andalusian hair, needed splendid, blood-flushed olive skin, needed a powerful red mouth and marble tits. Needed a Cartier lighter. She saw that she was being comic.

"I fume, Castang. I boil, and my lid clatters."

"Yes, well, turn the gas down."

"Are you telling me that you were called to Paris expressly to be told that the Minister would not feel happy . . . words fail me!"

Castang buys cigarillos in campaigns to smoke less; it's easier to count how many are left in the tin. Staring now in horror.

"Answer then, man." An impressive bellow for such a tiny woman.

"Madame le Juge – please," trying first one lighter and then the other. "You know as well as I do. The one wants money to modernise the police, and high time. The other wants more atomic submarines." A horrible snarling noise such as one might expect from a leopard poked with a sharp stick. "Come, we must be realists."

"Men! Forever talking of being realists. Childish trivialities and dangerous toys."

"But never underestimate departmental capacity for umbrage-taking."

She went and sat down and put her hands on the blotter.

"Monsieur le Commissaire, another notorious French habit is

134

never to keep things simple where a possibility of complication exists. I'm not going to worry about the War Ministry: trouble enough with my own. I too get murmured hints filtering down from the Chancellery. My one interest is a clear understanding between you and myself. We're obliged to work together: let's do so."

Magistrates and police officers – they're like cooks and waiters. No love lost between them.

"Jimenez," said Castang, giving it a Spanish pronunciation. He got a shocked angry look before she understood and smiled.

"True – if we go on screeching Monsieur and Madame at one another . . . let's look at what we've got. An army-caste family enjoying high official consideration and protection. The servants forming a similar block; the inference being that if so instructed by General Laurens they would conceal or deny essential facts – is that over-reaching?"

"Maybe but I don't quarrel with your synthesis."

"We have a magistrate and a police officer being urged to show zeal, and absence of zeal."

"Succinct," said Castang.

"A nettle that will have to be grasped sooner or later. Remains – within Lecat's immediate circle – the business entourage."

"I have a possible line of enquiry there, though it's not happy, nor am I sure it's lucky." He had resolved to tell her about the waiter's unfortunate accident. She listened quietly.

"I'm not sure I understand what weight you give to this."

"I'm not sure that I do myself. But when an informer falls out of a window the inference is that he learned that a trivial-seeming item of information had value and he was using it for his own ends."

"As a threat you mean, or putting the price up?"

"It would be both, wouldn't it? There's a direct link because Lecat was eating there with his office gang that last evening, and an indirect link: the autopsy on Madame Lecat showed bread and cheese, a slightly unusual cheese from Holland and they serve it in this place. The waiter didn't recognise a photo – or so he said."

"What inhibits you from enquiring into this? I appreciate your frankness but you place me in a false position: your suspicion of homicide was not made known to the Proc."

135

"The press is our greatest enemy: worse than Ministers. But it needs perpetual novelties: starved of those the interest dies down. A third homicide would be straight from heaven, just as their editors are showing signs of boredom.

"Apart from that Sabatier would have me for his breakfast. Paris shows me some indulgence and he's sensitive to that. As long as I don't upset the Army. I don't think it was Laurens; too gentlemanly and as I believe genuinely too nice. I suspect that Cécile may have influential uncles or whatever. High grades in the Légion d'Honneur; frowned upon to stir up scandal around such people.

"You see the bind I'm in? I'm pushed to get a quick clean result, and I'm held back from my one promising line of enquiry." Working up to a towering rage.

"Ssh," said the magistrate. "The judge must be scrupulous in avoidance of any act prompted by factors in her own personality. My teeth grate, blood of God: the law prescribes that I should question these people, ferret out their odious family concealments. That is where the heart of this lies, beyond doubt. And I have had the greatest possible prudence enjoined upon me. I know what that means.

"I see a weakness however. If Laurens defends Lecat it's in defence of his own family and caste; well and good. And he has this tremendous reputation for integrity. From all I hear and from what you observe it's deserved. It must mean a great deal to him. How does he reconcile the contradictions? That might suggest a possible approach." She sat back and pressed her fingertips against her eyelids. "I can't give you much more time, Castang."

"I'll have to find a bomb, won't I – something explosive."

Jimenez did not answer but made what could have been an anarchist face.

Miss Varennes had been given a little task.

"On the evening in question our friend was at a bordel in Brussels. No reason to disbelieve him but check it out."

"Brussels is over the line."

"Yes, and so is Lille: don't get on to Sabatier territory. But in the towns around here –"

"You don't seriously mean that Lecat –"

136

"I don't mean anything at all," said Castang crossly. "What I suppose is that like a lot of men of this sort he had huge energy, worked hard and played hard: it's a way of letting off steam. And he had ways of amusing himself I want to know more about. Whores come and go but —"

"They go more than they come." This piece of VV wit did not go down well.

"Make a little list," said Castang, "without alarming these ladies." And left her looking dubious.

She was still looking dubious.

"No great secret about one or two of these. Others are hearsay or guesswork – how many whores are there?" Exactly! Who's a whore? One reads that there are thirty thousand in the city of Paris, a figure that could be trebled without anyone contradicting and if you were to ask a cop he'd guffaw. It is a little bit easier in small provincial towns but still like asking how many moonlight jobs get done in the plumbing or electrical line.

"How many are there?" asked Castang.

"Hereabout, eight possibles."

"I don't want anybody else on this," Castang said after reflecting, "and we don't have a lot of time to spend. You take half and I'll take the other." VV, delighted that she didn't have to do the whole tedious chore herself, started to sing.

" 'Hitler – had only got one ball.
    Göring – had two but very small –' "

"Move your arse," said Castang rudely.

Club Ferrara in the Marché aux Grains, in Véronique's unexpectedly tiny neat handwriting. Mm, straightforward bordel and quite open; didn't sound up to Lecat's standards, but the nearest, and easily checked.

In the old town. He liked the medieval bits of these antique northern cities. So knocked about by sieges and bombardments that there was little left, but tenacious in survival, and touching. Insanitary alleys, steep and narrow, cobbled marketplaces with every second house a pub. The Club Ferrara was a discreet little neon arrow next the Seven Stars. A convent on one side and the parish presbytery on the other: religion and prostitution are cheek by jowl all over Europe – Bishop of Winchester's geese . . .

The day, since it was early afternoon, had just begun for geese. The bar was open for airing: airing it badly needed. A goose, languid, was doing a bit of dusting, making this look like terribly hard work. The décor was the usual aquarium, rigidly stylised in nineteen-thirties modernistic – original, quite likely. He asked for the head goose and she pointed five centimetres of opalescent fingernail at the ceiling: too much trouble to talk and he was plainly a cop.

The side door saying 'Private' led to narrow stairs, pitchblack until he found the pink lighting; a little landing and a plastic nameplate saying 'Jacqueline'. He was examined through the peephole. Inside, the smell of woman, bed and perfume was as suffocating as ether. The pink lights were cake-candle power. Ashtray, bidet, inhabitant; all embowered in pink satin. Laying eyes on Jacqueline only confirmed – nothing for him or Lecat either. This was the Chivas-and-Canada Dry circuit. Miss Bacardi-Coke was downstairs dusting and Miss Smirnoff-orangejuice still asleep on the floor above. Crates of cheap champagne, secret sip and surreptitious delight, the 'petite province' a mile off. A place for dealers from backwoods villages, bunny-fanciers, bank managers and sales reps. The girls have white skins and blue veins, mushy-tit and crinkle-thigh even by candle-light.

But Jacqueline was a pro. No secrets from the police, who kept her in comfort and she paid her way. Oh yes; we saw him here quite often.

A new Lecat, but not out of key, who came here simply for laughs. A coarse humour, harsh and mocking, angled to trip up, to humiliate; but not sadistic, not even really evil-minded: very Vlaams, that. He didn't screw these girls of course, he had better. Horseplay and tall stories, teasing other customers, some bottom-pinching and thigh-slapping, generous expenditure and big tips.

Anita in the Boulevard de la Meuse was highly modern, in a block of studio apartments full of anonymity and closed-circuit television and herself highly burglar-proofed. Nice to look at; a tall statuesque blonde who knew how to stay away from alcohol and cream cake: a light dry perfume and little makeup. A resolute keep-fitter; squash in the gym and exercise machines in the bathroom. And a computer terminal behind the navel. Click, airline reservation, click the superswift blowjob. Castang declined with polite thanks. She'd done one on Lecat once, and he slipped her a customer from time to time. She knew Mr Cesari . . . yes, quite.

The third was young and still fresh, pretty with gamine looks and a dancer's movements: vivacious. There had been a moment, and not long ago, when she had come close to a career, to making it. A Belgian accent and an attractive laugh, and who liked a joke. At that moment she had been through Lecat's hands. Now there was a hairline crack somewhere. What was it? She made good coffee and malicious conversation (funny on the subject of Anita). What was wrong? Obvious once one got it, so that he kicked himself for being slow: either heroin or cocaine. In another six months she'd be unrecognisable. A walking corpse right now, the shell still intact but nothing inside.

I have wasted time and got nowhere, thought Castang. Serve me right. VV knew better: he'd steer clear of the likes of these. I had seen him as casual, even careless. Prudent about entanglements, but restless and greedy. Cocufying 'some prig one knows' is always a good joke. A highly controlled man, but allowing the surplus energy to take any path that seems amusing. No Don Juan in the sense of an obsessive collector, but who seeks more women as he does more money, more power, more opportunity for manipulating others.

I may as well give up because time's running out. Lecat might have been content with a mistress in Paris, a nice Cloclo with a nice flat in the Ile Saint-Louis and an accommodating husband with a future in government: promising young man what! in Parliament, who'll know which side his bread is buttered . . .

Well, the next is the last and it isn't far away – finish the job. Josy in the Résidence Trianon.

So! Luxurious. Exclusive, very. They paid for service here. A concierge in uniform, and a security guard. One had to show 'patte blanche'. The phrase is taken from the wolf who put flour on his paw, to sweet-talk his way into the house of the little goats . . . Castang showed his white paw.

"I beg your pardon, Commissaire. You understand, it is for the protection of the tenants."

"There is no question of a scandal. Information only – informal."

"Fourteen C." A glance at the screen covering the basement. "Her car's in." The man would tip her off but no matter. He knew enough, already. A joy girl in this block was a young lady of independent income.

Josy answered her door with a sunny smile. She was just going to go swimming but it didn't matter. Would he like some tea? He would, very much. Quite the little hostess. She was very young, very pretty. The flat was furnished in expensive department-store taste, which was to say no taste at all. But she had a lot of flowers. And birds on her balcony. Which was likeable. And she would be worrying. Bitten nails. This last twentyfour hours she would have been biting a lot. All the goodies would get taken away, unless, unless . . .

"I haven't come here to be hostile. Nor to make miseries for you. I'll be wanting plain answers to plain questions. In return, no harassment. Fair's fair. It's a deal?" She gave him his tea but the look had narrowed at once: she retreated to a chair and tucked herself in.

"I don't know about any deals." It was hard to guess her background – they model themselves upon what they see on the television set. She chewed her lip and made her mind up. "If you want it straight I'll give it you. I've a very good friend."

"Yes? That's one of my questions. How many good friends? Just the one, or are there more?"

"This one will do, because he said to me, if ever I had any trouble just to give him a ring and he'd take care of it for me. So not to answer any questions because honest and you'd better believe it he can make trouble for you."

"Have you furry animals in your bedroom?"

"Never mind about my bedroom," angrily. In the same breath she decided that anger was the wrong tactic.

Her trouble here was that the thought was too obvious. Even if it had made snicking sounds, like the washing-machine when it begins the rinse, he could have pretended not to notice. It went clank Clonk, like steam-age railway points. "I mean, we're all right here. It's comfy on the sofa. It's hot, too. Whyn't you stretch out and

140

sort of relax?" Even without that whory, ad-agency word which never fails to irritate him it would have rasped sorely against his grain.

One of Castang's favourite fantasies is the little tiny brown girl from Bali who massages with her feet, walking deliciously up and down your spine. Nowadays it's mostly his bad arm which gets extremely painful. Vera is used to it and can nearly do it in her sleep; claims indeed that she does, sometimes. She can read at the same time, turning the page with her left thumb so as not to break the rhythm. But formerly, in criminal-brigade days, it was frequent enough for him to get home with every nerve and muscle so fatigued by tension as to feel his back had been flogged, and she would tell him to take his shirt off and stretch out flat. That's prone: supine is the other way round.

So that if young Josiane had been a little brighter; even just a little more experienced . . . Castang has nothing much against whores, even when they pretend that's what they aren't: they've been his bread and butter all his working life. They don't have hearts of gold, but most can be kindhearted on occasion and one or two can even be generous now and then, or sentimentalise enough about neglected children and poor doggies into believing themselves so. He had even known one with a sense of humour. Of a blackish nature but he enjoys black humour.

He does have a pretty ironclad rule about not going to bed with other women, even if that too has been broken the odd time. He isn't a saint in the desert up on a pillar.

If – ah, all those ifs – that stupid Josy had been a bit brighter . . . It was hot, and after a week of extreme strain his back was giving him hell.

Haven't we all had the experience of carrying a heavy suitcase too far? There comes a good moment when at last one gets it shoved up on the rack: slump back then and gawk out at the Gare de Lyon, and even that will turn into blue sea and golden sand, and a tall misted glass, and a topless girl on a beach mat.

The fool's second big mistake was getting too close. Said cat-on-mat is terrific from three metres off: silky hair and hard salty nipples and lustful little bows at the outer corners of the triangle. Closer up, the oil has plastered her navel full of sand and the hair stinks of sweat. Below that is a reek of chemical deodorant. There's a flaky crumb of pastry stuck in the corner of a fat greedy lip. Suddenly all you can think of is herpes.

Castang put his little cigar between his teeth and said "Sit up" brutally. A lot more harsh than he had intended. She was furious.

"Thinks I'm not good enough for him. I could have your crutch kicked in, pig, with one phonecall."

"No you couldn't then, Miss," restored at once to good humour.

"How d'ye stop me then, Fuckdust?"

"Because he's dead."

She burst out then into a noisy blubber like a fat child unjustly slapped . . . He is sorry for her now, but he's not going to get her a glass of water or wipe the saliva off her chin because he's doing his job. Poor cow, though. For the last twentyfour hours she must have been worried out of her pants. Wrong metaphor, that. Wondering what was going to happen now. The strain building up. And what came was a cop.

"This place isn't in your name. He paid the rent, right?"

"No it's his, or – I don't know."

"Have you any papers? What about the furniture? He buy it? Or told you to buy what you want and he'd sign the bill?"

"He – he –" But the sobs were dying down to hiccups. She'd soon be saying 'That's mine. And that, and those, I can prove it.'

"Any more? Jewellery or whatever? He was generous. In fact he didn't give a damn. As long as you amused him he'd give you a lot. Show me what you have." Wrongly worded again, Castang . . .

But it calmed her down pretty quick. Material considerations. "What about the car?" She'd defend her possessions tooth and nail, get away with what she could. It might be a month or more before accountants started poking about. She was welcome, for his sake, as long as she held nothing back of what he wanted.

"So who did he bring here? Men? Or other girls? When, where, who? – I want it exact. Dates, times, the lot. Where's your little diary?"

She had to understand: that was the bargain. He'd pester her no further. But he wanted to know. He'd keep on until he was satisfied he'd got it all. Give him any trouble and he'd take a stick to her bottom.

142

Castang ranged about. When he came to the fake silver tray with the bottles he twiddled till he found what he was looking for: a single malt. Everybody had it, since it became fashionable. He'd been drinking it since he could remember – when he could afford it, which wasn't often.

Something good, and they make a whore of it. The distillers had over-produced blended stuff, thinking the taste for Scotch would never stop booming. Mistake; the folks like their drinks tasteless, like their food. So that one way out had been an enormous publicity campaign for the singles. Over-producing those too, then: they didn't taste the way they used. Faking them up: corruption in this as in everything else. Lecat had been one of the great experts in pretending little country wines were Château Chenonceaux. Same story every which way you look. The devaluation in wine or whisky is the same as that in girls. Make them cheap, first. Sell them dear, afterwards.

And the way corruption works, Lecat hadn't even noticed. Cheapening everything you've cheapened, irremediably, yourself. He'd made whores of everybody, all those around him, as well as everybody who bought his lousy wine. Castang felt sick at last, for all his experience. What was he doing, drinking this trash?

He didn't have photographs, but by drilling at her he got physical descriptions that were unmistakeable, and they had better be because she didn't know it yet, but she'd have to recognise people, in Alice Jimenez' office. And before the Assize Court.

Cesari had been here. That lousy pimp had known enough to keep his fingers off private stock, but he'd been used for go-between jobs. Lecat must have had enough on him to send him up for a good stretch in jug: he'd been very sure the handsome boy wouldn't talk out of turn. Aurélie-Marie had not been here. Castang felt some slight satisfaction at that. Vanity no doubt, that his opinion was not shown false.

One or two youngish girls had been here, for games. Not – as far as he could tell – Miranda. Maybe her turn hadn't come yet.

Nor – he had a photo for this – had the wife. Madame Marguerite had been reckless when drunk and might have had a teeny habit. She had known quite a few subtle humiliations, but not this.

He wouldn't have had Cécile here! Something masquerading as

a laugh of a sour and inwards sort rose up in his chest and stuck fast in his throat.

Now come! The late Félix was a talented man but . . . But what?

A lot of glib patter gets on to policemen's desks and into their reading matter. Copies of psych reports: a long and dreary series because defence advocates nowadays are very fond of falling back upon psych. Get a plea in of diminished responsibility: it's an insurance policy. To forestall this, and also – to do them justice – in the wish to be just, judges of instruction will very often call upon 'the expert'. Who leads in turn to counter-experts. Newspapers print readers-digest stuff about psychopaths. And Castang's experience has taught him that the jargon might be bullshit, but every damn psych has its path side. Including his own.

He tries it on the girl, describing Cécile as he sees her, the tall handsome woman with striking bones. Dully she says no, no one like that. He realises that the way he 'sees her' isn't in the least like the same woman as seen by – try again. And this time she says maybe. But nothing conclusive. The girl is stupefied: he has given her a hard time and cannot press her further. So get out of here, because he's beginning to feel drunk on just one whisky, and nauseated to throwing-up point, on his own thinking.

# 13

He had gone on too long, and wasted – wasted? – the whole afternoon. It was after knocking-off time. What, a nice summer evening like this with lots of daylight hours left for work on all these homicide investigations, and the Police Judiciaire has gone home? You bet it has, without him to harry it. And his one idea by now is to knock off himself: his mind's going round like a mill and that he knows well is useless. His accelerator has stuck, his flywheel has dropped off. There's something wrong with the transmission of this car too; a nasty noise and a jolt as you change from third down to second: when is the ministry going to buy us some new cars?

Yes: VV has left a note on his desk saying No soap there, all blanks. And whipped off home before he could catch her. It was he who'd drawn the lucky number in the lottery, and he didn't feel lucky about it. Go home, you idiot, and unwind. Get drunk or something.

The flat is empty. Vera has gone out, taking the car and the children. Very likely to the swimming pool: there is a nice open-air pool, with grass and trees, extremely pleasant and he wishes he was there himself. Very likely VV is there too snatching at the opportunity. And didn't that Josy say she was going swimming . . .

The windows are all shut because of The Burglars and Vera has put the bar into the track of the sliding door on the balcony: there is a close heavy smell that includes fresh paint. Yes, Vera's naked girl. It is a good time for naked girls: they can lie about in this weather feeling comfortable. And pesticides are nasty toxic things, and aerosol bombs are bad too, but there are a lot less flies in summer than there used to be. The police are grateful; many a gruesome job involves garbage. And dead bodies.

Went and got a drink. Couldn't face whisky. Supermarket plonk and not thank heaven from Les Vins Barthélémy. Caves Coopératives. Saint Saturnin. Down in the Hérault. And I wish that's where I was. Don't be stupid, Castang. About thirtyfive degrees in the shade down there and thanks very much. He'd have a shower to wash the whores off and then he'd have another glass,

145

some more glasses of this nice plonk. He'd just look first to see how the picture was getting on.

Wow, progress there and rather good, it seemed to him. The girl had a shy, proud look. She was aware of her body, but not just lying there being pleased with it; admiring it; this is how you make the men jump through the hoops. She'd left innocence behind – maybe Vera hadn't quite got that – but she wasn't corrupt. You'd see it better if you had young Josiane posing next her . . . He stumped off towards the shower shedding clothes on the way but still disciplined enough to pick them up after him.

Policemen are a pretty low lot. Men are a pretty low lot. One was supposed to stride, down these mean streets, with an idea about one's purpose in life. Not too much bloody idealism. No ideologies. But some standards. A few poorly defined – but definite – notions, like not becoming corrupt and that starts at home.

He was vaguely aware of a good deal of noise, meaning the children were home, tired now and cross from a long time in the open air and the heat and playing in the pool. Presently Vera opened the door.

"Oh there you are. How quiet. Are you very tired? Are you by any chance pissed?" looking closer.

"Very tired and about half-pissed."

"I see." Fairly tolerantly. "Is there any left? As it happens I'm pretty tired myself . . . very well, it's obvious I'm not getting any help from you. I'll give them some cornflakes or something disgusting like that which they enjoy and fling them into bed but if you want to eat you'll have to forage for yourself. I'd rather like a glass of that myself."

People don't bribe cops much any more. They bribe governments instead – they're forever taking bribes and get awfully shocked if their humble servants do the same. That's in our civilised western countries. Places like Turkey all the money has gone on paying the generals and the colonels. Only a starvation wage left for the rank and file. Which is why when you show your passport to a cop you better tuck a twenty-dollar bill inside or there will be unforeseen delays. Treat people squalidly and they'll behave squalidly.

Moral corruption's something else. If people choose to think, or

146

to pretend to think (since it's against the evidence) that no moral standard exists, and that 'Get Rich' is the ultimate slogan, then everything's dandy.

The trouble there is that morality is a fact of life. Very well, it's the others who are immoral; it's never us. It's the Communists.

Vera who is just that bit too honest and has first-hand experience gets really mad at that one. Sit the generals down and make them eat it – wrap them round it – and she doesn't mean cornflakes.

No need to get emotional. A communist cop is no better than you, likewise no worse, on average as honest, and is generally managing on a lower wage. Nothing to choose between the ones in Czechoslovakia, who are pretty bad, and the ones in California. Some of both are pretty bad. And some of yours, too, my friend.

The din seems to have died down.

Vera came back in shortly after that. She didn't want any more to drink. Or maybe just to keep him company. Eating doesn't have to be a problem, if he doesn't object to deep-freeze pizza. One could always tart it up a little. She has drunk enough to feel unwound. The children were dead tired and have gone out like a light.

He has drunk enough to be talkative, to pour it all out, make a clean sweep. He is dimly aware that she is being quite incredibly patient listening to all this. She is sorry for him. That's all right: he is hideously sorry for himself.

"Take your shirt off and I'll do your back," she commands when she can get in edgeways.

"Never can make out, all this stuff about corruption. Should have thought it a pretty normal human condition myself. Every-thing gets old, rots, dies and smells bad: biological cycle. Look at art."

"Uh?"

"Each new movement starts off good with one maybe two original artists very strong and still a bit primitive; then there's a brief flowering period at a really high pitch, and quite suddenly they're gone mannerist and decadent: see it over and over."

"I suppose so. Ow. That hurts. Lower down."

"Was he a bad man, your Lecat? Really bad? Worse than the rest?"

"Not really. More corrupt, what does that mean? The rich are after power and they rot quicker. They rot on the way up, and being rich they spread rot quicker around them."

That sturdy plonk from the Hérault. Honest enough but rough country stuff and far too much of it. And already they're making like it's the Côte d'Or. Putting it in fancy bottles, and declaring vintages. Sent him to sleep though, and without any pills.

Bad angels woke him in the bad hour, before dawn. A bad time for thinking. The office is bad too. He should have a country cottage. Isn't that what everybody wants? The longing for somewhere pure and unpolluted; the illusion of escaping from corruption?

Cécile did not kill Lecat. She has an alibi; she was giving a party. Or has she? You give a party, you are present, very much so, at the beginning and the end, and people feel sure you were there all the time, and it isn't necessarily so.

He didn't like this at all. It was phony and over-complicated, like an English detective story.

You have to take it into account. If you can – and you can't. It's a dirty story invented by a cop and a prostitute. As against the simple, upright figure of Madame Laurens, ask who a judge and jury are going to believe.

Witnesses will say anything. Come to something they don't believe in, because they can't, and they'll swear blind it wasn't so against the evidence of their own eyes. Not just peasants, but the Establishment.

Lecat knew that. Charming fellow. Awfully nice chap. General Laurens says so. Brings money and prestige to the district. And he has close friends everywhere. The worlds of politics, business, banking and contracting, falling over to do him favours: you'll never know when you want a favour in return. (And don't ever think a Procureur or even a President of a tribunal is exempt from ambition.) There's no way you can suggest that this best of chaps was a sadist, a voyeur, a corruptor. Even if you bring proofs.

As for making indecent hints and nasty suggestions about Madame Laurens . . . 'Why, she's my wife's cousin!' The entire local power structure snaps shut and buries itself in the sand like an abalone. Who says so? That little policeman? He must be a Communist. Administrative measures of internal banishment

148

there with no time lost. Assigned to residence in Gorki. The goddam nigger-lover . . .

Improbable as it sounded it could have been so; it could be done. Not on a prostitute's word: that piece of dough could be made to say anything.

Lecat, so quickly bored – he is so much brighter, so much faster than anyone around – could find it amusing to seduce his sister-in-law. His wife had become boring. Girls were just girls; one has always two or three, and they're too easy. The army wife – very Christian, rather crude, pretty naive. A goody person, and married to that goody-goody general: now wouldn't that be funny! Soldiers, to Lecat, must appear childish and amusing.

How would it be done? Not with any crude lacing of drinks. With the power, in the long run, of a strong character over a weaker one: something Castang has learned not to underestimate. Because she seems strong but isn't, with her simplistic scale of values: patriotism and the immaculate conception: fleur-de-lysed flag and small intellect: a vague conviction that the ills of everything, everywhere, are brought about by Communists, Jews, and Freemasons.

Oh yes. He would enjoy her horrified reactions, the obstinate arrogance of her rejections. The transition from disgust to acceptance could be sudden. And there could be a culmination in taking her, probably when cockeyed, to the flat of his new toy, Miss Josy.

Castang! – this is the hour when one gets fantasies.

He rolled over, and went to sleep.

**14** Castang at breakfast, clear-headed, far from night-mares, had got rid of excrescences caused by super-abundant imagination. Whatever extravagant suggestions he found to make, to Alice Jimenez who might accept them, to an upright and uptight Procureur who wouldn't, the result would be the same. We want no inner certainties: we want visible, tangible, irrefutable proofs. To carry opinion with you, because being right, about some things, is worse than being wrong.

And how was he to go about this?

He got into his car, and drove to Lecat's palace, the House of Miracles. It is a very fine place. Works like a Rolls Royce, every part machined to micro-millimetre tolerance, and bench-run until the whole assembly goes like silk. He had made a huge mistake. He had been looking for grains of grit. Now he was going to take the machine apart again, and examine each piece afresh. But this time looking for something that seems all right, and has a bloody great crack in it.

He stood looking at the house. One got accustomed to that architecture; already he 'quite liked it'. Pretty garden: park, rather; it was a couple of hectares. Everything still running smoothly, on the impetus of the dead man. The maids working to the last instructions given, the cook cooking – who for? There were cars parked in front. He went to look for Violette the gatekeeper.

He found her as usual in her lodge, in her guard chair from which she kept an eye on everything, knitting. Life went on. There was a good smell, of a casserole in the oven, with a bone and a bit of bacon, and a little bunch of herbs tied in a thread. Her washing had been done and was pinned out: the white wash today, sheets and pillowcases shaken and stretched, hanging evenly, to bleach in the fresh air and make the ironing easier. That generation had grown up in the smoke and the coal-dust; as young women had known first the depression and then Hitler's war. They didn't really like gaily-coloured cotton prints on a bed, judging others in the terms of their own selfrespect. Shiny windows and white linen.

"And what's all this then – funeral games?" She twitched at the yarn to make the hank unroll evenly. In his childhood a small boy had still to hold the skein while his auntie wound it off into a beautiful even ball. Sometimes she had picked the wrong end, and if the skein was tangled the yarn would not shuttle freely between his outstretched hands. With her lip caught in concentration she would have to weave the half-formed ball in and out, many times when it was bad, before it again ran freely. And there too it smelt the same, the room behind the shop with roses on the wallpaper: casseroles and ironing and a coalburning stove that has been blackleaded. Stoves which came from this country between France and Belgium and are still to be seen in these houses where old ladies live out their lives. The modern enamelled cooker may be easier to clean but the metal's too thin; will never cook pastry as it should be: at once golden and tender.

Her voice was placid.

"Those are the business men. Come from Paris and the like. Lille and Lyon. To decide about the administering. And the inheriting, I'd suppose. That'll keep them there a longish while." Four polished steel needles, sharp and competent. Bluish-grey wool: socks for the gardeners. "They'll leave us alone, I hope and trust. It's cheaper to buy these now," her eye following his, "but I've had the habit all my life, I can't sit with idle hands. They frighten me those men because they only care about dividends. People's lives don't interest them. You, I'll say this for you, you think about life. Two deaths like that. People have their faults, no doubt. But who deserves killing?"

Castang nodded. He'd 'go bail' for this old lady at least, but for being a cop, who never goes bail for anyone.

He should have remembered that the cardinals would come, to sit in conclave. Auditors, the Man from London, and from New York; Man from Bank, and from Ministry. To elect a caretaker pope: the Investment must be protected. The small fry, like Guillaume, would not be present: on call if needed, at two minutes notice. Nothing for him there. Lives were his business and to these financial gentlemen, the interest there is only to prolong their own beyond what the actuarial tables give them.

"What have you noticed, these two days? Comings and goings."

"Them apart? Nothing unusual."

"Madame Cécile – for instance."

"Oh her – but that's natural. First her sister – and now the boss. Been in and out a lot: she's having an inventory made." Of course! Death in the family is tragic but the inheritance gives rise to much discussion, much scurrying. And listings. All those little portable items . . . The maids are trustworthy girls but . . .

Right, right! Castang likewise. Every item listed, and then the expert valuer, with his jeweller's loupe screwed in his eye, going over every small thing – the Judge of Instruction!

It's all right to *observe*. Questioning must come later. Rémy the cook put it to him straight, over the shoulder.

"Don't think I'm being awkward. But laying it on, pretty good lunch it's got to be. Twelve right now: more at short notice they tell me. That's not on, I say, this isn't a pub. Still expected to provide. Guvnor dead, brings the beetles out the woodwork, you'd never guess how many. Out of Rio – out of Seattle! Flying in from Tokyo and all wanting meals and drinks! So right now no time for the per-lice I'm afraid."

The maids were as curt. Perrine the housemaid 'up the wall'. Some of these people thought they had every right!

Victorine – "You guessed it, Mister. I've a list here like a whole roll of toilet paper. Middle of summer and frantic about her furs in cold storage. What's that notary phrase – testamentary disposition. Lot more fuss about their being dead than how they came there if you take my meaning. My own mother's in the hospital right now, and my guess is she's dying, these doctors don't tell you a straight story, I know damn well it's cancer, I ought to be with her right now and I'm pestered with stuff like where's the cleaners' receipt for that brocade frock, please Mister, I'm the maid, you got questions take them please to Madame Cécile."

Frédo, where is that bugger – the slimy, the subsequious? – is that the right word? – yes it is. Ho, gone to the airport, the whole damn day there, ought to have a camp bed. Some fellow flies in to Lille out of Paris and Frédo is sleeping with the Rolls on the concrete at Brussels. Wouldn't have happened while the boss was here and you had better believe it.

There is no point in bullying people who are doing their job. You are doing the same? You are only a servant too? Public servant, isn't that what they call the peelers? Get under the feet of these fast executive types you'll discover in what esteem they hold a PJ commissaire. They say shit, you say present, and then hold your tongue.

With this excellent advice to himself Castang plunged into the gentle midsummer smell of a garden. Old Georges was unfussed, but as uncommunicative as ever and still more military.

"Midsummer, chief, the grass has to be kept mowed." An officer of police, he had noticed, did not rank as army hierarchy. At best he was a senior non-com, and not something you say Sir to.

"Madame Cécile says this and that, she's the madam now. I take my instructions from the General, way I always have. He came over and told us to carry on with the making and mending, no matter who's dead. Even when you lose your battalion commander, you don't give ground. You hold on, until the General sees fit to issue new orders. So when I'm off parade, maybe then I'll have time for you."

These massive snubs were doing Castang no harm. He too could blow his whistle and scream. Call the whole lot out and have them lined up. Tallest on the right, shortest on the left. Marker stand fast. Ranks right and left turn. Form squad, quick march.

He too could get a bit of discipline into this useless shower. Much good might it do him!

He could use the alternate technique of the sergeant falling headlong upon the fatigue squad. Who're the musicians here? Right, I want three volunteers to move the piano – that's you, you and you! And on the double . . . A lot of good *that* would do him.

Jean-Baptiste, weeding flowerbeds, greeted Castang as laconically as ever but seemed a little more forthcoming.

"Weeds in June don't ask who died or got married."

"What's the old boy sore about?"

"Two of those banking types came strolling about. Wouldn't know a begonia from an adding machine. Nagging him. Staff officers, he says, who stay well behind the combat zone because of their nice boots." It was a renewed fascination to watch him work, himself as meticulous as any staff officer, choosing a long-handled hoe from the barrow as a golfer chooses a number five iron for a nice little chip up to lie dead a metre from the flag. Unhurried easy rhythm, blade just the right angle, just the right depth; feet planted in a stylist's open stance, a back uncramped, unstooped. Castang gardening got in a muck sweat with those damn dandelions that send their greedy great roots deep down and when changing position was liable to tread on the rake . . . The rake stood in the barrow with shaft at an angle to grasp when needed, with another hoe, smaller, short-handled for closer work: the number eight iron . . .

He stared, went on staring. Took a step closer: his mind had stopped freewheeling and was pointing like a gundog. Stupid great neddy, he told himself.

Castang had admired them all before, with the male pleasure in a craftsman's tools: forks with broad or narrow tines, sharp-bladed spades to cut turf, shovel heart-shaped for deep clinging soil or broad for lighter mould; the dibbers and planters: and all with their steel emerypapered and the shafts linseed-oiled at the socket. He picked up the little hoe.

"You're not using this right now?"

The long one, that could reach out and under the rhododendrons, paused for a fraction and the quiet voice said, "No."

"Mind if I borrow it? Quarter of an hour?"

A little longer pause: no workman likes lending tools, nor borrowing those of others.

"Suppose not . . . bring it back." He showed no curiosity. When Castang looked back from fifty metres he had raked the weeds and was gathering the pile between two wooden blades. Castang went on towards the toolshed.

It was an ordinary wooden hut, with racks for implements, a bench with a vice for repairs: a sparkplug spanner lay where old Georges had left it – the mower had given trouble. The door stood open. Pleasant smell of creosoted wood sun-warmed; grasscuttings, three-in-one oil. Castang looked at the door. No lock, but staples driven in each side; chain and padlock hung dangling. Careful chaps. Who'd steal tools, in an enclosed estate? – force of habit probably.

But a second look showed they weren't such careful chaps. The staple on the jamb side came out with a pull. He knew perfectly what had happened. They'd mislaid the key one day, and wrenched the staple out. Close up you could see the scratches, quite old, filmed with rust. Pushed it back in: who'd notice?

He examined his trophy. It was like a tiny mattock; on one side the broad-edged hoe blade and opposite that a narrow leaf-shaped blade with a rounded tip that interested him greatly. Now he wanted to try a little experiment.

He scratched, thoughtfully. Need something like a pumpkin, a marrow. Too early for them? Or a melon. Old Georges had melons; yes and brooded over them too – apple of his eye. A fuss would be made, explanations called for. Castang had no wish to make any, wanting neither to attract attention nor make an undue fool of himself.

He hid behind a tree with soft sweeping foliage that came down low. Is it a deodar? (He likes trees: one of his nicer aspects.) He began making snappy, wristy movements, one-handed. Lovely tool, went just where you wanted it. Balance as good as any golfclub. He stopped suddenly: he had just had an idea of singular brilliance. Hid the thing under the deodar, went up the steps to the terrace (politely wiping his feet), in past the swimmingpool, through and upstairs in search of Victorine. While he was talking to her in the bedroom a press had stood open that had caught his carpenter's eye with its beautifully made shelves and recesses, for scarves and gloves and belts and . . . an object he had noticed because he thought it comic.

He found her in another room, looking harassed. Cécile was nowhere about, for which he was grateful. She blinked at the thing under his arm, surprised and a scrap shocked.

"I'm borrowing this. I may damage it but I'll get you another. Don't cost much uh? Where d'you get them – hairdresser's?" She nodded speechless. "My girl will bring you a new one."

"What did you do with the – ?"

"Left it on the shelf." She stared as though he were mad: maybe so but he rather thought not.

He took the treasure back to the garden and looked for a suitable retired nook: found one, with a laurelly tree that had branches of the right sort. He had to wedge the thing so that it would stay relatively stable. He went back for his hoe, and contemplated both trophies with a view to his experiment – would it work?

155

What he had was a head. It was life-size and modelled smooth like a skull, though it had been given stylised features like a dress dummy. Which it was, more or less: in Marguerite's cupboard it had held a wig. The neck was squared to serve as a stand, and this he had jammed in a strong forked branch. The thing was polystyrene and would be fragile: he'd have to go canny. It mustn't be a blow. Or he'd demolish the object. A delicate flick, just to get the impact. If it didn't work? – why, he'd just have to confiscate the hoe. Have it sent down to the lab to be labelled and measured and photographed and niggled over. Taking ages, and Castang was in a hurry, and Jean-Baptiste would like his hoe back. He used it every day and cleaned it at each day's finish: microscopes would be no help.

Castang took several practice swings. Exactly like Severiano, the strong delicate Spanish artist: a tiny one just off the green, a feather-accurate pitch to within ten centimetres of the pin and it's been known to go straight in. He tried the branch again. Firm, elastic: a man's neck. Deep breath. Wrist. Click.

Worked like a dream. The branch gave, the head fell. Just like a real one. The polystyrene took the chop without crumbling. Sharp neat impact mark.

Of course he couldn't reproduce an impact on bone: the blade sank deep into this goo. Didn't matter: he had the exact copy of an entry. Size, shape, angle. He rolled the head in his jacket and headed for the poolside phone. Miss Véronique Varennes was typing up statements in the office.

"I'm at the house, Varennes, get your ass over here quick." He stretched out on a rattan chair by the pool and lit a cigar. Only two left but he'd deserved it.

"Photographs, VV, straightaway. The pick and this, handle it carefully. I'm pretty certain now that when we compare we'll find we've got the weapon we are looking for."

"Ho. Gardener?"

"No proof of that. Toolshed isn't locked. Anybody familiar with the place could have picked it up and brought it with him."

"Premeditation, though."

"That, yes; it's hard to imagine someone making an assignation in the toolshed and catching that up when words got heated – lose no time now, girl."

156

Rémy Mathieu had reached the strategic point in a cook's morning of being 'en place': the virtuous feeling that the house-keeping is done and the ship under way. All that tedious take-off drill behind one. The automatic pilot can be switched on. Time, in fact, for elevenses. He was sitting comfortably with his apron off, and a glass of something clear and amber which looked sophisti-cated and was in fact cold tea.

"Got a cup for me?"

"Sure. Sit yourself down."

"Big business happy?"

"Have had breakfast and are plotting takeovers in the library. Stack of shit. Expect a bloody good lunch as their due. And a bloody good dinner too. Where they stow it all away . . . Got to put up with them, same's I got to put up with you. Might go on for weeks." Castang nodded.

"But not with any luck. Think I found the assegai." Rémy looked mildly relieved: that's a little something to be going on with.

"Thought you were looking pleased with yourself. Good, as long as it's not my fish-slice."

"Curious?"

"Of course I'm curious. Caroline girl, that pot's boiling, turn it to tick and give it a skim. Another half hour I'll want you for the service. Tell Perrine to climb into her black frock, and tonight there'll be fourteen so put another leaf in the table. Here's the menu, see that she gets it laid up right."

"Wine?" said the girl stolidly.

"Roland's looking after that. Much too good for that lot," in a sour aside to Castang, "but the bankers are very hot indeed after the classified growths and carry little cards with the good years written out. What's your dangerous object then?"

"Gardener's hoe, a little one. I noticed it on Jean-Baptiste's barrow. Nelly I was not to think of it earlier. Looks right to me."

"Tchaa," shaking his head at the commonplace. "I search all over for my palette-knife and it's staring me in the face. They keep all their stuff in that shed. Wouldn't be difficult to get in there."

"You ever try?"

"Go there often enough when I want a lettuce or some radishes. If they're busy I don't even ask. Take a trowel and whatever I want. Everybody knows about it."

"That's what I thought. It isn't perhaps what a woman would think of."

"Who knows what women think of? Reminds me; Caroline, ask your father for a few spring onions and jog Perrine to look at the flowers if they need topping up. Well then, everything's jake, no, and you only need the fingerprints or whatever."

"That's right."

"Seriously though, it's a very queer thing. Who could have got in? The boss must have found out. Way I see it, he knew who queeked Madam, and said so; and got chopped for it. Okay okay, I'm not paid to think about that. My job's to get the grub on the table, and I'm a pro so that's what I keep in my mind. Forefront, anyway."

"Go on."

"What's to go on? Everyone's tense, nervous. I am myself, I keep dropping things. Not every day in every household things go all Agatha Christie." This lady, being full of ingenious contrivance, has great appeal to the French mentality. "And don't look at me like that – it isn't me!"

"No, I don't think it is so you should be safe enough," dryly. "I've got till tomorrow to find out."

"So go buy *True Detective* and see how it's done."

"You say Cesari will be in?"

"That's right. Perrine can serve it but the good stuff, he'll get it up and decant it. The guvnor used to do that. Now . . ."

"What will you do," asked Castang, "when this is over?"

"I've some money saved. And a bit of interest in a certain pub. There's always money in this business even if it is a lot of work. You know the old joke; there are two businesses worth having. Look after their mouths, or else between their legs. La bouche ou l'entre-jambe. So I'll stick to what I know."

"Like the Fox," suggested Castang lazily, and got a sharp look.

"Yes – like the Fox."

"With a few girls, for stacking behind the bar."

"Leave that to the Belle-Gueule," laughing heartily. Too

heartily thought Castang. He'd been a little too loose of the mouth and was covering it.

"Got to give you the shove now, Commissaire," he went on.

"Not to sound coarse, but I better start my motor. To wit, the soles." Caroline had come back and was standing dully. Mathieu turned to her with what seemed unnecessary sharpness. "The cheese then, girl. It needs time to breathe. What are you hanging about for?"

"Difficult customers," said Castang sympathetically. She looked at him listlessly. It meant nothing. As Mathieu had said they were all on edge.

"Accustomed to the best," said Mathieu sarcastically, tying his apron, slapping his toque on at a jaunty angle, "and the staff better give it them or they'll want to know what servants are coming to, nowadays. Vurry vurry exalted opinion of themselves, the financial gentlemen have."

"Couldn't run a sweet-shop, most of them," said Castang.

"That's right! As the boss used to say 'Weet je 't ook'," in imitation of Lecat putting on the accent to talk Vlaams. "Said they needed the *Financial Times* and the *Wall Street Journal* brought on a silver tray with the pages ironed. How to lose a million dollars and still make it look like paper profit. All right then, let's get it moving." Spry as a sparrow; when the work's got to be done don't think about homicides. Sensible man, thought Castang.

He drifted through to the diningroom. Perrine in her 'black frock' and a starched apron was staring vaguely at the table, yawning and scratching her behind with a silver fork: so much for bankers. Beyond was a little pantry, nicely fitted with marble shelves. Caroline was peeling the foil off a packet of butter. There was a little sink for washing sherry glasses. She had remembered the spring onions.

"Pay no attention to me," said Castang quietly.

"Mister, I'm just the kitchen maid." A plain face, gaunt. Bony hands and feet, thin hard legs, wispy hair. She was every housewife you see in the north, in a flowered overall and a headscarf over curlers, polishing the windows of the grimy little brick houses. They work all day, fast. They do a shift in the textile mills and still have their housework when they get home. They haven't the well-

159

fed look of the bourgeois girls sailing tranquilly to comfy desks. If they look pale and anxious they have reason: unemployment is high and money goes fast. But this one, he should have thought, had less reason.

"Rémy a bit rough with you, these last days?"

"Mister, don't butter me up, I don't like it."

"But you've worries about a future that's uncertain, is that it?" She looked at him with real astonishment.

"Who cares about the servants' future?"

"But it's my job, to think about things."

"You're a cop."

"It links together. I start by thinking of the funny things which go on in this house and which the servants understand better than anyone." Maybe he would have got somewhere with her and maybe he wouldn't: no way to know. The door opened and he thought it was Perrine until he saw the quick flicker of fear and he turned around slowly, lighting one of the little cigars.

It was Cesari, as usual got up to kill in one of his extravagantly dandified suits, standing all negligent with hands in pockets lightly not to spoil the sit. His voice had the insolence which goes with the part.

"Hallo, Commissaire – chatting up the maids? – oh oh. Caroline, the decanters there must be cleaned, not just rinsed." She put her hands in her overall pockets and squeezed them.

"Ask Perrine, I'm busy."

"Not too busy to gossip. I'm telling you."

"Go tell Rémy."

"I'll be wanting a chat with you when you've managed to get your wine poured out," Castang said. "We'll go somewhere for a drink. Down the Fox maybe. I'm beginning to get an appetite."

"I'm busy," taking his time and then making it contemptuous.

"You're busy as long as they tell you to be busy, at drawing corks and smelling them. So when I tell you to busy yourself you jump. Or I'll take you by the ear, in front of the girls." Behind big beautiful eyes a cool but unintelligent mind made calculations and Perrine in the diningroom dropped an ashtray.

"No, look," deciding against the heavy confrontation, "I'm truly tied up all day with business, so make it this evening."

"Certainly. It's a date," making it sound a pleasure. "Down the Fox. Plenty of time then. For a serious chat. As long as is needed. Write it in your diary." Where had Varennes got to? There were too many people here.

In the hall one of the businessmen was returning from a trip to the lavatory. This monster gave him the hard look and asked "Who are you?" abrupt and challenging.

"No business of yours," said Castang politely. He opened the front door and there was VV just arriving, as though come to the party with her contribution of a melon in a plastic bag.

"That the head? Slip upstairs and give it to Victorine. Don't get raped on the way by any of these bankers. I'll be out in the car. We'll go and have some lunch." Light lunch. There was a lot to do. He hadn't in the least wanted to frig about drinking in the Fox or anywhere else nor to waste time upon Monsieur Cesari, who wasn't a person of overwhelming importance in anybody's eyes but his own. This evening would do nicely, and he'd give himself the pleasure of a nice bottle, some really good cheese, and Cesari for dessert. Which would give Inspector Varennes time for a pretty thorough heart-to-heart along with Mademoiselle Josiane. Meantime, it was too much trouble to go home. A beer and a sandwich. The Judge of Instruction. But first, the verifying of his battle-axe. Not a handy thing to go carrying about, but he couldn't go to Alice Jimenez with his ridiculous games. Whacking at a polystyrene head of all things . . . He couldn't tell how much legal finesse would be involved. They might need a disinterment order, for the physical comparison with the original wound. A pretty forensic point. Would photos suffice, for an expert being crossexamined in the Assize Court? It was not like the familiar comparison-microscope problems with ballistics or the like, for which the police lab will suffice. To identify a gun you have only to fire a bullet and put it alongside the original. Pickaxes are altogether more complicated. Nothing for it but his old pals in the pathology department.

"Not again? And what's *this*?" Castang carrying his plastic head in plastic bag, and a garden hoe in the other hand: yes, it was a sight for sore eyes.

So that by the time he got to the 'Fox' . . . Early for them, but for him it should have been the end of the day, and time for the domestic bosom, and the day was nowhere near ended yet. It made a break, and it meant time to unwind, and a drink he had been looking forward to for an hour and more. Jimenez had been meticulous, not to say pernickety. He had told Varennes to join him here.

"I'm off duty," sulkily.

"You are when I say you are. I'll buy you a good drink and you can have the pleasure of tickling Monsieur Cesari's handsome –"

"Wouldn't even with yours let alone with mine," snappish.

Saturday night in the old town, but quiet this early. A few eating at the tables along the wall, drinking at the long bar. What am I doing here snuffling about? Anybody with sense is out enjoying the fine weather. In the garden pottering, looking to see what sort of shape the tomato plants . . . in a boat, I wish I were in a boat. The Polizei (Commissaire Richard's portmanteau word for the guardians of the law in all their varieties 'too tedious to enumerate') spent so many hours stuck indoors in smells. It is aired here and the food is good: it is still a stuffy, smelly . . . how long this might have gone on for, nobody knows, but the 'patron' saw and sailed over to him. Biggish man like a weight-lifter or shot-putter gone to seed; the fat that used to be muscle hanging in heaps on jaw and shoulder. Great bags under sharp pale eyes. But the bulgy belly was still hard; the shuffling step not yet flatfooted.

"Evening, Commissaire. Nice to have you back. Like the table in the corner? Quiet, and you can see what goes on." Sly, like Alfie Hitchcock. "And what can we find for you to drink? You'd like to eat? There's a lovely fish, cold." Waiting upon the great man's pleasure with a napkin over his shoulder. The flattery was skilful.

Castang loves 'nice fish' (just like Gollum, Vera says) but in order really to enjoy it he needs to concentrate upon it, and he'd better have something he can eat without noticing. And a Cahors? No, a madiran, from the Basque country, in memory of Richard. The patron beams.

"Then bring two glasses, patron: we must drink to that."

Richard one day had been discovered reading the American magazine that says it forms-world-opinion, unashamed. 'Preens itself upon being required reading for people On the Way Up.

They tell me that the Polizei is both macho and sloppy. Do we on this account hold our sides and fall about laughing?' French senior officials are much given to the rhetorical question. 'Do we deride the complacent superficialities of this hairdressing-salon reading matter? We do not! I walk in and discover Mossieu Lucciani playing with his Python Threefiftyseven. Keep all this masturbation in check, Castang.' Sniff: the phrase 'macho and sloppy' hung in the air.

As for Castang's police positive, thirtyeight, excellent model from Smith and Wesson, it was in the office drawer for good and all, gathering dust. One must learn to walk without the crutch.

The bottle of madiran arrived with a flourish of napkin and the patron did his act of smelling the cork with closed eyes and expression of ecstasy. It's pleasant stuff but as the French admit they have an awful lot of Viticulteurs. There are precious few vignerons left; the farmer who really knows how to make wine and takes the trouble involved. The patron winked, poured out and sat down. They raised their glasses and solemnly admired the colour. The patron is of the generation which inevitably says 'Tchin-tchin'.

"I was sorry to hear about your waiter."

"Yes. He was a good boy. Lousy luck."

"He served me," says Castang putting country bread in his mouth. "Alert. Good service."

"I train them," modestly. "We have good food, good wine. Spoilt unless you have good service." Drinking.

"Very true," sententious. "They have to look. And listen." Drinking. Castang took the bottle and poured them both another glass. "I'm interested, patron, in a lady."

"That is praiseworthy," gallantly.

"I think she was here. There was a coincidence about cheese."

"Ah yes, our cheese is famous."

"I'll show you her picture. There was talk about this lady. But this, of course, is just between us."

The patron put his elbows on the table and made a little steeple of his fingers, speaking behind them.

"I think I recognise her. Not a regular customer."

"But you might remember. Not being regular. While reading the newspaper you might think 'Tja, she was in last night.' Now that would be a help. Even more of a help might be who with."

"It sounds logical," with a French respect for logic. "There is a difficulty. Were it a badly served table I might have occasion to take notice, to tell the waiter psst, you, pay attention. And I do not always have the leisure – the pleasure – to sit as I do now. When it is late and we are full; you understand, the kitchen gets snowed under, my wife with the bills . . . it is such a pity, this waiter . . ."

"Very true," said Castang pouring out more wine. "I say, this is good. The waiter is alas dead. This means – sorry to appear hard-hearted but you understand – he no longer has my interest. He was paid to notice things, I mean that's what you paid him for, and it was to his advantage: got good tips that way. But that no longer interests me. Damn," looking at his cigar tin. "Empty. You don't have these? Might I have a packet of Gitanes? And," emptying a dribble into the two glasses, "I almost think we'll need another of these."

"My turn," said the patron politely. "Might I borrow the picture again, a moment? My daughter, you see, it's just possible," bearing away the dead soldier.

The girl came two minutes later, with the packet of cigarettes, the new bottle.

"Complimentary," she said smiling. "Would you like to order your dinner?" producing her pad and pencil. A nice girl, of nineteen or twenty. Fair ringlets, pale shell-rimmed glasses. "Was it the fish, after all? It's a turbot, with mussels and shrimps and things, awfully nice." She wrote out the order, tore off the top copy, slapped that on the table. The photo of Marguerite was under it. "Your friends were in the other corner as I recall. The table for two, there. Didn't she have a blue frock? I don't remember much but it was just wine and some cheese, I seem to think. And wasn't she with a gentleman? I don't think I know him though I think I know most of the regulars. Sort of elderly. Distingué. Hard to say," whisking off with a pert little grin behind her glasses.

Elderly? Distinguished? What the hell . . . ? He smiled beatifically at the girl bringing his dinner. Dirty old man. Greedy, too; helping himself to more mayonnaise. Castang ate; enjoying it. Drank water, drank more madiran, belched slightly. Wouldn't have got this from Vera. But had steered clear of trouble. No mention of his great friend Mr Campbell. Alfie Hitchcock had understood that he wasn't trying to be sly or hassle anybody. He hadn't tried to be secretive. Just kept his information back, as a prudent man would, until he could either sell it or present it as a favour. You don't give things away, in this business. A drink and a packet of cigarettes, that costs nothing. But in return for keeping Paddy Campbell from falling on them like a ton of bricks, this is what we have to offer in return. So he made a good supper.

"Evening, Monsieur Castang." He looked up. She was ready with the name – one must never forget names – and the profession-al smile. Aurélie. One did not forget Marie there behind, but in the eye of the beholder after a few glasses of wine they blended. A blue and white summer frock, very dashing: high heels and a little Italian bag.

"Join me then. Or is there a party?" Some vinous enthusiasm, some cop nosiness, but of no great account. "Have you eaten? A cognac then?" She shook her head smiling but slid into the chair opposite.

"Never any hard stuff. A coffee though if I may. I only wondered whether Roland might be here – I was working late and wanted a word, about those financial people at the house. We're hoping they'll leave things as they are. No, I don't smoke either, thank you. They do incline to meddle."

"I'm expecting Master Roland myself. Stick around and we'll work on him together."

"I know you think him odious, but to me he's just a colleague. An insecure person behind all that show, or is that cheap and glib?"

"Quite likely true and one would still prefer his being insecure some place else. Indiscreet but it's a relief to put the job aside sometimes. You got a friend?" sliding it in paternally so that she was still smiling when she started looking angry, caught it, blushed a little, and settled for a smile.

"Not right now and haven't you asked that before?"

"I'm always forgetting what I've asked before," mendaciously, "and forever indiscreet. Thought you'd have some chap maybe. Most girls do. Two filters, Miss," at the passing waitress. France has now the espresso habit but in the North you can still get a real cup of coffee.

"What's this then, an offer?" She wasn't being roguish; the tone was telling him to stay off her patch of grass. The Basque wine is easy to drink but he hadn't had that much of it. And unguarded bonhomie is a Polizei technique.

"Mustn't get that paternal." Rather true: she was an extremely attractive girl but he could see Vera's sardonic look, counteraphrodisiac. "I'm not aflame with fantasies. As you'll know, they get in the way of work." She nodded, seriously.

"It's very indiscreet to ask, but you've taught me – does it get anywhere – your work?"

"Ye-es." He had determined to play her gently. "You know France – never make anything simple while there's a chance to complicate. Homicide enquiries are simple as a rule; if there is any rule: somebody was in the grip of an overmastering emotion. But Monsieur Lecat was a pretty complex personality."

The coffee came. Neither touched it: the metal filters are very hot. Everybody's in a hurry now, and the espresso, forced through under pressure, goes with this. People are too impatient to let a filter drip through in its own time.

"So I don't know all that much about him yet," went on Castang, lighting a cigarette. "Be interested in your view of some aspects. A womaniser and what does that mean? – liked them, and being in their company? – I do myself. Great deal of energy, and people call that being highly sexed. Bit superficial perhaps. He manoeuvred people, a manipulator. Girls unwound and rested him, maybe.

"Or did he have a sort of contempt for women? Your conventional womaniser, like friend Cesari perhaps, tends to humiliate them for a variety of shrink reasons. Self-aggrandisement, some sort of vengeance. How did you read him?"

"I didn't pretend to know him," she said. "I saw a lot of him, yes, but I'm a small wheel in just one of his interests. I keep my ideas to myself." A bit flurriedly she flipped at the hot lid, but the water was only halfway through. "You are polite – and I suppose you make efforts to be sensitive and I'm grateful for that. You don't seek to brutalise."

"I'm not a comic strip," to help the awkwardness, "viewing all the girls' tits strained against torn scraps of flimsy fabric."

"Okay," laughing, relieved. "As a sort of salesman I make a

166

goodish living and like that for the independence it gives. People do find it hard to accept that one doesn't use sex as bait."

Castang flipped the lid on his filter which was almost ready. People asked to talk about others may be reticent, but they're mostly ready to talk about themselves. Natural; to them that's more interesting.

"Ready," lifting the top off on to the little tray. "Sugar?"

"I take it without, thanks."

"Take it without what?" enquired VV's voice, in her accustomed vein. "Warning? Precaution? Thinking?" He'd forgotten about her. The interruption was tiresome. But there she was.

"Sit down then, Véronique, and get yourself something to drink."

"All this coffee – I need something harder." Noisy girl. It wasn't the moment to tell her so. He had missed another moment too, perhaps.

"I must go," said Aurélie looking for her bag.

"No no," said VV, "stay where you are; I've been hearing about you." Castang had to let her be, because plainly she had got hold of something. "I'm thirsty, I'd like a beer. That address you gave me . . ." Yes. Josiane. "Out of fags again," helping herself to his. "A Pilsener, love," bawling at the waitress, "and a packet of Marlboros." Castang, whose bill it was, reminded himself to stop buying his staff's cigarettes. She was a bit over-excited, all set for a pounce.

"He had set her up cosy," addressing Castang. "A Rosemarie gag." The famous Nitribitt, for thirty years the synonym for the call girl used as listening device. Industrial espionage is too heavy a phrase. The beautiful Russian in furs . . . No, but the pillow talk of the exhausted executive can and does give useful pointers to his frame of mind. Castang had guessed it. There wouldn't have been much point to Josiane, otherwise.

But it works both ways. The original setter-upper can in a careless or irritable moment drop clues. And that, to the Polizei, is of more interest.

"He'd got tickled by something new," went on VV, "and she was young enough to feel narked about that. You'd know about this, wouldn't you, love?" at Aurélie, who said nothing but listened with strained attention. "You made a good job of hard to get and his curiosity got piqued. Little bit of a challenge. Oh good, I needed that," with a powerful swig at the beer put in front of her.

"Good guess too," addressing Castang, "about this lousy little pimp Cesari. Running errands on little details the big shot couldn't be bothered with. And he's been trying to make this number here for a long while. Bit of a conflict there. No, that's wrong, my guess would be his boss made him swallow a lot of castor oil and be fervent about the flavour." She took another swig.

"Brings me back to you, love. Monsieur Lecat-Deceased wouldn't have tried for anything crude like a bounce on the office sofa, which everyone would have got to know about. Maybe he thought of something sly. This girl's tales aren't the most reliable under the sun. She's scared of losing her nice flat, and she was a bit shaken," showing her strong white teeth in a grin, "and she gets loquacious, and anxiety makes her inventive. So I come, hurry on down, the boss here wants a chat with boyfriend-Cesari, and who do I find but you? So we're looking forward to hearing more, love, and you telling."

Aurélie was looking pinched around the nostril but keeping herself under control. Castang smoked in silence. He'd thought himself doing quite nicely in the paternal role, but women can be crude with other women. He couldn't have stopped VV anyway: she felt sure she'd got hold of a good key. And she might be quite right.

"So," said Inspector Varennes, "I don't know about the evening engagements. Rather like some supper myself, looks like I might not get time later on. I think you'd do well to forget any plans made, love, because you'd be well advised to come back with me to the shop and dictate your memoirs sort of freely into my machine. Going to be a hot seller, but we don't want the juicy bits leaked to the press before we get them. I'll ask for a take-out sandwich," she told Castang.

"Is there no protection from all this abuse and these insinuations?" asked Aurélie. "So the public's right, and all cops are crude bullies – when they aren't hypocrites. Don't I get a chance to explain myself, or do you only listen to words put in my mouth?"

"Inspector Varennes is a little nervous. She's tired too and has had nothing to eat. She won't put any words in your mouth. Neither will I. She's right, simply in thinking your best policy is to abandon concealment. This isn't the best place so I'll pay my bill, when you've got what you want, Véronique. We've a job though, which is to gather in Prettyboy; the animal's keeping me waiting."

"Bet your life, but I'm not settling for any corned beef sandwich: what was it you had?"

"Fish," impatiently, "but get some chicken salad or whatever and have it put in foil."

"Bitch!" said a voice. Not loud but very distinct. VV looked up, sure that this meant her. Aurélie, aware that it meant her, tried to keep still, and not to look up; to give herself a countenance by pretending to drink coffee from an empty cup.

Castang looked up but in no hurry. Recognising the authentic note of the Prettyface he didn't want any dramas in a café by now crowded. The patron was two tables off. He wiggled the fat forefinger.

"No row. Let me beg that there should be no row." It is a pity that Castang finds Dickens unreadable and that Vera, who always says she does not get enough to laugh at, was not there.

"Bitch," said Cesari again. "Cuddling up to cops now. Telling them your life story . . ." Aurélie looked stunned.

"There'll be no row," said Castang comfortably. "Stop making an exhibition of yourself. Now that you're here at last you can come with us." He is busy paying the reckoning. Miss Varennes, mind on her stomach, is fussing about her parcel.

"Oh *can* I?"

"No two questions about it," not even looking.

One can't add it up. The shrink deals in abstractions; vanity, immaturity. Yes but when, how, at what moment? In a concrete situation, arriving suddenly. Even the Polizei, experienced, gets caught out.

Fear? Certainly fear is the source that energises violence. But what was there to be afraid of? In Castang's eye, nothing much. Thinking of garden hoes, he had not seen the Belle-Gueule wielding one. Not his style.

Vanity? He wouldn't have instructed VV to go out and pick this man up. It is the sort of man who cannot abide any sort of physical challenge from a woman. But from him . . . Cesari is a young man;

tall, active, muscular – pretty. While he is a funny little middle-aged man with an awkward left arm. And far from pretty. The chap would go on being convinced of his own superiority.

It was for sure that Castang made a mistake, but it remains hard to explain quite what that was. True, the Roland was a bit drunk. And vain, frightened, stupid. Alcohol mixes as badly with vanity as with sleeping pills. That is about all one can say. Violence comes fast and does not think.

A step took Cesari behind the girl's chair. The hand came out of the pocket fast, the knife opening in the same rapid movement. His other hand dragged her by the hair to her feet. The knifeblade pointed in just under her right ear. He moved bringing her body to cover him.

"Stay still," he said nastily.

Of course they stayed still. Castang is carrying no gun and wouldn't think of it if he was. Gunfighting in crowded public rooms you leave to John Wayne. Véronique is wearing a big gun, with a loose cotton jacket to conceal it; a great pest in this hot weather. But she has sense enough not to go waving it about. Everyone else, disappointed of a juicy scene the moment before, had gone back to the serious business of eating and drinking, and now they were all looking intently the other way, like elderly ladies confronted with a flasher.

"You won't even reach the car," said Castang sadly in the silence. What does the imbecile think he's doing? Taking a hostage? What for? Like so many others he has watched too much television. These clowns will do anything to get in front of a camera. And everybody's always so eager to oblige them.

Apparently convinced that guns and cameras were trained on him Cesari walked backward pulling the girl with him. Reaching the door he made her open it. As he stepped on to the pavement a hungry python wrapped itself around his neck and pinned his wrist.

"What did I tell you?" said Castang. "Silly little boy." A bit providential, it's true. But what a lot of trouble it saves.

Pythons are not as a rule white, hairy, and reddened by sunburn, but this one was made up of both Paddy Campbell's solid arms. And it's choking the Belle Gueule, so that the hand loses grip and the knife falls on the pavement. Castang would like to say 'Cut!'

170

"Do hurry up with the dindin," he says instead. Véronique has ordered a complicated meal in anti-hamburger protest.

The Corsican terror was on one knee wondering where his next breath was coming from.

"Half-assed little squit," said Inspector Campbell. He is under six feet tall and Cesari well over, but he is a python in a bad mood.

"Whereabouts were you?" asked Castang. "Don't kick him, it's bad for his teeth."

"In the kitchen having a sandwich. Chat there with Sydney Greenstreet. When I saw this yobbo acting up I snuck out in the alley. Pushing people out of windows, hey? Kiss that pavement, boysie, you're the Pope on a visit."

"Let him up now. Where's that girl? Damn Varennes thinking of nothing but her belly."

Aurélie was gone.

Angrily, Castang put the knife between the pavement and the gutter and trod on it, breaking the blade sharp off.

"Here I am," said VV breathless with her parcel.

"Fucking late in the day," said Campbell, cross.

**15** "I don't know when the fellow fell out the window. So I can't say what I was doing then, for chrissake be reasonable."

"You're going to be reasonable," said Campbell. "You've got all night to be reasonable in. And tomorrow's Sunday. All that nice legal time before I have to turn you over to the judge. The Commissaire here will tell you whether that's exact, just in case you think me a nasty man and don't believe what I say." Castang has had occasion enough in the past to voice his dislike of police brutality. Campbell is near fifty – that's a bad age for a cop. And he's had an old-fashioned upbringing. It is true that the police are much less inclined than formerly to beat up suspects. Judges of instruction are less likely to look the other way. Doctors less ready to accept tales that the fella-slipped-against-the-table. But we mustn't be boastful.

"Put him somewhere I can't see him," said Castang. "I'm tired of looking at his stupid face. Put him in a cell. You can smack your lips and carve him at leisure. Having him around makes me feel stupid: he's infectious. Take away his fancy tie and his Gucci belt and his Dior lighter."

Mr Campbell escorted his prize into dry-dock and Castang yawned hideously. He knew that it wasn't clever to be brutal, even at the expense of this jerrybuilt stud. He has moments of backsliding and isn't proud of them. There are excuses to be made, and at least he doesn't make them.

"He knock off that waiter who was Paddy's private source?" asked VV, who was eating with her fingers.

"We can trust Paddy to find out. And if not – might be more interesting still."

"You don't think he did for Lecat?"

"I don't think anything at all, I'm too tired. I don't imagine it as likely. Might turn out handy to pretend we think so for a day, to gain a little time. We're as short of that as I am of sleep."

"I feel better now I've eaten," says VV who feels apologies are due for her stupidity.

Campbell came back and sat, putting his feet on the table. Big feet; his way of saying he intended to make sure nobody was going to slide bananaskins under them. In this position he lit a cigarette and enquired "Anything I ought to know?" of the company at large.

"I know a lot but nothing much adds up yet. And nothing much to help you with as yet. Sorry, not clear. Like one of those stupid films where everything goes on in the dark and you can't hear a word anybody says. Over-ingenious, trying too hard to be clever. I'm not clever at all; might feel a bit brighter in the morning.

"I did find out what killed Lecat; little garden hoe out of the toolshed. Whoever that might be could be smart and could be stupid: to my mind didn't care one way or the other. I shouldn't think your boyfriend there would be either smart enough or stupid enough. He could be playing crafty in order to create confusion so I'd rather leave him alone and try the girl. Probably she just went home. Frightened, and didn't want to get mixed up in further complications, sensible of her. Going home myself.

"I'll want you in the morning, Véronique. You might check up on her as you go home, it's on your way."

"We'd have heard what she knows but for that idiot's posturing. She was getting ready to spit it out."

"She'll do in the morning, and if you want a word, Paddy –"

"Equal shares," said Mr Campbell.

"Ho," said Vera. "And here is milord! And what is this house then, the night-shelter for clochards? And I'm the mattress, no doubt?" It didn't need to be made plainer. In a stinking rage. He had forgotten to ring.

"Vera, please . . . I'm sorry; I didn't think."

"You're sorry, and you didn't think. And that's the end of the matter and I can kindly keep obedient silence."

"Look, I've said I was sorry. I was preoccupied."

"Preoccupied. Busy. Too poor to buy a telephone."

"I was in the wrong. What's the point of arguing?"

"So shut up. No I won't shut up. Monsieur le Commissaire has been detecting things. Sitting in some pub." How has she guessed? "I can stay babysitting until he comes lurching in at midnight and don't strike a match anywhere near his breath."

His turn for the suspect to be interrogated.

There is really no way out of this. It is ridiculous to bang on the table and roar that nobody's going to talk to me like this in my own house. It will also increase the lady's sense of grievance, and reinforce her determination not to be intimidated.

Making explanations is as bad. That way you give her more points to score off, and more to nag about. Never explain.

The reasonable man, having admitted he was in the wrong, might reasonably remark that nagging any further will only put her in the wrong too. All one has now is two wrongs. This appears logical.

Women have no use for being logical, or reasonable. Five thousand years of that, they say, have landed us with an atomic bomb, and thanks a lot.

The only possible remaining course is to keep silent and let it blow over. Bring her flowers in the morning. It will probably start her off again but at least you're trying.

Castang thus is silent. He is taking his shoes off in a heavy atmosphere of criminal guilt when the phone rings, and for once he's grateful. Varennes, in a loud squawk.

"Not home. Hasn't been home." He tries to think, dully, gets nowhere with that.

"Come over here," he says at last. Vera, maddened, slams the door. Oh well, children will sleep through a thunderstorm. Air raid too, come to that.

Comic contrast. Vera and Véronique. Big strong girl with the gun on her hip. Big red nose and bony knees. And his beloved wife, limpyquimpy with her hair – which needs washing – in a plait. Her jeans need washing too.

VV feels herself upon quicksandy bottom. A commissaire is nothing much: you learn how to handle them. But the commissaire's Madam you better look out for. She'll have you down the shit-chute in no time flat. As the Psalmist remarks, a whore is a deep ditch. Yes, but Memsahib is a yawning pit.

"I'm awfully sorry," says VV, pacifically.

"Are you still working? What a shame!" Vera all smiles. This disregard of logic should properly have left Castang openmouthed. "Would you like some cocoa?"

174

"Ooh I'd love it," said the Empty Stomach with perfect sincerity. "I'm sorry Commissaire, I thought I'd better –"

"Shut up and sit down," says Castang who has put his shoes back on again: socks a lot more dubious than his wife's jeans. And down plumped his Big Bayerische Maid, eyes going like ball-bearings. VV True Detective. The six weeks he'd been here, nothing said about private lives.

A nice room: a nice flat! Well, on a Principal Commissaire's pay one could do it. She liked a modern flat herself. Lived all her days in these tatty old buildings you never got the dirt out of.

That eggshell lacquer's nice; the off-white good with the dark marine blue. Doesn't she make a pigsty of it though! Two small children by the look of things. Went about it late: they're neither of them that young any more. She'd look all right dressed up.

Lot of books: a nice Bang-and-Olaf. We knew he was long on the Culture stuff. In fact a hell of a lot of Art. Is he a sunday-painter on the sly? No it's her; paint on her pants. Landscapes and flowers sort-of-stiff, oilpainted. Lots of drawings, charcoal and red chalk and a jamjar full of pencils. A naked woman on a big canvas, youngish girl. Don't ask me to pose, I don't strip that well. Lots of lamps, plants, pots: junk everywhere and all over dust. Doesn't seem to worry her!

Slav. Those funny eyes, and the facial bones, and the accent's a bit weird too. Polish or Hungarian or well, I've a Flamande granny myself and that's why I've these big bones, a draught mare pulling a beer wagon but wherever else I've got it I've no hair round the fetlocks. She's nice, though.

"Schnaps in it," said Vera, crinkling, handing Castang too a mug in silence. Peace-offering: he kept quiet. The mug given VV had the Cerne Abbas Giant on it (brought home from Dorset to amuse Vera). And Varennes was plainly worried by this: Memsahib taking the piss out of her by any chance?

"I say! Introduce me properly."

"He's cut out on a chalk hill, in England."

"As long as he stays there menacing the Brits; with a dick that size I wouldn't want to meet him on the street. Only boys running the risk there." The firm and universal European conviction that the English not only have tails but are pederasts one and all. English people who talk so loudly about Frogs and Krauts would get a surprise to learn the opinion that is held of them . . .

"Ow, hot," went on VV. "I better tell you then. I phoned her, no answer. Rang her bell, likewise. Looked for her car: nowhere. Think she's done a bunk? I thought it, maybe, important enough to tell you."

"Ay Maria!" said Castang. After reflecting he reached for the phone. Mr Campbell, holding a prisoner, was obliged to pass the night in the office . . .

"Paddy, the girl has vanished. One doesn't know. It's just as likely that she put her head under the bedclothes, deciding that it's a nasty existence out there. Until I lay hands on her you treat Pretty Boy according. Her initial tale was that she thought him the dog's dinner all along. I think I like it better that they did have a brief passage which quickly went sour. Anyhow, play him by ear till we find the songbook. Ciao."

"You want to put an alarm out?" asked VV.

"No. Or anyhow not yet." His mind had slowed to a thick crawl: his words trickled out, sticky over his lip: he felt as though he were riding a bicycle under water: he tried to make sense. "She might have gone home to her parents. She might be with a girl friend. Somebody she trusts. What grounds have we? She's a reluctant witness to something or other."

"She could have killed Lecat."

"With a garden hoe she happened to find in the tool shed?"

"Funnier things have happened."

"They have indeed, right there in that house. They all know more than they let on. Nothing salient, maybe. Little bits of the jigsaw, there's nothing for it but patience. You may as well go to bed."

"Tomorrow's Sunday."

"That's right. So you're hearing the sermon now. Do not commit adultery. Don't covet your neighbour's wife. Start playing about with people's basic beliefs and you can end in front of the Assize Court. Or with your head knocked in. And all your family extremely reluctant to admit they knew anything about it."

*

Just like any other day. An alarm clock goes off. You get out of bed piece by piece, in wooden movements like a deck-chair unfolding. Not very supple yet. Set the coffee machine going; go shower; shave: lubricating movements these. Tuning the eyes and ears – and feet – up to concert pitch. Brush your teeth and empty the spit out of your trumpet.

Early church bells made their Sunday lin lan lone. A Sunday had advantages. There wouldn't be any judge of instruction, Procureur or Divisional Commissaire ringing up to nag at him.

The coffee-maker had finished slurping and piddling: its little red eye stared at him peacefully. The US Air Force, no?, had got into trouble asking for a coffee-maker with preposterous specifications: working upside-down at thirty thousand feet.

"What are you laughing at?" asked Vera behind him. But her voice was gentle.

"We're all modern now. Rockets and whatever. So why haven't I a spy satellite that would roll round the hexagon with a camera to pick up missing witnesses?"

"You are a bastardly and offensive person." She put a hand gently on his forehead. "And I like you."

"On a Sunday too? Have some coffee." They stood in sunshine on the balcony. Over the way the butcher's girl was winding up the metal shutter, her bottom waggling as she did so. Two doors down the cake shop was already displaying a windowful of luscious sticky temptation. Come to church, dear people, but don't leave your money behind.

"I love a Sunday morning in summer. I wish I could paint that. The special air."

"A pity for me to have to go out and spoil it."

"She's necessary, this girl?"

"I'm afraid so. She might be a quark or whatever makes the other particles behave oddly."

You can't see it, and you know it's there. The dust motes, the sunshine itself and the air have a different feel, a different texture – and the sound, of the bells travelling . . . you begin to understand physics, and without physics there would be no metaphysics. Something happened about fifteen hundred years before Christ. Nobody quite knows – a meteor, a comet? It changed the magnetic

177

poles, the climate; put us out of kilter, made nonsense of the Laws.

"And you just have your Big Maid."

"And my feet."

"She is a nice girl. And will it be enough?"

"It had better be," putting down his cup.

The premises of the PJ are those of any dingy office: if there are any barred windows they're at the back. It is a Sunday; no cleaning woman has come to open up and air: there is a stuffy smell, stale paper, stale tobacco and stale people. In the little back room there were quiet sounds from the old sofa kept for kipping purposes: Mr Campbell, the sleep of the just. Ranged round the typewriter were a heap of interrogation forms; 'procès-verbal'. Wooden officialese, bureaucracy's stilted phrasing, that Richard used so to complain about. But Inspector Campbell is an experienced officer, and this heavily worded mass, caked together with verbiage, may sink in the oven. But the cake when baked will be legally impeccable. Careful notes, all properly initialled and countersigned. Time and length of interrogation: detainee's rights respected: pauses for rest and food (Chinese and beer; expense note appended).

And some neat police work. The Pretty Boy (he wouldn't be quite so pretty this morning) had produced an alibi for the estimated times of the alleged window-pushing, which was going to be subjected to some minute verifications. Yes indeed, thought Castang, recalling Mr Canetti the cellarman, oldish and quiet, so harmless there in his corner – and another Corsican . . . Unpicking a faked-up alibi is tedious work, but Paddy was using it skilfully, as leverage to build an indictment for conspiracy to defraud. But of Lecat, not a word!

Mr Campbell, prudent man, had no intention of getting involved in compromising affairs. His superior's can, and let him carry it!

There was a note on his desk, in neat, unexpectedly beautiful handwriting.

'3 a.m. Concluding nothing, but prima facie indications strong towards suggestion that the lad had cut in on their racket and was proving greedy. Motivation removal of denunciation threat. No connexion connection demonstrable with current affair. Hypothesis that the lad had approached Lecat scouted as preposterous – RC.'

178

To be sure, my dear Robert, quite so.

While he was flipping through the typed pages of interrogation the tap of steps in the day-room made him look up: Inspector Varennes looked fresh and neat and like somebody who has slept well.

"Any good?" catching sight of Castang's wrinkled nose above typescript.

"Departmentally good. Ssh, the young lad is sleeping. Let's make a start: the house again first and I'll fill you in as we go."

"Lovely day for tourism," starting the motor.

". . . and it would be nice," concluded Castang, "to know a little more about this alleged time of waiting at the wrong airport. Campbell hasn't caught up with him yet. Slimy man; do him good to feel the hot breath of Nemesis on his neck."

The gates of course were shut and VV had to ring three times before an irritable Frédo appeared in pyjamas.

"What d'you want to go pestering people for on a Sunday morning?"

"We see no need," said Miss Varennes carnivorously, "to be the only people pestered. Let's make as much misery for everyone as we can. We only exist to persecute the innocent. We get all our pleasures from that."

"If you can't take a joke," recoiling from the big girl's ominous advance.

"Have you had breakfast?" she enquired kindly.

"You got me out of bed," the grievance reviving.

"Good: one should always have surgery on an empty stomach." Castang moved on before the nice nurse began asking about bowels. He was leaving Frédo in safe hands.

He stopped at the lodge. Spotless as always. He knocked, heard a grunt, went in. Old Georges, in his Sunday suit, sat at the kitchen table. A tin in front of him, a packet of Dutch shag. Smuggled no doubt. He'd been rolling his day's ration. He looked up at Castang speechless; an expression of sullen obstinacy, of 'Don't think I'm going to say a word'; and resignation too. No good mornings, this bright sunny day.

"I want your wife," said Castang. There was a pleasant smell of the Sunday cooking, already in the oven; one of the oldfashioned country dishes, carefully assembled and put to cook slowly on a low fire. Tja, police work is much the same: there are things you can't hurry. There are ghosts of smells of floor-wax and stove-polish, of old selfrespecting people. And an unmistakable smell of calamity. It is, if you like, metaphysical. Oh, it can be physical enough, hanging about perceptible in any police station; a smell of fear and sweat and stale underclothes.

Violette was in her 'loge', dusting television screens which stared at him there in a shiny row. We see everything, they said. And we'll see nothing, when we don't want to. The old woman too was in her Sunday dress, with her Sunday apron atop, and the same expression when she turned; of having expected him for some time: unsurprised, knowing it had to be gone through.

"Good morning. And where's Caroline? I'd like a word. We got interrupted yesterday." She didn't speak but the face changed. It held an appeal, now. Don't torment me, it said.

"And Jean-Baptiste? Not out hoeing the weeds, on a Sunday."

A long silence, while Castang felt sorry for her, but the pleasure too of finding at last the right log, that when shifted will make the entire jam shake, and slip.

"You'd like coffee," she said politely.

Castang sat at the kitchen table, recognising the need for ritual. Of making as it were common cause against catastrophe. A wrist as controlled as the rest of her measured the coffee into the filter paper, swung the boiling kettle over, tilted the exact dose, just to moisten.

"Caroline's up at the house. These gentlemen," without enmity or even resentment, "they expect their comforts and their service whatever happens." She poured the water with care. "A heartbreak for her. My daughter. A good, quiet girl. And now . . . I see that you know already." He didn't, but he was making rapid guesses.

"I didn't know. But a word she said yesterday . . ." There is no point in saying anything.

Old Georges came in carrying the little tray with the goldbanded decanter, the 'carafon' of ritual occasions. He walked in a flat-footed shuffle, big shoulders slumped as though it were a great weight. His accustomed allies, God, his gun, the General, availed nothing. Big scarred hands concentrated upon filling the tiny glasses to the exact brim with the clear white spirit. Castang did not in the least want the little-glass of peasant hospitality but said nothing.

"Jean-Baptiste – he was like a son to us." The sharp delicate scent of distilled damsons floated on the air. The two men looked each other in the eye, nodded, drank the single shot off. The old man breathed heavily. Violette put a cup of coffee in front of each.

"Caroline," said Georges, as though the alcohol had undone a knot in the tongue, "is no great looker. She'd make any man a good wife. And he has to fall for looks." He seemed to be wondering what it would be like to be young and fall for a girl with looks. Violette, thought Castang, had been a fine-looking girl. The old man grasped the decanter and Castang shook his head.

"She came up here last night?"

"Thought nothing of it," said Violette. "She's often here on errands. That Roland was always after her." And Lecat, thought Castang, seeing more logs slide, freeing the flow of turbulent water. "And Jean-Baptiste never said a word. How was one to guess? She just came like, and the two looked at each other. Not a word said."

"And they're gone together. And where? But that you wouldn't know."

"No!" said the old man violently, pouring himself another glass of the damson schnaps and tossing it straight back. Just as well It's the truth, thought Castang: you'd be packing your gun.

"I want," he said, "to avoid any more calamities."

The old lady made up her mind, holding the porcelain 'sunday' cup in both hands and staring past the rim at a far past.

"Rémy Mathieu, he might know." Castang nodded.

"Take anything with him? Mind if I look at his room?"

Everything there was as orderly as his tools. Shoes stood polished with trees in them. The gardener might just have stepped out for a Sunday paper, for the football results. Castang went on up to the house.

At either end of the long kitchen table work was going on in silence. Mathieu was skinning soles – so simple when a professional does it. Castang admired the technique. The knife clipped the tail square and scraped back enough for fingers to take hold and whisk the tough black skin straight off; a rough tearing noise. The knife nicked each backbone through just enough for the head to come off when cooked, trimmed off the little side fins in two exact arcs.

Caroline sat with bunches of spring vegetables before her and a basin of water: between thumb and finger a little knife 'turning' the carrots and turnips. Exactly like knitting: snick snick snick, and plop, in a rhythm as regular as rain from a leak in the gutter. Her face was expressionless and she did not look up. Two professionals.

His cooking too had to be done gently. In however much of a hurry he must appear unhurried. VV could wait. Which would be nice for Frédo. Mr Campbell might well find juice in that; it would do him good too. Castang took a chair and straddled it. In the centre of the table sat a whole loin of veal, boned and the bone replaced, the loin rolled with its kidney and the surrounding suet beneath, tied with mathematically even turns of string.

"A beautiful job," he said appreciatively.

Rémy dumped the skins in the bin and threw the soles in the sink.

"You come rolling on back, don't you mate? Taking cookery lessons?"

"Beats me how they eat that much, taking no exercise."

"You take up finance for a living, and you'll see. Come to the point." Very well. He would behave as though the girl was not there.

"Aurélie. And Jean-Baptiste."

"Ah." Plop, plop, plop, steady and unaltered.

"Ah," said Rémy. A quick flickering look. Surprise, respect, fear? – no, just a quick look. Reading meanings into people's complicated emotions is foolish.

"You knew. Guessed, at least. I like a man who shows loyalty to his friends. I could peg you, for withholding information. Charge of obstructing justice."

"Yes." Hot and cold tap, to get the fish smell off. Drying his hands with care, lengthily. "Jean-Baptiste was by way of being a friend of mine. How d'you come to add it up?"

182

"We have the Pretty-face in the cooler," with deliberation, "on another charge. He made a fuss. Aurélie was there and took fright. That was last night. This morning, I talked to Violette."

Rémy opened the small fridge and took out a bottle of white wine.

"Bit of juice for the motor," filling a mustard glass. "Like one?"

"No thanks. I ought to say I don't want to start a big scene. Mobile brigade, riot guns and tear gas. Unless I have to."

Work went on. Caroline was doing beans now. Snap, snap. Mathieu assembled things: peppercorns, and white-wine vinegar; a packet of butter; eggs. "That for a hollandaise?" asked Castang, curious. Mathieu nodded, silent.

"A cook – or a cop – we both have to work on a Sunday. No choice about that, it has to come up on the table. I'd like to leave it till tomorrow. Let them anyway have the day and night in peace. But I can't. And I don't want the press. Or turning out the gendarmerie. If you know where they are, tell me. Easier on them."

"And if I don't know, you peg me for obstruction, that it?"

"People don't trust us and I can't blame them. No, I won't peg you and I won't peg the girl. You've only my word. Honour, like the general says."

The butter went on the piano of the stove to clarify. Supple wrist movements separated the yolks from the egg whites. The crushed pepper in the vinegar had gone on the fire to reduce.

"She used to come into the kitchen to watch. Rather like you. I got to know her a little. She's a straight girl. And not horizontal." It hurt having Caroline there. Not that one would notice her.

"Pretty Roland tried to make her."

"That's right. And while on the subject," said Rémy, "so did the boss. Pretty funny character that. In streaks, like bacon."

Castang nodded.

"Too bright and too smart, and found it too easy to cook people."

Rémy glanced at the clock, picked up the roast and put it in the oven, checked the thermostat and said, "You said it."

"Where would they go?"

A big diamond-shaped pot came out. A turbot poacher, with a perforated tray inside, to lift out the fish unbroken. One can do twelve soles in it, in a mixture of fish-bone stock and white wine.

Fifty different kinds of 'sole normande' but they all start the same way: slow. Caroline had put butter and sugar into the mixer at slow speed, to cream it.

"You know the Somme estuary?"

"No."

"Your big girl might. Sand dunes. Bird sanctuary. North side of the delta. Marquenterre, it's called. Never been there myself; deserted sort of place. She told me once she'd a shack out that way which her father had, weekends. Don't know where. I better ask you to leave now because I'm going to be busy. Maybe it's an obstruction. You can please yourself about that." Castang left; Caroline concentrating upon her cake, Rémy whisking the eggs in the reduced vinegar. Delicate business over a low fire, till they double in volume. Clickety-click, went the whisk in the copper pot, like a train running over points, clickety click. Let – us – honour – if – we – can, The – ver-ti-cal – Man. One of Vera's English poets. Good appetite, friends.

> Though we only value
> The horizontal one.

Véronique was sitting in the driver's seat of the car, having a smoke. She threw the butt out of the window.

"Dirty girl," said Castang.

"You took a hell of a time."

"And you?"

"Yes, by the time Paddy comes to pick him up he'll be jelly."

"Cooking takes a long time."

"Where do we go now?"

"Abbeville on the main road. And from there on we don't know but we're going to find out."

"Abbeville on a Sunday morning!"

"I might buy you lunch. A sole maybe. In a normande sauce, with shrimps and things. You'd like that?"

"It's an added inducement," accelerating.

Abbeville is on the Picard coast. A hundred kilometres from the industrial north. So that Castang has time to think. But he doesn't think, he refuses to: now that he has something to do thinking would only lead him astray. Disjointed interior monologues you can't call thought.

184

He had never lived near the sea. It was not part of his being. He took an unromantic view: a dangerous place, which might drown you. Uncomfortable as well; hell of a lot of wind. Furthermore expensive; too many tourists in summer and not enough in winter and both ways the prices go up. Melancholy too: the sea is depressing.

The publicity people invented fancy names for it. The Azure Coast, appalling place to which rushed enormous crowds of people like lemmings, suicidally. This was thought a great commercial success so that more names were invented. The Roussillon was red so they called that Vermillion. Sea around the Breton peninsula is bright green, or was before oil spills: this was called Emerald, by people who'd never seen an emerald. Well, you could hardly call it the Deepfreeze-Peas Coast. And the Channel is called Pearl or Opal, he couldn't remember which, since there's fog all the bloody time.

He hadn't often been to sea; mostly been sick when he had. Small boats moved about so, in several directions, all nasty.

Now he'd remembered another rhyme, taught him by a nice English woman named Emma, wife of a nice man called Geoffrey. Owl . . . owl. And the pussycat went to sea, in a beautiful pea-green boat. Shrieks of laughter because it had been a Royal Navy fishery-patrol thing, very English all round.

Vera, who being Slav had never seen even the Euxine before coming to France, had started a painter's love affair, conducted under difficulties.

"One wants transparent, quicksilver, liquid: one has these horrible muddy chemicals, good for pea soup and darkblue mud. Mm, Joyce says it's snot-colour, I do so see, but what I want is the real, the literal meaning of the word ultramarine they print so nonchalantly on the label." She had been working hard on the technical problems. Valenciennes is the town of Watteau but she wanted the car for days in Holland, and the Family van der Velde.

Vera, delighted as she was with this beautiful and baroque North, had seen nothing yet of its coastline: no more had he. Castang improves himself along the road with the information Miss Varennes can give him.

The Somme coast is low and sandy. Such harbours as there are remain small. So hurray, it is largely unpolluted and has scarcely any population. Inland lies a placid, mercifully dull farming country. From Boulogne to Dieppe there is a blessed absence of commerce and industry. The government of the Republic would simply love a big factory here for nuclear waste, so cross your fingers.

In summer, naturally, hordes of tourists from the Far North come stampeding down the main road. There is nothing to look at but television so that they hurtle on south and west. God be thanked. Even Le Touquet is only insufferable for a few days in the year: 'Paris-Plage' was only invented because the railway-line runs close by. The regional authority in Amiens sits in interminable discussion of how to make money (should have gone running to Félix Lecat), dreams of Disneylands. Doubtless the last piece of European coast still left unravaged will not survive much longer.

Abbeville, at the head of the estuary, is a nice small town and Castang should have been glad of it. But getting any information from bureaucracies is apt to take three days at the best of times, and on a Sunday . . . Still, they did get something to eat.

The Police Judiciaire is a bit over the edge, here . . . Authority for the Pas de Calais region ends in Berck, a few kilometres north. Strictly speaking, Castang should be consulting his dear colleagues of the Picardie region: PJ Amiens . . . He hasn't done so because he wants to keep his business private. He is not much worried. It is a bit of a handicap not to consult the local gendarmerie, which knows the topography. In Abbeville he learns that the object of his interest is a small piece of land, bounded by the coast, between the Somme and Authie estuaries; amounting to twelve kilometres by five. Very small indeed, until you start looking for two people who may or may not be inside.

An inland road, narrow but navigable, leads to the sprawling village of Rue, a scatter of bricky cottages. In the fields here and there is a massive farmhouse in a Norman kind of architecture with external timbering and a high slate roof, sheltered by trees. The fields are carefully drained by ditches and a winding little stream named the Maye, whose estuary forms the bird sanctuary. Between here and the coast lies the Marquenterre. There are two roads coastwards from Rue.

186

Castang fumes at not having a proper map. Open are tobacco shops of the sort that sell newspapers and Agatha Christie paperbacks – and maps: as always the map wanted is the one nobody has in stock. And even the most rustic of constabulary will be curious, and eager to feed official interest with paperwork. *What* – exactly – were you up to there? will enquire (some three months later) the Préfecture of Amiens. And *Why* has official notification not been made through the proper channels, may we *Ask?* Perish the thought.

"Quend," said Véronique, getting back into the wagon. A tiny hamlet, minuscule seaside resort.

And here – suddenly – they were in the dunes. Instead of ploughland and poplar and the ubiquitous pollarded willows there were little hills of sand and the characteristic maritime growth of scrubby pines. Along the road appear caravans and camping sites and wayside hutments selling icecream or pommes frites. The road ends in a street of little houses crouching low, plastered white against the sea and the salt wind. Blue shutters closed . . . a paved carpark facing a tiny beach. There's nowhere else to go. A kilometre north is another hamlet just the same; Fort Mahon. To reach that you need to turn back to the crossroad in Rue . . . But in Quend there is a map. South of here – so the map says – there's nothing. No roads. Dubious paths, among dunes with folklore names like the Flea, or the Wine Hole.

More than forty years ago the German Army sat here, defending their Atlantic Wall. Quite a lot of German Army, with many hidden gun emplacements and great rolls of barbed wire, and behind that strong groups of tanks and artillery. It had been deluded into belief that Allied landings were due here in the Somme area. History tells us that this delusion was of material help in forcing the Normandy landings, which were more lightly defended.

One wouldn't much have envied troops trying to force a landing here. The German Army knew its business. Many a spiky trap lay hidden below the tidemark; and many another above. In the dunes to this day are powerful works of massive concrete buried to their firing-slits in the treacherous sand. Most are now invisible, drowned under the shifty, tricky dunedrift that would have drunk the blood of the invaders.

Into a road or two you can get a car – for a little distance: it is marked Private, and Sans Issue: blind path. For there are houses here, ferociously private, and short of getting up close one would scarcely guess their presence. Your average dune, a rounded ridge of three or four metres height, is an effective barrier against seeing over the other side; and nine out of ten it's just another dune.

Even in the month of August, and this was only June, tourists would not trust their duck legs in here. Anything more than fifty metres from the security of the automobile, the mussel-shell with its reassuring radio and picnic equipment, its delicious stuffy homey smell, they lose faith. The moment the auto is no longer mobile neither are they. What! Go floundering through this infernal sand, encumbered with parasols and folding chairs, enchained by whining brats and nagging mum? Not as much as a Coca-Cola or a portable barbecue in sight? Not on your Nelly!

The privacy of the inhabitants, a troglodyte lot, is thereby assured. Of course the English will poke their noses in anywhere with their rucksacks and flappy macs and huge hairy legs but they are intimidated. Right of Way? Coast Footpath? Those reassuring Brit notices chanting of Afternoon Teas and Public Convenience? Nix! You're in France. Navajo Reserve. The natives are hostile; will sell you pots for exorbitant sums but don't go looking for Toilets.

Thus it has to be said that Mr Castang, Commissaire Principal, Police Judiciaire, got as buggered as the Brits. Even with his pocket compass, his Véronique (full of complaints, so that he had a strong inclination to fling her down upon the sand and jump on top and fuck her). Even with a tough constitution, sensible shoes, some experience of terrain off a macadamed road, and native tenacity, he gets good-and-bogged. All the merciless afternoon they poked and pried; floundered. Sweated, cursed, and slapped at midges. The only clue they had was the make and number (professionally noted by Inspector Varennes) of Aurélie-Marie's car. They lost their own car twice. The domain-demesne of the Marquenterre has adequate natural defences, as well as any made by man, during or since the little upheavals caused by world wars.

"You don't have to dig a grave," said VV. "Just launch me, and the tide'll do the rest."

Castang felt the same. Being told to look for needles in a haystack is a commonplace. Where it gets hard is looking for a piece of left-handed hay.

**16** A hut among sand dunes. It is not far from the bird sanctuary, and towards evening you hear the crying of birds. Castang – who is not far away – supposes they might be curlews. He knows nothing about it. Pressed, he might suggest sandpipers. Oyster-catchers? They're all seagulls to me, said VV. Nice birds, he said, getting like Gollum again.

The sun was well over to the west. It was unsurprising that it had taken them so long. Bureaucracy had missed this hut. It had no postal address. Electricité de France had never been near it. There was water there, and nothing else.

If it hadn't been a Sunday they'd have found it in the Land Registry for her grandfather had bought the piece of ground around nineteen-twenty. For twopence-halfpenny because who wanted it? Sand if fertilised with seaweed and chickenshit will grow good potatoes, but who's going to bother? He had built the first hut: he was a hunter, and came here in winter for the wild duck, and the geese.

An exciting business, thrilling as a tiger-shoot but a lot colder. You have to get up before dawn, with a lot of sweaters under your oilskin, and in waders your feet freeze off. You dig a hole in the sand and hide in it: the birds are sensitive and suspicious. They come from the north, migrating. They are a difficult shot. They come fast, and the dawn light is tricky, and probably you are too cold and stiff by then to shoot well. Just as well for them, or there wouldn't be one left. They are too thin and tough – and fishy – for eating so why shoot them? Well, you don't eat tigers either.

The quantities of duckshot buried in the sea and sand must be enough to poison any small forms of life, scratching a humble living.

Aurélie's father had forgotten all about it. The Germans forbade access to the coast. But approaching middle age, pottering at weekends, he found he had the title to this piece of land. The Germans had knocked the hut down for firewood. He had no interest in ducks but it became his 'place': a weekend cabana. His wife had not appreciated (the men like playing Crusoe but it's the

190

wife who does the work) so that he used to go by himself. *Bricolage*, a French word for a very French occupation; building something hideous, illegally: the hell with the Authorities. He worked for one of them, which helps account for it.

He'd built the shack afresh, using anything he found cheap: wood, brick, breezeblock. Builders' scrap had provided a door, windows, a stove; in the long run anything you wanted. It had become quite elaborate. And quite often he had brought his small daughter. She was no trouble: she played about, while he was working.

'Aurélie' turned back into Marie here. She had left it very much as she found it again, in adult life (after quite a happy and fairly ineffectual life her father had an easy, sudden death, never knowing what hit him). Going out there, she found it in perfect order, Frenchly fenced, barricaded, padlocked. Her mother had never set foot there, did not even know where it was . . . She made it a little tidier, a little cleaner. Filial piety? She wouldn't have known: it never occurred to her to ask that sort of question.

Ever since, she had come here five, six times a year; for no particular reason but that she likes it: she leaves here refreshed.

Always she had come alone. There wasn't any 'psychology' about this. It was instinctive. She feels herself a normal and balanced young woman, which she is. She has learned to be wary, and in general to distrust people. The shack; the sea, the sand, the wind – there was never distrust here. She has nothing but happy memories. A dune shelters the hut from storm, and acts on warm days as sun-trap.

And now – extraordinary and violent sensations beset her. So many, so hurried: she has had no time to think. She does not want to think. She knows that tomorrow she must, but this is not just a Sunday, this is a dream. She knows this – as one does – but she is going to stay in it for this day, this night.

She had brought a man here. She had slept with him. That fact, alone . . . A man she was frightened of, knowing the thing he had done. She felt fear. But not distrust. How extraordinary, and how laughable, to see him here, himself laughing at her female ways of fixing things that needed repair, to hear a confident voice say 'I'll see to that for you' . . .

191

It was madness. She suddenly lost all power to reason: she only knew she could not endure this another instant. Without thinking about it she went to him and said 'Take me away from here.' Was it shock? She was supposed to be – she is – an experienced, even sophisticated young woman. She has never thought much about 'emotions'.

She had slept with him. This she had not done before. It was not painful, humiliating. The excitement was momentary and rather artificial. Well, she isn't used to it yet. A man had killed for her. This man. And that has not shocked or frightened her as much as it should – perhaps that is the effect of shock, that she doesn't care, that she feels numbed. It all has to sort itself out and that is why she came here. They had nowhere else to go so that was . . . Anyhow it is a dream.

The proof is that this is a day such as one rarely sees on the north coast: windless, perfect, the sun golden, now westering going a deeper, gentler gold. She is here on her own terrace and she hasn't a stitch on – another proof. She has never done that before.

True, it is safe here. Nobody comes. Once or twice she has seen people who had rambled in by accident along the old and now barely distinguishable track her father made ferrying stuff in. Once she saw a gendarme, a quiet elderly man who gave her a half grin, half salute. She is not frightened of them . . . It is in a way disconcerting to have no clothes on. He has nothing on either. He had asked her to take all her clothes off so that he could look at her. Why not? With her he is not violent: he shows her only gentleness. And it is hot. She has a straw hat.

Is it part of the dream or can it be real? – that contrary to everybody's suppositions she has never before trusted herself to a man. But now . . . who is this man? Is he 'hers'? She is terrified of waking up, of coming back to a world she knows to be as cruel as it is crooked, and filled now with fearful consequences. How is it possible that she is not as terrified as she should be? That she feels a strange confidence?

The sun on the creosoted planks of the 'terrace' is no longer so hot. The smell is wonderful.

Castang reaching the top of the dune ducked, and let himself drop, sliding back until the sand makes a hammock for a weary body. He is more relieved than he can show. A PJ Commissaire, upon learning the identity of a killer, has failed – we are waiting for your explanations, Monsieur Castang – in the most elementary of his duties; that of ensuring the immediate apprehension . . . a rivulet of sweat went clear down his spine. He'd be feeling a lot stickier than he does right now. Am I hearing you aright and you didn't even notify Lille?

They've made it! Thanks to the month of June sunset is still some way off. Castang contemplated Véronique, who was a little behind. She sat up. Cross mumbling gave way to a satisfied puffing sound. She looked to see whether sand had got into her pistol.

It is like the wolf legend. Wolves do not attack humans: Red Riding Hood has much to answer for. So ingrained is the terror that grabbing for the gun has become second nature.

"Let's have no fucking bang-bang," said Castang tartly.

"I could do with something long and misty and lots of ice. Any chance of the apéritif on the terrace?" It occurs to Castang, who has forgotten all fatigue, that the word is comic. *Aperio*, Latin for open. He remembered Geoffrey Dawson drinking beer on a hot day in Munich, lazily remarking that in Europe it opened your appetite whereas in England you got given an aperient to open your bowels.

"We'll ask for an invitation." On the little rectangle of planking laid across old railway sleepers Marie is sitting in a faded canvas deckchair. She is naked: it is a pretty sight. And where is the man? He is there – his trousers hanging on the window sill.

One is not going to shout 'Cha-a-arge!' over a twenty-metre stretch of soft deep sand. One is going to walk down politely.

Marie let out a short harsh shriek. The reaction was not slow. Took four, five seconds – as many steps in the sand. The man in the doorway was carrying – pointing – a weird, oldfashioned shotgun. VV's big pistol jumped like a grasshopper.

"No!" said Castang, his fingers weighing on her wrist. She stopped dead, outraged. Silly situation.

An old duck gun. Long single barrel. Ornate lock with a hammer. Hammer back. Damn cowboy. VV would have blown you in half. It might have gone off, at that. Blown us in half. Charge of duck shot, at ten metres . . .

Hell, this isn't any garden of Eden. Though I'm sure as hell the serpent. I'm not going to bite. Just tempt.

"Drop it," said the man. Jean-Baptiste had been a soldier and knew how to hold it. People who have killed are apt to feel they've nothing to lose. It was a nasty moment.

"Give it me," said Castang softly. He took it gently by the barrel, looking at her, his mouth going 'Douce – douce' . . . He held it reversed, butt foremost, and said conversationally, "Where d'you find that extraordinary thing?" Marie was looking wildly for her clothes. Jean-Baptiste kept the big gun steady. "I don't have one, myself. And there are no more of us." Twenty years Castang has been a cop. Twenty times give-or-take he has had guns pointed at him. One has to learn not to look frightened because fright is contagious. Frighten the wolf and it cannot stop itself snapping.

"Even if there are," said Jean-Baptiste slowly, unemotionally, "we can do a bit better. Equality, like. You take your clothes off. You too," jiggling the barrel at VV.

Not in the script! Castang has a vision of Geoffrey Dawson dissolving in the giggles? From somewhere, presumably late-night television, he had thought of Edward G. Robinson creeping out unaware that Bogart is watching from the cabin roof. With that matchless cringing whine. 'I'm coming out now soldier. I ain't got no gun.' Now you don't tell Edward G. Robinson to take his clothes off.

Inspector Varennes is boiling! That's what comes of these loony pacifist gestures! This clown thinks himself funny! Tying us up or something tricky out of some fuckass movie even if he doesn't think it funnier still to blow our heads off and bury us in the sand, nobody knows we're here, but nobody . . . And that fart Castang doesn't look like Bogart with or without clothes. If I can get a bit closer . . .

"Darling," said Castang, "I'd no idea you looked so like John Wayne."

Marie, self-conscious, had bolted into the hut. Jean-Baptiste couldn't care less about having nothing on. He grounded the shotgun only after recovering the pistol and making sure there was no sand in the action.

"Less bad. Equal terms like."

"Afraid not," said Castang. "I haven't killed anyone in months –

194

have to look in my diary." He got a long cool look, but no further reaction. "I'm really thirsty as hell, might I ask for a drink of water?"

Marie came back wearing a shirt and shorts. He still had VV's bare ass to look at but it wasn't the consolation it should have been.

"I'll sit down if you don't mind. Something I'd like you to think about. You're in some trouble, all right. At present I could still say it's relatively slight. It could get much worse. I'd like to see it cleared up while it still is slight. Is the glass of water too much to ask?" plaintive.

"Sorry," said Marie. "I'll get some."

"Were you hoping to go free?" he asked conversationally of Jean-Baptiste who was playing idly with VV's pistol, not pointing it at anybody but to show he was in command.

"We've a fair chance," said Marie with defiance and handing him the water. She didn't throw it over him. She'd brought a glass for VV too.

"What's wrong with your arm?" asked Jean-Baptiste.

"It's patched up. Not really good for much. Fellow shot it. You see why I have good reasons for disliking guns."

"Who shot you?"

"A crooked cop."

"You mean you aren't?" cuttingly. So take your time, answering.

"You know why the blacks call us bananas?" in a drawl. "Because we yellow, we bent, and we come in bunches." It is an old joke by now. Well: we have only a couple of jokes but at least they're good ones. It served. He isn't disarmed but let's hope he's defused. "It's too often true. You can feel easier – only the two of us, and with no trousers. Good moment to start? Look at it quietly. I said there, you were in some small trouble. One mustn't exaggerate this. See it this way; you killed Lecat. Millionaire, lots of press with cameras and microphones. But it isn't the first time someone got killed. Nor will it be the last. And probably he was a shit and you lost your head."

"He was trying to make Marie –"

"I don't want to know. Save that for the judge; she'll listen. What I'm trying to get at, let the temperature fall. I have to arrest you, with pants on or without, I've no choice. Let a week pass and papers forget, people forget. Way of the world, today's big drama wraps tomorrow's leeks."

"What's all this bullshit – cops saying now let's kiss and make friends?"

"Oh crap, you get a good lawyer. It's all the same to me. Can't you see? I walked in quietly, didn't bring a squad of riot police, I didn't want the riot. I'm glad you've had a good day. But while I sit here talking . . ." He looked at his watch. "Come eight o'clock and it's near sunset now, if I don't phone in we'll find every crossroad full of cops and machineguns. I don't want that any more than you do."

"If I just knock you on the head," said Jean-Baptiste reasonably, "we can be out of here in ten minutes. Nobody the wiser. If you had a squad they'd be here by now. We can be in Boulogne in an hour. Ferry, main road, anything we like. Long gone before they find you. Nobody comes here."

"Oh dear jesus," exasperated, "you don't believe that comicstrip stuff. That's for children, the stowing away. Lookit, you're on every telex from Iceland to Istanbul. You go for fake papers, the fellow who sells them to you sells you to the cops in the same breath. Easier for him and double the profit. Don't think of yourself, think of Marie."

One doesn't ever know if it's going to be a chink. Criminals when they rob the till, and shooting a few onlookers makes no difference, are behaving selfishly. They have no interest whatever in their wives, their children, their girlfriends or their dear old mum. It's me, me, me, every step of the way.

Castang has been banking all along on it's being different here. A gamble, yes.

What to do with Marie?

But this chink is the only one.

Véronique has had the sense to keep still and stay mum. She was taken aback to hear him talk about a homicide charge as a small affair. He would have admitted later to a slight exaggeration. Not a lot. He can think of a great many crimes worse than homicide. A bit of professional deformation, he'd call that. He doesn't even think of it right now. He's thinking of the job, and to his credit he is thinking too of Marie. She hasn't killed anybody.

196

So is that sentimentalism?

"You better get your knickers back on, girl, you look nice like that but it won't do for business." While Jean-Baptiste is busy thinking . . . getting back into his own. It wasn't disagreeable but the sun is going down.

"Why should I worry Marie? I've no charge against her. I don't even need anything from you but the formal bit of paper, that you bashed Lecat because it seemed a good idea at the time and you prefer to say nothing more about it right now; didn't have anything to do with his wife, did you?" You only had to look to know that he had no interest in Lecat's wife, and never had.

Marie was staring at him with wide stunned eyes but intelligence was coming back to them.

"What you have to do is as hard as it will be for him. You have to go back to being Aurélie. For as long as it takes him. You do it well, and you earn good money, and he'll need that." He reached out for his shirt: there must be some cigarettes in the pocket. But Jean-Baptiste was still holding the gun.

"Where he goes, I go," she said with decision. He pretended to take this literally, pretending to think about it.

"Who's got a light? All right, I agree. My responsibility only goes as far as tomorrow morning. I can give you the night together." It was VV's turn to look at him with wide eyes and he didn't look. That is to say that he stared her down while addressing the man.

"I have to put you in a cell, I'm bound to that. Lot of regulations. Like I should take away your belt and your tie; they're frightened you might commit suicide. You won't because you've everything to live for, meaning her. A Sunday night, nobody's to know, I'll put her in with you. But get dressed now because we want to stop for something to eat. I'm beginning to starve."

Jean-Baptiste looked at VV. He held her gun in both hands. Then he joined his middle fingers together inside the trigger guard and spun the gun round and round. He laughed then.

"Nice pair of tits," he said politely, and gave her her gun back.

"They're her own too," said Castang looking at Marie.

"Will you please do that?" she asked.

"Without strain," he said with matching politeness. Monsieur

Sabatier had better not hear about it, but he thought he knew how to keep Paddy Campbell's mouth shut.

"A detail here and there," said Castang. VV was driving the car and they were sitting in the back. Aurélie was in her own car behind them, alone. It was understood that she didn't feel much like talking. The Sunday evening road was full of people coming back from the seaside.

"Why'd the Pretty Face heave that waiter out the window?"

"He did?" Jean-Baptiste sounded surprised.

"Him or his pals."

"They had a lot of crooked deals going for them," uninterested.

"We had a theory for a while that Lecat found that out."

"He'd have them chopped up raw if he had."

"You get to hear from Marie?"

"I don't suppose she knew anything about it. No – Rémy Mathieu got a wink from Canetti one day down at the Fox, said he didn't want to know." Ten kilometres passed in silence.

"Georges and Violette – they didn't give you away, you know."

"I didn't think they had."

"Even if it was a bit rough on Caroline."

"I never promised her anything. Old Georges knows that. I've never put a finger on her. He knows that too."

"He'd have busted you if you had."

"Too right he would." And another ten slipped past.

"A thing we'll have to watch is the Press."

"Tell them the truth," said Jean-Baptiste without inflection. "That I bashed Lecat because he was trying to make a whore of Marie."

"They won't print that. Lot of crap about jealousy."

"Let them print what they like." The eyes that met Castang's were calm. "He offered her the job he thought she couldn't refuse. In Amsterdam and a flat to go with it. An exclusivity. His!"

"The judge of instruction," said Castang, colourless, "is a woman. Tell it her how it happened, hold nothing back; she hates that. She gives me a rogation warrant, for the Dutch police. We'll confirm it that way."

"What'll I get? No bullshit."

"You got any previous? In the Army? As a juvenile?"

"No. The General will speak out for me. He's like that: you can rely on him."

"With that – act of passion. Sudden, no premeditation, heavy provocation. They won't like you taking the hoe. But if we show Lecat up, and we've a girl he put in a flat here. You've pretty good witnesses. Call it at best two, at worst five. Count on three, you won't be far out."

There was nobody in the office. Mr Campbell had taken his prize off to Lille. Castang sat VV down behind the typewriter: 'make it as short as you can.' On his table was a summary from Campbell: his rabbit had cooked till the meat came off the bone . . .

A longish stew there, but a juicy one. A judge of instruction in Lille and another in Belgium. A couple of Common Market bureaucrats would be losing their pension rights, too. Passive corruption, falsifying of official papers, conspiracy to defraud. Oh yes, a five-to-seven there in the offing. And fair enough. Some nice newspaper pieces too. Do Mr Campbell's affairs no end of good. Not exactly subtracting from Divisional Commissaire Sabatier's comforts, either.

On the subject of comforts they had stopped at a roadhouse because Castang was complaining that he was too hungry to think straight. The two of course had no thought of food: the idea made them sick. He'd answered with the classic quotation: 'if you can't eat you can always drink!' He and VV had had andouillette, which he loved. They tried to serve frites with them. An argument followed because there was no mashed potato. There wasn't any watercress either. What can you expect of a roadside pub? They all drank a good deal, so that it was to be hoped that no zealous Sunday-evening gendarmerie would smell VV's breath on the way home.

And Castang had thought of telephoning home. He wouldn't just be late: he wouldn't get home at all. He couldn't leave a prisoner in the office overnight (there would be no mention made of the second).

"Good, that'll do nicely. You sign, I countersign. Véronique, you get home, and think of getting Aurélie out of here in the morning before that nosy old Madame Metz gets here. And she has to go to

199

work. As though nothing whatever had happened. You understand? You won't see him for a few days, girl, but the judge will give you a visitor's pass for the parlour."

He got the duty-room sofa to sleep on. He did not sleep well. Apart from the creature comforts.

Madame Marguerite was as much an enigma as ever. Not even the most rabid prosecutor was likely to imagine that Jean-Baptiste was in line for that one!

There will be a considerable temptation once the dust has settled to classify it. On the shelf: we haven't found out and nobody ever will. It is a comforting if unworthy statistic in the entire world's police forces. Between forty and fifty per cent of criminal affairs remain unsolved.

The alternative (improving the statistics) is to say Lecat did it. And maybe he had. It would be nice and neat. The accused, being previously deceased, cannot be brought to justice. Trial cannot take place. QED. Everybody will be pleased . . .

He isn't there to contradict.

It will employ a lot of lawyers in highly lucrative fashion.

It's what the family, led by Cécile, wants to believe.

Not to speak of the Chancellery of the Legion of Honour.

It would save us all a great deal of trouble.

Lecat, who was a schweinhund anyhow, has a broad enough back to carry it.

He could see Mr Campbell nodding appreciatively, saying 'Now you're talking sense.' Commissaire Sabatier, delighted. Even Mademoiselle Jimenez, to whom justice is a bed of thorns, can probably be talked into it, once the Proc has done a bit of thinking.

And as for himself . . .

Is it exactly because Lecat was a schweinhund that you can't do this? Bit of a parallel here with Mr Klaus Barbie. You have gone to great trouble to get him extradited. You must bring him to trial and make sure he has the best damn defence there is. You can't put ground glass in his pudding just because you're scared of what he might say. Cops have too often shot people before they were tried. Jacques Mesrine, machinegunned at the wheel of his car, haunts the Criminal Brigade. The phrase 'getting mesrinised' has entered the vocabulary. It is too easy to say 'he did it' when he's no longer there to speak for himself.

Hideously early on Monday morning. Castang is swallowing ratshit coffee and aspirin. His eyes, says VV, are like pissholes in the snow. So, says he, are yours. Marie has gone back to being Aurélie, and Jean-Baptiste has been given breakfast. VV's next job is to get him a razor and a toothbrush and a change of clothes from his home and to tell the two old people that least said soonest mended: neither Caroline nor Rémy Mathieu were likely to prove talkative.

The phone rang. Madame le Juge. In no friendly frame of mind.

"My patience, Commissaire, frays to breaking-point."

"I was just about to –"

"Is in fact ex*haus*ted." With a stab like a knife on the second syllable.

"I was just having breakfast!"

"Reporters are ringing me up, needling me. You made an arrest on Saturday night and I'm neither able to confirm or deny."

"Yes but –"

"I haven't been *told*!"

"It was Sunday!" in the outraged tone of the Lord's Day Observance society.

"Piss on that noise," said Jimenez in Spanish.

"Madame le Juge, at the moment you reach your office I will have the man who killed Lecat outside it with a signed confession in his hand. A simple, straightforward act of passion. *Furthermore*," bellowing to override acidulated notes in a high soprano register, "Divisional Inspector Campbell has a complete and far-reaching case for the homicide of the waiter at the Fox. There are charges of fraud and attempted fraud. Also conspiracy to defraud. Active corruption of governmental and intergovernmental functionaries. I forgot attempted extortion and proxenitism. Oh I also forgot trafficking in import and export licences. Further charges may be laid as accessory before and after the homicide."

"Will you shut up!"

"Just trying to tell you you'll get your picture in the paper."

"Castang, are you showing insolence and derision towards a magistrate?"

"Look Jimenez, it's favourable. The courageous and farseeing publicspirited incorruptible gangbuster judge is going to be on midday television. She's got her man!"

"I'll see you in one hour's time."


"I'm sorry," said Castang, "there are photographers outside." Jean-Baptiste, face set, held his hands out to be manacled, in silence. "I don't like them any more than you do. Parasites. Bloodsuckers. Surrogates for the morbid voyeur. We have to put up with them. I'm ready when you are."

There was a good deal of pushing and some microphones got held out.

"Statement, statement." Varennes and young Louppes hustled Jean-Baptiste into the back of the waiting car. Castang cleared his throat pompously and stared wooden at the camera.

"Article Ten of the Code of Criminal Procedure imposes secrecy upon the instructing judge and all functionaries under the authority of the Procureur, because of the presumption of innocence towards a man untried and so as not to prejudice the rights of the defence.

"I am aware," over the sounds of anger, "that Article Ten is also held not to apply to journalists so as not to prejudice the freedom of the Press." The quacking was now furious. "So Article Ten is bullshit," getting in and winding up the window, "but it's all we've got." They'd cut all that. One must never say anything but the approved euphemisms. No such thing in public as a shower of shit. Only a certain number of points remaining to be clarified.

# 17

"So on Saturday night," said Vera, "I catch a glimpse if obscured by large numbers of young women, and throughout Sunday there is no glimpse, and on Sunday night I sigh in vain; like Mariana in the moated grange he cometh not, she said, you tell me you are snoring drunk and stinking like a badger on the office sofa; and what am I now to say beyond something profoundly original like Men must Work and Women must Weep?"

She wasn't in a bad mood at all. Simply taking the piss, in quite a gentle way. This is a concept difficult to put into French. I'm having my urine pumped. Dreary connotations of prostate and catheter. Useful phrase, taught him like most of his English by Geoffrey Dawson and one did so wonder what the origin could be.

"What else could I do?" Five notes of a banal little melody, like all theme tunes.

"Well, you could take me to the seaside for a start. I'd quite like a little cabin near the bird sanctuary. Just what I want for drawing and your new girlfriend would lend it me."

"I don't think I could ask her that," very seriously, "it's her special place and now it's all she's got." Vera burst out laughing and he understood he'd been had. A rigid and compartmentalised French mind.

"She's an upright girl. Integrity. So has he, really. Lecat was just an ordinary criminal. Unusual qualities of quickness of mind to add to ruthless egoism. Sharp intelligence. Big doses of whipped-cream charm for any pill somebody might find bitter. What way could a simple honest man combat that? Hit him on the head. Bad but what choice did he have? So I have to peg him for homicide – what choice have I?"

"No other. Up against cold iron. Like all the rest of us." She had brought him a cup of black coffee with whisky in it, and it was cheering him up.

"You should have seen old Vayvay in her bare bottom, perfectly hilarious. In fact the only thing there funnier was me. But if she starts making a good story of it," menacingly, "I'll tighten the bonds of discipline round her jockstrap.' Vera was frowning, not quite convinced that the spectacle of the Commissaire and a female PJ inspector, frolicking about with no trousers on the beach, was not indecent as well as vulgar. There are moments when cold iron of a puritanically czech sort places restraint upon her healthy sense of the ludicrous . . .

"It's no good asking you when you are going to take days off?"

"Except that I've now a reasonable understanding with that mistrustful bugger Campbell. Fadasse" – this name for his prede-cessor can be spoken in English as well as in French – "used to take off for weeks on end and leave Paddy in charge. Natural enough that he viewed my arrival with small enthusiasm. Do better now, but this minute –" He looked at his watch and his face fell. "Not much time now, and a sea of paperwork to look forward to."

"Have a wash anyhow, and shave. You'll feel better. You should be a private eye. They go to bed drunk, and when they wake up the current biddable mistress who never menstruates is making them a colossal breakfast. She doesn't have to nag about the mess; there just has to be a kind motherly black woman who cleans the bathroom."

"No cold iron in that kind of book," resisting the temptation to use the electric razor. "The readers wouldn't like being reminded. Under the tough surface everything is BarbCart-land . . .

"Violence is as sentimental as Mothers' Day," buttoning his shirt. "It doesn't do to remind people that they live their entire lives with slave-rings round their necks."

And for that he got a kiss.

They would sentimentalise the June day, grumbled Castang; to himself for there was no VV to grumble at. A northern June is by sacred tradition a wet and chilly horror: a good one is something to complain about because it takes one by surprise. There had been thundershowers during the night; thunder too, which he had been too tired, perhaps even too drunk to notice: he'd slept like a log on his sofa . . . Fine again this morning, with nice little clouds and a breeze blowing warm from the south west. The rain had laid the dust and freshened the foliage, darkening now from the delicate greens of spring.

Roses everywhere, in hideous profusion. He hates roses. Like huge horrible cactus dahlias, great fleshy gladioli, they are much too big; coarse things with vulgar flowers. On a par with the top-heavy lumps of concrete. Thank God there is still much of the old soot-darkened brick, and old overgrown ramblers, bearing little, single, delicate flowers. The countryside looks lush, flushed. This soil has been watered with too much blood. Thank God for the huge open sky of Flanders – made for the tall northern baroque which he is learning to understand. This countryside shows fearful witness to greed and oppression. Twenty centuries of pillage and rape. Is there anywhere to be found a land more unquiet, that has suffered with such patience? But how lovely it is.

And here again is this extraordinary house. How did that escape, one would like to know? Four, five generations of blitzkrieg generals had camped here. But the licentious soldiery had kept its loutish hands off. Light and elegant and French in ordered symmetry, harmony of proportion. Artifice, coquetry; very ancien régime. So wrong and so right, unnecessary and indispensable. Deceptively simple, small and open, this stronghold of privilege and good manners.

"General Laurens, please." The maid was polishing the intricate parquet. Through open doors he could see the grey and gold, the pictures by Nattier and Van Loo – were they? Why not? Everything was so perfect. Much too perfect, and he had to put his great peasant boots into that.

"The General's in his study. Please come through." A strapping Vlaams woman. There was no sign of the women of the house. Out riding, still? Getting on for lunchtime. Never mind – he could do without the women.

"Ah, Commissaire, good morning, and a lovely day." It was everything that could put one's teeth on edge, from the horsy English cut of the jacket to the too-perfect narrow ankle-boots. You're just jealous, Castang told himself, an obsessive shoe-polisher. Laurens' tone was as always kindly, unaffected. "Have a spot?" holding up a whisky bottle. He should say no, and felt drained enough to say yes.

On the label in oldfashioned copperplate was written 'Jas & Geo Stodart, Distillers at Forres, Dumbarton & Glasgow'.

"What funny names. Are they Scotch?" And why was he reading

them so carefully – were they a clue? But it struck him suddenly that the General was offering him whisky because he himself was feeling the need.

"Not particularly, as far as I know. Antiquated abbreviations of James and George. Rather sly of them so neatly to balance the Jacobite and the Hanoverian." Castang didn't understand, but there was so much else he didn't either.

"I felt bound to come to see you – no, nothing with it; straight if I may."

"Hard man!" humorous.

"When one has to be. Owe it to you to give you a warning."

"Really? Warning of what?"

"Just common courtesy to tell you, instead of your getting it garbled on the midday television."

"I'm afraid I'm not following . . ."

"Sorry, I'm back to front as usual. We've arrested Lecat's killer. I won't say assassin; it was a matter of passion. Over a woman."

"Women are the very devil." This strangely hanoverian, one might say early-victorian truism, as though uttered by Jas or Geo, Laurens delivered with solemn emphasis, as though he were the very first man to make the discovery.

Heartfelt, thought Castang taking a gingerly sip of scotch. He hadn't had much breakfast. The General looked like a man who had got through porridge. He'd had a hateful greasy croissant that VV had gone to the baker for, and he'd rather a stale crust any day.

"And who is it?" asked the General.

"Oh, one of the servants. As one might expect." A stupid phrase, and arrogant-sounding, which he at once regretted. "The gardener."

"Jean-Baptiste? Poor chap, poor chap. I'm not altogether surprised. Under that calm exterior . . . Those very controlled types, you mustn't push them too far . . . Lecat must have been out of his mind!   What woman for heavens' sake?"

"Very pretty girl and gifted, runs the wineshop in the town."

"Trouble-maker, eh?"

"I don't think it would be fair to suggest anything of the sort."

"I've laid eyes on her, I do believe. Agree, striking-looking girl."

"Yes. Well. Straightforward enough. Once I had it sorted out."

"Poor fellow. What can I do, I wonder? Poor old Georges and Violette looked upon him almost as a son: an orphan, you know. You did quite right to come and tell me, Commissaire: it was thoughtful of you . . .

"Tell me, Commissaire, the crime of passion, that's an antique phrase, but unless I'm much mistaken would still carry weight with a jury. Not a crapulous crime. Not a base or mean-minded man. There'll be a disposition towards indulgence or am I quite at sea?"

"Lecat was attempting to prostitute the girl, which will weigh with the instructing judge. Unless the prosecutor shows an unexpectedly vindictive turn. He hit him with a garden hoe. In combat against a man of such power, resource, cunning – what else could he do?"

"Would you agree to testify in that sense?"

"I'll say that he made no trouble, offered no violence, and has a sense of honour."

"Splendid," said the General, pouring out more whisky.

"Wo there – easy does it."

"The death of poor Marguerite, in this light . . . Lecat had much charm, much talent. Too much, I suppose we must say. She'd hitched her wagon to his star. She'd keep faith. But if he tried over far . . ."

"So that you account for things . . . ?"

"From what you tell me it's clear. She must have found her loyalty strained beyond endurance. Some particularly outrageous escapade such as this – she threatened Lecat with exposure and a damaging scandal."

Castang drank his whisky and held his palm over the glass.

"No more, thank you." Enough time had been spent with the cut glass. "This explanation has been put to me. I have to say that it does not altogether satisfy me. I've some reason to suppose that it might not satisfy the instructing judge."

"I see." The General wandered across to the chimneypiece, where he stood busying himself with his pipe. "With respect, Commissaire – in judicial matters, would your opinions – thoughts, sentiments – um, dictate the decisions taken?"

"Not on every occasion," said Castang, trying to take the same care with his words. "Like any police officer I am under the authority of the Procureur de la République. An important official who naturally delegates. Nine times out of ten, knowing little or nothing of the facts, he accepts the conclusions of an investigating officer.

"He doesn't have to. He could refuse the conclusions and override the findings. He might claim a particular knowledge of facts which it was thought meet to withhold for political reasons. I mean in the interest of the State. Suppose that persons were concerned who hold, or have held, positions of weight in public affairs."

"Really?"

"We had a case not so long ago in which the enquiry was conducted by the gendarmerie, in a country district. The Proc felt that perhaps this enquiry might have been conducted with a little too much regard for the force of local opinion. He asked for a second enquiry by different officers. Who arrived at different findings." He kept his voice slow and colourless. "In a matter such as this, involving a man of affairs with considerable financial interests, one might bear the hypothesis in mind."

Laurens suddenly took the pipe out of his mouth and said, "Come down to brass tacks." The sun, streaming through the high window, struck the whisky bottle.

"Pretty good one right there," said Castang. "Look at that. Lovely colour, huh? Gold. I don't have the words, I'm not an advertising agency. Gold stuff in a whisky bottle. Mr Stodart from Forres, Dumbarton and Glasgow, who sounds impressive, says it's whisky. We believe him. In that bottle and with that colour it's got to be whisky. My point is that it could perfectly well be horsepiss."

"Not if you pour it out," said Laurens smiling.

"That's what the cop does. He pours it out. Lookit," slow and painful, "if you poured a glass of whisky into a little bottle, and stuck a label on saying 'Albumen, Sediment' everybody would think it was urine. Nobody would think of smelling it or tasting it.

"But that's what a cop is trained to do."

The General went back to his leather armchair. He hitched his trousers and crossed his legs.

"Put a stop to the fencing."

"When this affair became known, my superior in Paris called me for a private word. To shed a bit of light on what he told me I went to the Hôtel, Palace, what's it called, of the Légion d'Honneur. Very few people, we could say nobody, would be prepared to believe that whatever is in that bottle," tapping it with his fingernail, "is not whisky." Silence. The General relit his pipe.

"Leave the metaphors aside. Speak in plain terms."

"I don't have evidence," said Castang. "Without evidence no judge will pronounce an inculpation. Without an inculpation nobody will examine witnesses. For example a waitress in a pub, who served cheese and a glass of wine to a lady in the company of a gentleman, described as elderly and distinguished. In the context of Lecat's death there'd be formal interrogation of servants and employees."

"I see."

"Nobody would do anything so silly as to pour out a glass of this and say in extreme surprise that it is piss. If I were to say so they'd look at me and tap the finger on the forehead."

"I see."

"People will be quite ready to admit that Lecat felt such shame at a threat by his wife to desert him and make public his moral turpitudes that he could not bear the threat to his honour and killed her. Whereas you and I know that he would have laughed in her face."

"I see," said the General.

"I've taken up a lot of your time and I apologise and I'd better be going. I hope I've done as courtesy would demand of a public official."

"I am grateful, Commissaire, for your visit."

Castang turned at the door.

"You don't judge a soldier, do you, even when you've known him a long time, till you've seen him under fire, am I right?"

"Mr Castang —"

"Yes?"

"I'd like to think over what you've said, during the course of the day."

"Certainly."

As he came out he was surprised by Cécile in the passage. Still wearing riding clothes. She said good-morning; have you been talking to my husband? One or two polite formal remarks were passed before she went on up the stairs to change before lunch. Peculiar expression on her face, the peculiar feature of which was no expression at all.

Castang glanced back at the door. Tall and heavy, of some fine-grained colonial hardwood and so well made that you'd be hard put to slide even a razorblade between the door and its frame. Voices had not been raised. Hm. He went on down the hall. The hair prickled on the back of his neck.

**18** There were work details at the office, where the Big Maid was typing away at paperwork with long strong fingers and an expression as though about to vomit. He made his arrangements, told the good Madame Metz that he'd be at home for the rest of the day, and drove back to the Bosom in time for lunch. His small daughters were gleeful at seeing him but got told to go look at the television instead, a thing normally forbidden and now accepted with humiliating delight. The Bosom, so known since it tended to flatness, made cold soup on hot days but more generally salad, believing that heavy meals at midday were unhealthy and sent one to sleep. He ate the salad and fell asleep anyway on the big sofa in the livingroom. Quiet descended. The smaller child was bundled off for a siesta and the big one to nursery school.

He was woken by Vera, wearing a disgusted face much like VV's, holding out the telephone towards his nerveless hand.

"A teenage fan," she said. "I'll make some tea."

"Wah?" but she was gone. "What is it?" irritably, in the vague belief that it was VV.

"Mr Castang?" What was familiar about that high young voice? He woke up then abruptly and said "Hold the line"; sat up, focussed, and said "Yes".

"Is there anybody listening?"

Tiresome mystery. Tiresome voice. Put together, tiresome Miranda.

"No."

"I have to see you." That too was a tiresome idea, but could not be dismissed.

"I'll buy you a cup of coffee," hoping that it sounded a little more enthusiastic than he felt.

"No no. Not where I could be seen. I mean – it has to be secret and – after dark. Look – you know our copse. The woodland near our house. There's a bridle path where we take the horses, you could get the car along there. But go very quietly with the lights out because – I'd join you there; d'you understand? There's a place the far side with poles cut to make jumps. But not a word to anybody; you'll be sure not to say?"

"I understand."

Inaccurate, but one thing he did understand, and that's beware of assignations. Specially after dark. Specially with nicely brought up girls. Isn't that what they tell the diplomats in Russia? And, come to that, anywhere else? Always bring a witness, chap, because of this eager little CIA man clutching his camera.

The house had been a manor. The surrounding and even adjacent farms had been sold off perhaps, but rights had been kept. This pleasant countryside of low wooden hills and pastoral watered valleys was nice to ride in, nice to shoot over. A traditional landscape still of hedgerow and spinney and 'our copse'. Might there be foxes still, even rabbits? Pheasants. Hares. Other delectable creatures for owners and farmers to shoot at.

"Come come. Nesting season. You don't shoot in June." But neither he nor Witness had any country lore. They were street-bred, urban folk. They felt this sort of covert country to be a dangerous place. Rustlings in the undergrowth might betoken the CIA or a boa constrictor.

"I bet the farmer does. Pigeons and uh, rooks and things, as well as nasty beasts. No close season on cops. Even if we do nest from time to time . . ." They were puzzling over the map. The National Geographic Institute does a 4 cm. to 1 km. A bit better than an inch to the mile but not much: it's no great help.

"Well, if you think . . ."

"I don't know what to think." Crossly.

"We can get a bullet-proof vest from the riot squad."

"Too hot. And the idea is ludicrous. I get it only because I have been shot at too often and the idea doesn't appeal."

"The novelty wears off."

"A dark shirt: no point in making it too easy. Is there any moon?" A calendar was consulted.

"A tiny one."

"The bleating of the goat excites the tiger."

"Come on – you don't really imagine –"

"Of course I don't, dammit; it would be completely crackers.

But all these people *are* crackers. It stinks of conspiracy."

"We take precautions," said Witness, who was quite enjoying herself. "What next?"

"You can spend a year with me, on an uninhabited tropical island. So get dressed for the part."

They were in Véronique's flat, which made it easier to pick over the wardrobe.

"You at least mustn't show up. I may be goat, but you stay snake." A pair of black trousers in imitation leather and a cotton shirt. Her fair hair was a problem, but in the office they'd found a silk balaclava such as is worn inside a motorbike helmet. For the 'horrible great nose' they found hideous dark suntan makeup 'as bad as being bootpolished'. She had a torch, night glasses, and –

"For once I think the gun is indicated." Of course the over-whelming odds were on nothing happening at all, and a drama that only existed in Miranda's imagination, said Castang, now again cheerful (she did look hilarious in the snake-costume). Still, they're a very odd family.

Buried nice and flat in the back of the car, Snake kept complaining of asphyxiation, cricks in neck, near-total paralysis, and the gun sticking in her kidneys. The big wrought-iron gate was not locked: perhaps Miranda had seen to that. The announced bridle-path took them off the approach road just as they came into the sight-line of the house. If anybody there had a sharp eye out . . . A windscreen will catch even a small amount of light . . . They circled round a good deal before he brought the car close in to the copse at the wrong side of the clearing where there were jumps-and-things.

Snake crawled out, groaning and complaining that she was nigh pissing herself. Taking up quarters in the wood made a perfect cacophony of treading on dead sticks, and getting unhooked from bramble bushes, not to speak of emptying her infernal bladder – she was capable of sitting on an ants' nest – so that Castang felt a colossal fool. How could he ever have imagined that they could move about unnoticed in the countryside at night? The Polizei's problems with a nervous bladder, compounded by a dry ditch containing nettles, were more trouble than the whole of the concrete jungle in which it moved with such practised skill and speed.

This is just morbid imagination; the memory of an old wound which throbbed reminded him how vulnerable he was. There is nobody about. They had taken care to be early.

Miranda though was punctual. She came flitting along the edge of the copse as easily as in broad daylight. But once his eyes had got used to it there was an amazing light from the sky. Even in shadow her bare arms and legs seemed white instead of tanned. Her skirt and blouse had leafy patterns.

"There isn't a soul about," in a natural voice. "I know all these paths by heart. It's lovely out if you don't mind bats and things."

"Which you don't?" It had plainly never occurred to her that a middle-aged bureaucrat would see anything untoward in meeting people at night in a wood.

"Of course not. Let's get in the car though: it'll be comfier than sitting on a log. No, in the back's better." She might have been doing this all her life.

The seduction had throughout appeared a great deal likelier than the ambush; itself little more than the memory of a most unsatisfactory homicide investigation a year before, when a poacher had been shotgunned in a wood at night and they never had established whether it really was assassination. What took him aback was her losing no time at all. He hadn't got the window rolled down to let a bit of air in before she was snuggling up! Why should he feel shocked? – he was an experienced officer. Even if he'd already learned that Miranda's imagination was more lurid than his own he was taken aback by her saying so baldly "I want to make love – that's what I came for."

"Just for that?" Of course girls offer themselves to police officers with in general a bargain in mind: it happens all the time but rarely so bleakly . . .

"Only a few buttons." And it was in exactly the voice of a young girl saying 'Yum, strawberry tart.' Castang was flustered. Some hours later it would be Vera – a woman of austere morals but less surprised – who remembered Ray Chandler's phrase about the girls who are already in bed while you're still struggling with your collar button.

"Hoy – take it easy."

"What's the matter? – anybody would think you were shy . . ."

"It's better when it's slower!" She had undone his shirt. She had her own shirt open to her waist. Holy cow! wailed Castang internally – and in the back of a police car . . .

What worried him more was that old Snake-stick down there was showing symptoms of upheaval. While still feeling surprised he is getting lubricious. He wants to tell himself he's not old enough to be subject to these fantasies concerning teenage girls. And instead of telling himself anything of the sort he's aware of adrenalin and hyperthyroid or just call it horn, floundering and wallowing in that ribcage of his she's playing with.

"Just a hook and eye," said Miranda, from down a long tunnel full of ghost-trains. He had a mouthful of hair, and behind that an ear. The ear must be getting plenty of his heavy breathing. His hand reached the hook and eye. She started to wriggle out of her skirt.

This – slightly snaky – movement reminded him that the situation was inconsistent with the behaviour expected of state functionaries in the performance of uh, their performance. Look, it's another whorelet. There are so many already.

One wouldn't have put any money on virtue remaining intact, though. The odds weren't good enough. In fact, Vera would say, not laughing much either, One will get you Twenty (Archie Goodwin talk) that virtue would Not remain intact. Come-come, said the suspect attempting disculpation in the face of this severe judge of instruction – you've forgotten the Snake.

Snake, in between trying to get a better view (why is the word voyeur always of the masculine gender?), had been looking around carefully to see whether, and anticipate where. There's going to be a candid camera, she thought. Much neater than shotguns and nowhere near as risky, and a great deal more devastating. This is going to be Jam.

But procedures are getting steamy, and no Canons are appearing in the undergrowth. All this foreplay lark is going on too long. Nor does she like the role of voyeur. All Véronique's instincts are to participate. What! Sitting here with ants crawling up my leg waiting for the springs to start squeaking?

215

She gave a smartish tap on the roof with the torch, damaging the paintwork but it was that way already.

Snakestick subsided in a hurry. Miranda, terrified, opened her mouth for an enormous yell which he was just in time to stifle.

"Stop that!" said VV roughly, forgetting what an appalling sight she must present. "Out!" jerking at the collar of the girl's shirt which slid back over her arms so that she could not clutch at her skirt. But VV was too keyed up to have time for the niceties.

"Git!" with a foot threatening a kick in the bottom. "Home!" The girl ran, in a stiff knockkneed shamble, holding the skirt in a bundle in front of her.

VV pulled off the black balaclava, which had been driving her dippy, shook her hair and said "Ouf." Castang had got out of the car and leaned his elbows on the roof: he said ouf too. She sympathised. Americans say empathise but it's just fellow-feeling.

"It's happened to me," she said with unexpected tact. "When I'm very tense, with fear or maybe pain, I get madly sexy. Do you feel very bad about it?"

"Not any longer."

"Good," with a return to the usual manner, "because I wasn't about to propose a substitute. Let's get out of here because I'm thirsty as hell. There was no tiger."

"Small," he said. "Kittenish." He had his hands over his plexus, digging the fingertips in, breathing deeply.

"Scratched you, all right. Like me to run after her and ask her back?" This did him good and he stood straight. They didn't look at one another. Both got into the car. VV started the motor with unnecessary noise and drove – rather too fast with lights out – back along the bumpy track. I underestimate girls, he thought. She got so rough back there. I wasn't the only one breathing heavy in the bushes.

He caught a glimpse of the house, dark and still, as they turned down to the gates. That household is full of frightened people. We read it all wrong. It was never meant to be a trap; that's all out of key. It is likelier and more natural to see it as a crude, childish effort to shield or protect. 'You can have me, but don't pursue us.' She had not thought it out. Impulse, in a mind stuffed with fantasies.

VV dropped him in his street.

"I want to get home in a hurry and have a shower," in a light, harsh voice. "So I'll thank you for the exotic evening." In the light – unflattering – of streetlamps he looked at her a bit unprofessionally.

"The thanks are on my side."

"On both, mate. You could have had me, back there, and you know it. I'd have been on the shitlist then, wouldn't I?"

"One does what one has to. Isn't much choice, sometimes. Think ourselves lucky." The car whisked off round the corner and Castang plodded towards his home. The sweat ran off me: I'll have a shower too. Close shave twice over, and neither of those girls is exactly horrible in the clutch. Let me seek my dear wife.

Vera was of course in bed, and equally of-course awake. Since the beginning of this marriage, when he had been a junior inspector, called upon to do tricky and often dirty jobs which were occasionally dangerous, and now and then took place at night, she had trained herself not to get into a stew, not to work herself up, not to gnaw herself with worry: call it what you like it's never easy, whether or not a girl has had an extremely disciplined upbringing, which she had. If she could not stop herself getting into a stew she planted herself under the shower. She tried turning it hot and she tried turning it cold. She had tried all sorts of things from masturbating on: a mistake, and one still did. Later, she managed to go to sleep. What help was it to a man to find her waiting up? It only meant two of them gummy next morning.

Nowadays Monsieur le Commissaire is a respectable citizen and doesn't go out much at night. If he does though, that means something nasty in the woodshed. It is preferable then that she stay awake. It is also preferable that he tell her about it. Not that she's going to do anything in particular. Just that she's like kings-and-queens under constitutional government – she has the right to be kept informed.

He does inform. She is good then at keeping adequate control over herself. There is no room for sentimentality about police work. His imagination (unrecommended to those seeking a cop-career) gets him into trouble. She's not going to say Poor You, or rush to pull her nighty off and cuddle the poor lorn man. Laugh one can and laugh one does.

The English taste for ironic understatement is sometimes neatly underscored by a sarcastic use of the opposite: any agitation, however mild, making itself felt within a bureaucracy, is termed a mad panic. Such was now creating draughts in this remote outpost of the Police Judiciaire. Telephone calls from the Proc, quite fulsome; from Divisional Commissaire Sabatier: the Loyal Subordinate stuff had gone down rather well and Inspector Campbell had also been given feathers to stick in his hat. A call to the Sous-chef, in Paris, who listened; said 'I like your reading. I hope it's the right one.' He didn't say that it had better be the right one, but the sense was conveyed.

Session with Mademoiselle Jimenez, on her best behaviour: there were no emotional ejaculations in Spanish. Quite the contrary; all in French of a professorial kind, with a bit of a pointu accent like a minister when he sees a microphone. She'd been on television and hadn't quite yet shaken off the mannerism.

The staff needed taking in hand: there were everyday affairs to be seen to. Inspector Varennes was lolling about saying she wished she were at the seaside. Madame Metz was hideously fluty in a high coloratura register, as though cast as the Queen of the Night and every time the phone rang Castang had to use a little finger to wiggle his eardrum.

The business gents . . . the moment stuff started coming out about love-nests all those bankers and financiers had decamped in a hurry and were being incommunicado elsewhere.

"General Laurens on the line for you."

"Castang here."

"Good morning. I'm at Lecat's house. I'm clearing up what might be called intendancy details. I've sent the servants home; on leave as you might say, telling them to stand by if needed for further questioning."

"Perfectly correct."

"I'm given to understand that the examining magistrate will be coming here, to verify certain details."

"That's to be expected."

"Yes. Her secretary tells me that she'll pay a call this afternoon."

"Yes. So she told me."

"I will stay on, of course. I've the notary coming, for some legal bumf. Thereafter I'll feel – that these affairs are left in order."

"Quite so."

"Since from lunchtime on I shall be both free and alone – I was wondering whether you'd care to run over. I'd take it as a favour."

"Shall we say towards one o'clock?"

"That would be most kind." The General's habitual expression of an oldfashioned punctilious courtesy.

Castang sat awhile.

"Varennes."

"Sir."

"Make it a quick sandwich; I shall be needing you. At the Electronic Palace."

"I thought all that was finished."

"Not quite. We have a call to pay on General Laurens. One more river to cross. Vive la Compagnie."

The pressmen had all departed and the siege was over. Even the electronics were switched off and the gate yielded to a push. Nobody asked their business. Even the front door of the house stood open. Inside was silent and full of sunlight. Castang made a tight, lipless mouth. He prowled down the hall and through to the pool, back to the kitchen. Everything tidy and unoccupied. He took one of his little cigars and lit it. The 'salon', the library, Marguerite's morning-room. Nothing and nobody. He drew on the cigar and started slowly to mount the stairs. VV the regulation two paces in the rear in case his train needed carrying. On the landing of a sudden a door closed. He looked up and found himself facing Cécile.

She was conventionally dressed; the middle-aged lady of good family: clothes of excellent quality, rather dowdy but 'good taste'. On a hot summer's day a flowery cotton frock with no unbecoming display of vertebrae or armpit. Her legs were bare, tanned and shapely. She wore high-heeled sandals. Her naturally greying fair hair was neatly done. Her finger- and toenails were painted pale pink. She carried a soft Italian handbag on a shoulder sling.

When she looked at him the whites of her eyes showed all around the iris. These eyes were completely crazed. She started to talk and didn't stop. As she talked she advanced, haltingly, and as it appeared without purpose. As she came down, step by step, Castang retreated in the same rhythm until halfway down, where she stopped. VV at the foot of the stairs effaced herself like a well-trained footman.

"So, you are there. The ill-omen bird. A vulture with its neck stretched out, eager to gorge on carrion." She giggled as though amused by the theatricality of this utterance, the banality of her own rhetoric.

"A stupid bird. It knows nothing, it understands nothing. But attracted by the smell of death, comes to profit by death, to fatten on death." The mad eyes focussed momentarily and she giggled again. "Bewildered. Can say nothing, prove nothing." Castang, the cigar between his teeth, let the ash fall on the staircarpet. Her eyes followed it. "Dirty!" as though to a careless child.

"Recognises corruption itself corrupt, like all police. Able to smell it.

"Lecat, the filth, began the corruption of my daughter. You completed it, or tried to. Oh yes, I saw you, I saw her, I know where she went, I understood, the sneaking backstairs seducer with the ignoble purpose of getting a young girl to talk. But she could not talk of what she does not know, she could not grasp how the filth seduced my sister, my baby sister, who forgot her family in the pride of her vanity.

"Nor could she tell what her own father did." Cécile stopped. Her voice lowered an octave. She became confidential. "I would kill her myself rather than that she should find out that that impeccable gentleman, that perfect officer, universally respected, loved, admired, has never been able to keep his hands off other men's wives. Ended, even, bedding my own sister." More of the high toneless mad giggling, like meaningless machinegun fire far outside the house. "I'm telling you, aren't I? But it won't go any further."

She must have a gun, Castang thought. She is going to proceed to a wholesale execution of the corrupt. She has killed Laurens and I'm next. He had a most unhappy remembrance of a mad woman in Germany who had taken him by surprise. He hadn't got shot. But another woman had: it wasn't 'good police work'. He had of course no gun. Had VV hers? Had she perhaps taken seriously his injunction to bear in mind that guns were never of any use? Ironic, and possibly nugatory adumbration of what is loosely termed process-of-thought.

"Where is he?" shouted Cécile. "You want to see him. He's upstairs. Washing his hands. He's forever washing his hands. It'll take him a long time." Merry laughter.

"The filth knew. He was a clever one. Forever at the trick of seducing wives himself. Recognised it when he met it. Thought it funny. He thought everything funny that was vile." When she stopped to think Castang could not help doing the same. About saving his own skin, but oddly too wondering whether Lecat had in fact bedded Cécile, to set off this insanity.

"He saw advantage in it. When did he ever do anything without seeking profit in it for himself? Street arab, little underbred barrow boy that grew rich on cunning and thievery but richer on our good name. All these years I have kept it quiet. Years of patience and suffering." Down went the voice again from the high pitch it had climaxed at, to a churchly murmur. "I offer it up, for all my sins, and for those of all the faithful departed." Castang's face must have shown that he recognised an antique, honourable piece of wording because her eyes snapped at him.

"You laugh at that. We know what it is to keep faith, we have done so since the Crusades, we have kept our honour in the face of the Jews, the Arabs, the Communists, the freemasons, the politicians who have sold and debased our country, our royalty, unsoiled for twenty generations but what would you know of that, who would not even recognise your own father? You might recognise the filth you live in embodied in a filth like Lecat. What a turning of the tables upon him that he should be cut down by a faithful servant! But what could you ever grasp, of faith and truth, or purity or honour?"

Not 'fluting' like Madame Metz. And the Queen of the Night, rocketing in firebursts off her high notes, is quite coherent in her conventional wicked-fairy style.

"But the time comes when it shall all be paid back. The time is here. That miserable, cringing man of mine. Whom I married, in

221

the belief that he was one of us. Who spread corruption round us but never could alter my purity. He would have gone on and on, until his reckoning came with paralysis. He would have profited by the corruption of his own daughter. He could never – could never – could never . . ." She was looking at Castang as though for her cue to the next line.

He didn't have any line. He felt sorry for her – what use is that? What good are police officers? They have to act their role of course. Cécile was crying now, standing still and silent with the tears oozing from her closed eyes. He had a woman police officer with him. Her role to do a bit of comforting, and he stood there while Véronique did it competently enough. Glass of water, etcetera. He watched while an unobtrusive hand patted the handbag. Of course there was no gun in it: that had been only the memory of the woman in Munich. And of Alberthe de Rubempré; quite a different pair of shoes and a dangerous, distorted woman. This was only a poor wretch who had found herself strained beyond endurance. Days of knowing the truth and struggling with it. And guessing the outcome she had been upstairs and what she had found there had put her over the edge – was that it? Was he going to find what he had expected, upstairs? VV was coping. He looked up, up the stairway to the landing, and his heart bumped him, sickeningly. Laurens was standing there looking down at the scene. Holding himself tight, unsure of his footing as though each tread might slide or tilt, Castang climbed the stairs. But Laurens stayed still and waited for him.

The General's face was as though mummified; dried and sunken, a yellowish white colour. He was wearing his English jacket tightly buttoned up. Even the collar was turned up, as though he felt the draught. His hands were driven down into the side pockets, bunched, bulging them out. One bulge was far too big. But Laurens did not try to resist.

"No no no no." A little querulous, as though in rebuke. Castang took possession of the bulky object. A ·45 automatic, the old US Army model. The big, slow, stupid bullet.

"I was too late," said Laurens in the voice of reproach, at work improperly done. "I wasted too much time. I couldn't let her find me like that." Looking into the policeman's face, asking him to understand. For he must surely know also that a gunshot suicide is a horrible sight; that one should, even in death, have consideration for others. "And now that you've heard it all from her, what would be the point?"

Castang glanced down, over the stairwell. Véronique was managing nicely. He took Laurens by the arm and propelled him towards a bedroom which turned out to be a bathroom, but did it matter? Laurens sat obediently on the edge of the bath. Castang sat on the lavatory and wedged the big pistol in a towel-rail.

"Tell me the truth. You will have to tell it to the Judge, but tell me anyhow. It will serve, you see, as a lesson."

"She told you the truth." Castang made himself breathe slowly, keeping his voice uninflected.

"To sleep with your sister-in-law, that's hardly the concern of the police. Even if it's relevant."

"Commissaire, if I wished – if I determined to kill a fellow being, I would not do so with a pillow. She did not deserve that death."

Castang pointed with his finger at the pistol.

"You were prepared to leave the impression that you had done so."

"You remarked, yourself, that it is in combat that one judges a soldier."

"I say a lot of silly things."

"My honour was lost. My wife acted, you must understand, out of a sense of honour. As for you – you felt a certainty that I had killed poor Marguerite. That was a small thing left to me, that I could maintain, at least, that appearance. And I could ensure that the essential witness – myself – would remain silent.

"I was cowardly. I delayed. My wife guessed my purpose and came here to stop it. I ask you to remember that she has been loyal. She has not been faithless."

He was still sitting upright, straight-shouldered. It is Mr Castang, a principal commissaire of the Police Judiciaire, thought of as a relatively competent officer, who sits bent forward with a crossed leg. The elbow rests on the thigh. The chin rests on the cupped palm. It is the pose of Rodin's 'Thinker', but he was not perched, surely, upon a lavatory seat? Not while thinking. It was at best a reverie. There are still people like this, who will kill for honour.

Others: themselves. Decidedly, Lecat had married into the wrong family. Who could blame him for that? Hadn't he paid too, with his own life? What difference is there between the honour of the General, and that of his wife, and the honour of Jean-Baptiste, who is a gardener? An orphan of the Public Assistance, defined in France as a Pupil of the State? They have both taken the same means of wiping out dishonour.

The Polizei had made a dog's dinner of this. Vera would have done better, no doubt of it.

It now remained to be seen whether the Law would do better. For a start, Miss Alice Jimenez.

But one can certainly trust her to do better than me. I sat there waiting for Laurens to be conventional and Do the Right Thing. Where had he got that ugly great thing from? A present, no doubt, from some sentimental American general.

And he had hesitated. With, one could only call it, a remnant of common sense.

Cécile had caught up with him. The poor girl, spitting out her pain, shouting no matter what.

But she is not mad. The famous, the too famous section sixtyfour of the Penal Code, which provides that a person clearly deranged at the moment of a crime's committal is not thereafter to be held answerable before the Assize Court: this does not apply. Though there will be lawyers enough, experts enough, to argue the contrary.

And the Chancellery of the Legion of Honour? They may be taken aback to find themselves dealing in honour. Wouldn't that be a change?

The two of us sit here. Quiet. Downstairs sit the two of them. Big VV, clumsy and delicate, crude and sensitive: and Madam General. She will have removed any tubes of pills there may be in the handbag: she will be saying Drink this; nice water. Bless the girl.

Bless all good awkward girls. Véronique, and Vera, and Alice, fighting all day for justice against rows and rows of lawyers and cops and magistrates. And bless awkward Cécile too, and Marie.

What an awful shit the women do create, to be sure.

And how very very poorly the men do come out of it.

Still – what else could we do?

Bip-bip, the doorbell; sharp and bossy. Madame le Juge and her clerk. All right Alice, we're coming. And please do now like your namesake, Larrocha. That great big black piano appassionato; hit it very, very gently.